THE ONE DOLLAR HORSE

The
ONE DOLLAR HORSE

Lauren St John

Orion
Children's Books

First published in Great Britain in 2012
by Orion Children's Books
This paperback edition first published in Great Britain in 2013
by Orion Children's Books
a division of the Orion Publishing Group Ltd
Orion House
5 Upper St Martin's Lane
London WC2H 9EA

1 3 5 7 9 10 8 6 4 2

The Orion Publishing Group's policy is to use papers that are
natural, renewable and recyclable products and made from wood
grown in sustainable forests. The logging and manufacturing
processes are expected to conform to the environmental regulations
of the country of origin.

A catalogue record for this book is
available from the British Library

Printed in Great Britain by Clays Ltd, St Ives plc

ISBN 978 1 4440 0636 0

www.laurenstjohn.com

www.orionbooks.co.uk

For my editor, Fiona Kennedy,
whose faith & support changed my life

1

C ASEY USED THE twin points of her horse's ears to line up the jump, like a sniper lining up a target on a gun barrel. Even from a distance it looked enormous: Everest in miniature. An artistic flower display attempted to make light of it, but the blossoms and shrubs did little to disguise the reality of Badminton Horse Trials' most notorious fence. The Wall of Fear was the nickname given to it by riders who'd fallen there. If she survived it, she'd be well on her way to winning the greatest championship in three day eventing. If not . . .

'Rhythm and balance, rhythm and balance,' Casey told herself. 'Trust your horse, trust yourself.'

The fence seemed to grow in size as they approached it – a towering monster.

'Come on, boy, you can do it,' Casey urged, driving her horse on with her legs and seat.

But Patchwork had had enough. Already today he'd been required to cart around a brat who wouldn't stop kicking him, a woman the size of a double-decker bus and a boy who had refused to share his Polo mints, and he had no intention of hurdling the abomination before him. Spying a direct line from the school to his stable, where his dinner was waiting, Patchwork veered around the jump, ramming the assembly of junk with his shoulder as he went. The din could be heard three streets away.

From the direction of the office, Mrs Ridgeley's penetrating voice started with a yell and built to her trademark roar. 'Who moved my flowers? *Where* is my good chair? Where ... ? Casey! CASEY BLUE! IF YOU'VE BEEN RAIDING MY OFFICE AGAIN SO THAT YOU CAN PRETEND YOU'RE RIDING AT BADMINTON, I AM GOING TO MURDER YOU!!'

Hope Lane Riding School was known to all who passed through its rusty gates as Hopeless Lane, albeit not within earshot of Mrs Ridgeley. The potholed road that ran alongside it was indeed called Hope, but anywhere further from a place of optimism could scarcely have been imagined. Situated between a toxic wasteland and a row of businesses in various stages of decrepitude – a second-hand electronics shop, a Chinese takeaway, a barber and a car wash which was, Casey was convinced, a front for a stolen vehicle operation – the twelve horses and three donkeys, overlooked by the listless trees that guarded the stable-yard, represented a last ditch stand against the city's concrete advance.

Barely a kilometre down the road lay the green and lovely contours of Victoria Park, where the young professionals who'd become Hackney's fashionable new residents sipped flat whites at cool cafes, shopped for funky clothes, visited art galleries devoid of paintings and bought exotic fruit and veg at crowded ethnic street markets, but the money and buzz had not yet filtered down to Hopeless Lane Riding School. Or, for that matter, to another of Hackney's hotspots, the infamous Murder Mile, a thoroughfare frequented by gangsters, drug dealers and a rich array of immigrants, legal and illegal.

An invisible wall seemed to separate the two worlds. A sliding door. Sometimes that door would open a chink and Casey would catch a glimpse of how the other half lived and entertain ideas of how she might join them. But an instant later it would slam shut again, as impenetrable as a bank vault. Casey would be reminded that this was where she belonged: at 414 Redwing Tower with her father, barely a stone's throw from Murder Mile, at school, and with the horses of Hopeless Lane.

And yet hopeless was not at all how Casey viewed the riding centre. Beneath its shabby exterior and sagging stable roofs it *was* a place of hope and sanctuary for many people. For all her bluster, Mrs Ridgeley (no one had ever dared to call her by her first name, Penelope) was a good and even inspirational leader to the motley collection of waifs, strays, disadvantaged and broken folk who were bussed in by well-meaning charities. Others wandered, bemused or simply curious, into her stable-yard. More often than not they left uplifted, ready to fight another day. One such person, a woman who'd found the strength to walk away from a life of petty crime after falling in love with riding, had remarked to Casey that Hopeless Lane's owner was the patron saint of lost causes.

To her instructors – Gillian, burly but big-hearted; Hermione, who had long dark tresses and the air of someone who expected to be tapped on the shoulder any day and informed that a mistake had been made and she was actually a princess; and Andrew, a drippy boy who was in love with Hermione – Mrs Ridgeley was a mother figure.

To Casey and the other volunteers, she was part mentor, part tyrant.

'CASEY BLUE!' yelled Mrs Ridgeley. 'Where are you hiding?'

'Can I help you, Mrs Ridgeley?' Casey asked innocently, materialising out of the shadows with a grooming kit. She'd persuaded one of the other volunteers to whisk the piebald cob back to his stable while she took advantage of the winter dusk to sneak the flowerboxes, chair and foldout camp bed back to the stable owner's office.

Mrs Ridgeley glowered up at her. A wiry woman with jaggedly cropped yellow hair and skin like an ageing peach, she barely came up to Casey's chest. But what she lacked in stature, she made up for in sheer force of personality.

'Don't come the innocent with me, girl. I know your tricks. I've told you before that I don't mind if you want to have a trot around the school on Patchwork at the end of the day once the paying clients have gone. It matters not a jot to me if you want to exhaust yourself coaxing him over a pole or two. But I will not have you misusing stable property in order to playact these ridiculous fantasies of yours.'

She followed Casey into Patchwork's stable and watched critically as the girl cleaned his feet with gentle efficiency. At fifteen and a half, her youngest volunteer was tall for her age and almost boyishly strong despite her thin frame, but the strain of the past year showed in the pallor of her face against her tangled brown hair. At first glance she was resolutely plain. A thousand people would pass her on the street without noticing her. It was only on closer inspection that you saw that her intelligent grey eyes burned with an intensity that was quite unsettling, and that there was a blue ring around the pupils, almost as if nature had intended them to be the colour of a sunny sky, but a storm had moved in.

Beneath those eyes were purple smudges, betraying many nights of lost sleep. Hardly surprising with what she'd been through. Goodness knows what her home life was like with no mother and *that* father.

Mrs Ridgeley's voice softened. 'Casey, you're one of the most talented volunteers we've ever had at Hope Lane, and if you work hard and stay out of trouble I give you my word I'll try to obtain some sort of grant for you to do your BHSAI exam when you finish school next summer. You have the potential to be a fine riding instructor one day. We could do with you here. But this nonsense about jumping ever more crazy obstacles has to stop. Or else . . .'

'Or else what?' Casey asked nervously, straightening up.

Mrs Ridgeley pursed her lips. 'Oh, never mind. Patchwork needs grooming and I need to lock up. Turn out the lights when you leave.'

Running a brush over the cob's dusty black and dirty-white hide, Casey reflected on Mrs Ridgeley's offer. She was well aware that it was the best she was likely to receive. Trouble was, it wasn't what she wanted. As fond as she was of Patchwork, she knew she could never be content with a future riding horses like him – stubborn, lethargic and hard-mouthed. She had no interest in notching up a dizzying number of hours attempting to communicate the finer points of 'throughness' and rising on the diagonal to parents and kids who only wanted an hour away from their troubles. She didn't have Mrs Ridgeley's leadership qualities, Gillian's passion for teaching, or Hermione's fondness for being adored by dozens of pony-mad children.

Casey dreamed of soaring over heart-stopping fences on a horse of fire. Of performing incredible feats to win the greatest prizes in eventing: the Badminton Horse Trials, the Kentucky Three Day Event and the Burghley Horse Trials. Together they made up the most elusive goal of all: the Grand Slam.

Of course, to do those things she'd need lorry-loads of money, gleaming, specially bred horses, the finest tack, clothes and boots, the best instructors ... the list went on. All of which lent weight to Mrs Ridgeley's argument that she should let go of her 'ridiculous fantasies'. She was almost sixteen. Practically a grown-up. If her teachers were to be believed, it was time to be sensible and focus on a realistic, achievable career. Unfortunately, conforming to what was expected of her had never been Casey's strong suit.

'Five minutes till lock-up,' called Gillian over her shoulder as she passed.

'Night, night.'

'See ya.'

Casey presented Patchwork with his goodnight carrot and gave his granite rump an affectionate pat.

'Not that you deserve it,' she told him. 'With the teeniest bit of effort, you could practically have stepped over that jump. It looked scary, but it was not even half a metre. A four-star horse, a *Badminton* horse, would barely notice something that small, but then those horses have wings.'

The piebald chewed without acknowledging her departure. Too long ago to remember, he'd had the spirit snuffed out of him by the learner riders of Hopeless Lane and he was committed to spending his last years doing the same to them. If a grenade had gone off in his stable, it's doubtful he'd have flickered an ear.

It was a Friday night. Beyond Hope Lane, London's East End seethed and crackled with an energy that was both intoxicating and sinister. Bursts of music – Arabic, Bollywood, African and cheesy pop – came at Casey from doorways, along with wisps of illicit smoke and snatches of foreign languages. Food smells assaulted her senses: Lebanese, Korean, Chinese, Caribbean, Thai, Greek, McDonald's and every possible variation on fried chicken.

Mouth watering, Casey jogged to shorten the fifteen minutes it usually took to reach Redwing Tower, the January wind freezing the small part of her face not covered by her sweatshirt hood. On the front steps of the grim, grey tower she called home, a group of boys were wrestling and swigging from cans. She waited for them to leave before letting herself in. Redwing was, as her father liked to say, worse than some local authority housing and not as bad as others, but she generally found that the fewer people she encountered on a party night like Friday, the easier life would be.

When she reached the fourth floor and set off along the corridor to No. 414, she had the sensation of being watched. The hairs prickled on the back of her neck. 'I won't look, won't look, won't look,' she told herself.

Looking was weak. Looking was cowardice.

She was putting the key in the lock when the sensation became overwhelming. She swung round. A net curtain twitched but otherwise the corridor was empty. Nothing and no one was there.

Casey sighed. It was nearly four months since her father had been released from prison, but the unspecified fear that had been her shadow while he was gone had been slow to loosen its grip on her. She stood in the darkness until her heart rate returned to normal. Turning the key, she let herself in.

2

'HI PUMPKIN. PERFECT timing. Dinner will be ready in ten.'

Casey couldn't help smiling. Her father knew almost to the minute when she'd be home each day. On Tuesday, Friday and Sunday afternoons she was at the riding school until shortly before 6 p.m. On Mondays, Wednesdays and Thursdays she was at school until 5 p.m. Saturdays were less predictable because she worked at the Tea Garden from 8 a.m. till 3 p.m. before heading over to Mrs Smith's for coffee and homemade chocolate shortbread. Most days it was still warm from the oven.

Once she and Mrs Smith started talking, hours had a way of vanishing, and by the time Casey got home she was usually so stuffed with Welsh rarebit (posh cheese on toast) from the Tea Garden and Mrs Smith's wonderful biscuits that she was incapable of eating another morsel. Saturday evenings were, by long-standing agreement, Roland Blue's night out with the 'boys' (none of whom were under fifty). That meant that Casey had the flat to herself and could lounge on the sofa for hours on end contentedly watching horse movies like *Secretariat* or *The Black Stallion*, or re-watching DVDs she'd recorded of the three disciplines of eventing – dressage, showjumping and cross-country, interspersed with the odd soppy romance.

Despite this unvarying schedule, Roland Blue always made out that her arrival ten minutes before dinner was ready was a matter of the most delightful chance, all the better because he'd been so busy himself that it had only just occurred to him to throw a few ingredients into the pan. In reality, Casey knew that the opposite was true. Her father's days were mostly spent scouring the classifieds, or walking the streets looking for jobs. In jail they'd encouraged him to get a book-keeping qualification, overriding his protests that no one would employ a convicted thief to do their accounts. But so it had proved.

Roland Blue had since abandoned his attempts to get book-keeping work and was prepared to do anything 'short of street-sweeping and slaving over a deep fat frier', but four months after his release he was still unemployed. On several occasions he'd been on the point of being hired when he was obliged to come clean about his criminal record. All of a sudden he was too qualified for the position, or not qualified enough, too experienced or not experienced enough, too old, too slow, too laid back or too uptight. Twice he'd been told he was too greedy after refusing to work backbreaking hours for half the minimum wage.

Over the months, he'd grown desperate. His confidence was paper-thin. Casey's homecoming was the highlight of his day. As much as he tried to act casual, happiness was written all over his face. His inability to hide his emotions had not stood him in good stead in court, but it was one of the many things Casey loved about him.

'Back in a mo, Dad. Washing my hands.'

At the kitchen table, Roland Blue, a tall man with a slight stoop who tended to dress in a worn denim shirt and jeans, like a country singer who'd fallen on hard times, was ladling steaming creamy pasta into a bowl. He was not the world's best cook but he enjoyed it, spending ages poring over recipe books he picked up in charity shops for a few pence. Jamie Oliver, Madhur Jaffrey, Gordon Ramsay: he liked them all. Since money did not exactly grow on trees at No. 414, many of the recommended ingredients were missing. It had become a standing joke between him and his daughter.

'What are we having tonight, Dad?' Casey would ask.

'Vegetarian cottage pie.'

'Anything missing?'

'Only rosemary, tomato puree, redcurrant jelly and, uh, the cottage. Couldn't afford it, house prices being what they are.'

Spices were missing from Madhur Jaffrey curries, icing from Delia Smith cakes, and as many as twenty ingredients from Gordon Ramsay recipes.

Tonight Casey asked, 'What are we having, Dad? Looks good.'

'Jamie Oliver's macaroni cheese.'

'Anything missing?'

'Only oregano, mozzarella, parmesan, mascarpone and fontina cheese. Had to make do with bog-standard cheddar livened up with nutmeg.'

Casey took a mouthful and savoured it, even though it was, in truth, fairly bland. 'It's delicious, Dad. Really yum.'

'Do you think so?' Roland Blue asked modestly. 'Took no time at all to throw together.' He reached for the pepper grinder. 'How was your day?'

Casey shrugged. 'School was school. Patchwork was Patchwork. Mrs Ridgeley told me I should stop dreaming impossible dreams about becoming a champion eventer and focus on doing something practical, like working towards an assistant riding instructor's certificate.'

Her father put down his fork. 'Will that make you happy?'

'It's a great job and the instructors at Hopeless Lane seem to love it – well, apart from Andrew, who's really only interested in Hermione – and at least I'd be working with horses, but ...'

'But what?'

'But nothing. Mrs Ridgeley is right. I should forget

about my stupid fantasies. It's just that . . . oh, Dad, you know that more than anything on earth I'd love to be flying over mad jumps on a horse with wings and competing against the world's greatest riders, but those kind of things never happen to girls like me.'

Her father's face changed. He leaned forward and wrapped both of her hands in his big brown weathered ones. His eyes, as vividly blue as the Atlantic, bored into Casey's serious ones.

'Don't ever let me hear you talking like that. Your mother would turn in her grave. Anything can happen to a girl like you, anything you dream of. Maybe not tomorrow or next month, next year or the one after that. But if it's in your heart and you work hard enough and believe enough, you can accomplish anything. I know you can.'

Whenever her father spoke like that, which he did often, Casey felt guilty for thinking, But what about you, Dad? What happened to *your* dreams? All that wishing, dreaming and believing and look how it ended up.

But she'd instantly repel the thought, because that was the sort of thing her dad's sister, Erma Delaney, would say – had, in fact, said with monotonous regularity during the course of the eight months she was charged with taking care of Casey while Roland Blue was detained at Her Majesty's pleasure at Wandsworth Prison in south-west London. Eight months of her life that Casey would never get back. If it hadn't been for Mrs Smith and the horses of Hopeless

Lane, she would, she was sure, have gone insane.

Erma was a kindly bully who spent most of her time killing with kindness her long-suffering husband, Ed, and deadly dull daughters, Chloe and Davinia, in Inverness, Scotland. When Roland had been arrested Casey was only fourteen and Erma had flown down to London in a flap to save her niece from Social Services, who'd swooped in and were all set to drag her into care.

'You're a dreamer like your father,' Erma had told her. 'No, don't smile at me. Don't take it as a compliment. It's the opposite. Dreams give people false expectations. They give people ideas above their station, lead them into trouble. Your mother was a dreamer too – hardly surprising, given she was American. It's genetic. I blame Hollywood. People are brainwashed from the cradle to believe that anything is achievable by anyone. Your mum learned the truth the hard way. One minute she was footloose and fancy free in New York, dreaming of becoming a writer, and the next she was head over heels in love with your father, dirt poor and living next door to gangsters in a council flat in Hackney. That's what happens when you dream.'

Casey had heard this rant so many times that she no longer had the energy to get annoyed by it, or to defend her father by pointing out that he'd held down a respectable job as a gardener at a local college while her mother was still alive. She said mildly: 'Mum and Dad were so in love with one another that they didn't care how or where they lived as long as they were together. Dad says that when their eyes met across the snowy piazza in Covent Garden, he turned to his friend and said: "That's the girl I'm going to marry." It was love at first sight. I think that's romantic.'

'Love, schmove,' Erma said dismissively. 'When I married your uncle I barely liked the man and we're still married forty years on.'

Only now you can't stand each other, thought Casey. But she didn't say it. What was the point?

'You're doing it now, you're away with the fairies,' scolded Erma. 'Snap out of it, girl. Wake up and smell the coffee. Wait till you're out of school and queuing for unemployment payouts. Then you'll get a reality check. You need grades in this world. QUALI-FI-CATIONS. If you carry on dreaming you'll end up where your father is, behind bars. That's where *his* dreams got him.'

With the exception of a couple of deluded, tone-deaf girls in her class who were one hundred per cent convinced they were going to win a reality show and become overnight pop sensations, her father and Angelica Smith were the only two people Casey had met in the entirety of her existence who not only believed in the pursuit of fanciful goals but actively encouraged her to do the same.

'Earth to Casey. Earth to Casey.'

Casey giggled, suddenly aware that she'd gone off into a reverie in the midst of her conversation with her father. 'Sorry, Dad. Long day. Okay, I'll hold on to my dreams until I have to get a real job. Badminton here I come.' She gathered the plates and filled the sink with soapy suds. 'You haven't told me about your day. How did it go?'

Her father beamed. 'I have some news. Good news, for a change.'

It was only then that Casey realised that he'd been bursting to tell her something from the moment she walked in. 'You've got a job!'

'Well, no, not yet, but it looks promising. I have an interview to become an apprentice tailor. The money is terrible, but the prospects are fantastic. Good tailors are like hen's teeth apparently. Your old Dad might end up on Savile Row. Imagine, Case, I could hand-stitch riding jackets for your competitions when you become famous.'

Casey reached for a tea towel and began drying up so that she could hide the conflicting emotions she always felt on occasions like this. On the one hand, her father's enthusiasm was so infectious that it was hard not to be swept along. At the same time, a voice in her mind that was almost parental wanted to caution him to slow down and not leap ahead quite so much. To remind him of past disasters. But he believed in her and she wanted desperately to believe in him.

She turned with a smile. 'That's wonderful, Dad. You'd make an amazing tailor and they'd be idiots not to hire you. Have you mentioned—'

His face fell. 'That I'm a convicted burglar? Not yet, but I will. Casey ... Casey, I was wondering if you'd accompany me to the interview? Not into the room as such, but to the tailor's shop? It would help, you know, to steady my nerves. It's at three fifteen p.m. tomorrow. I know that your afternoons with Mrs Smith are sacred, but hopefully you wouldn't be more than a few minutes late.'

He looked so earnest that Casey immediately rushed over and gave him a hug. 'Of course I can, Dad. No problem at all. I wouldn't miss it.'

3

I T WAS ROLAND Blue who spotted the one dollar note lying in the gutter. It was folded in half so all that was visible were the words '*In God We*' and part of the Great Seal of America. It was not until he opened it out and handed it to Casey that she saw the whole motto, *In God We Trust* and, on the front of the bill, the green countenance of George Washington, the first President of the United States.

'I wonder who dropped it here,' said Casey, dusting it off. 'It's a bit unusual, finding a US dollar on the streets of East London, especially in a back alley. It's not really a tourist destination.'

'It's a sign,' said her father, taking the note from her, tucking it reverently into his pocket and resuming his long stride down Half Moon Lane.

Casey hurried to catch up with him. 'What kind of sign?'

'A sign that your mother is with us today and that all will be well and I'll get the job.'

If a stranger had overheard him talking that way, especially to his daughter, they'd doubtless have disapproved, but over the years he and Casey had found it a huge comfort to imagine that Dorothy was watching over them. Casey had been two years old when her mum went into hospital for a routine operation to remove her appendix and never came out again. She'd suffered a rare reaction to the anaesthetic and died on the operating table.

Aside from faded photos showing a laughing woman with curly brown hair, Casey had no visual memory of her mum, only a feeling – one of warmth, security and gentleness. It was perhaps for that reason that if she saw something unexpected that made her spirits lift – a spill of rose petals, her mum's favourite flower, on a crowded pavement; a pretty feather on a grimy windowsill; a robin singing its heart out on a grey morning – she liked to think of them as love notes from the mother she'd never known but who she felt was always with her.

And so she had no objection to her father seeing the dollar that came from her mum's birthplace as a good omen. She was inclined to believe the same thing. Forty minutes later it had all but been confirmed when Roland Blue came flying out of the Half Moon Tailor Shop and whirled Casey round until she was dizzy.

'Okay, okay, I get it,' she said laughing. 'You're happy. You got the job.'

A tear spilled from her father's eye and he brushed it away roughly, embarrassed. His big hands were trembling. 'Phew! I've not been that nervous since I asked your mum to marry me. The worst moment was when Mr Singh offered me the position before I'd had a chance to tell him about my prison sentence. I debated whether to keep quiet in the hope I'd get away with it, but I didn't want to do that, to start on the wrong foot. It would have preyed on my conscience. I stuttered and stammered, but I finally managed to get it out. Told him every detail. As you can imagine it came as a bit of a shock to him. The blood sort of drained from his face and he was silent for the longest time. Then he told me that, as a young man, he'd been in a lot of trouble with the law himself and that if he hadn't been given a chance he wouldn't be where he is today. He thanked me for my honesty and said that the job was mine if I wanted it. I start on Monday. '

Casey was so proud she was almost in tears herself. It felt like a new beginning. A fresh chance.

She squeezed his hand. 'Congratulations, superstar. I couldn't be happier for you. Make sure you have a celebratory drink with the boys tonight. Right, it's nearly four o'clock and I need to get to Mrs Smith's for tea. Let's go left up this alleyway. I think I know a shortcut.'

That was it. That's why they were there – in the wrong place at the right time, or the right place at the right time, depending on how you look at it. Afterwards, Casey couldn't stop thinking about how the odds were trillions to one against them being in that exact spot at that exact moment. That if they'd passed that way a few minutes earlier, or if Mr Singh had been a more pedantic interviewer, they'd have been too late. Years on, it would still send chills through her.

The smell should have been the giveaway. The air was rancid with it. An unholy mix of fear, sweat and death. But it was a Saturday afternoon, a time when the streets often reeked of human excess ('*Eau de Weekend*' Roland Blue called it) and the pair were so deep in conversation that they were as oblivious to their surroundings as they were to the first flakes of snow. It was only when they heard an unearthly scream that they stopped in their tracks.

'What in the name of all that's decent was that?' demanded Roland Blue. 'Sounds as if someone's being murdered.'

Casey's whole body had turned to gooseflesh. She knew at once what it was but she didn't want to believe it.

The scream came again, this time followed by the unmistakable clatter of hooves on concrete and men yelling. Up ahead on the right, a high wooden gate, signposted BJ Enterprises, was struck with force.

'I think I'd better investigate,' said her father. 'I don't know what's going on in there, but it doesn't sound good. Case, you wait here.'

'There's no way I'm staying behind,' Casey began indignantly, but before she could get any further the gate crashed open, spraying splinters. Out flew a vision from a nightmare. Half horse, half skeleton, its dull grey coat streaked with blood and white lather. The creature paused momentarily, as if startled to find itself free, before bolting down the street in their direction, pursued by three red-faced men.

As the horse tore towards them, Casey, frozen on the spot, had a split second to take in that although he was so emaciated it was a miracle he was even standing, his eyes, sunken deep in his skull, blazed with a terrible hatred.

Do something.

Casey didn't at first realise she'd spoken out loud. But, of course, nobody was about to do anything, because the horse was thundering along the tarmac in a blur of speed, the men were stopping and throwing up their hands, and her father was as stunned as she was.

Do something before he reaches the main road.

The horse was almost past her when she leapt for his swinging lead rope. It burned through her hands but she threw her whole weight back, forcing him to a swerving, clattering halt. He reared, wrenching her from her feet. Hooves flashed. She had the sudden understanding that he could kill her, yet she felt peculiarly unafraid. Somewhere, far away, her father was shouting her name. Everything hurt – the rope ripping through her palms, her body slamming against his bony side, her left ankle as she crashed down to the ground – but still she held on. The horse gave a final, defiant scream, but he was weakening. He staggered, his strength almost gone.

Casey snapped out of her trance. Recovering her balance, she moved as quickly as she could to take hold of his headcollar. He flinched, nostrils flaring. For an instant his wild eyes were level with hers, and into her mind came the quote, its author unknown, that Mrs Smith had cross-stitched, framed and hanging on her living room wall:

'. . . and he whispered to the horse, "Trust no man in whose eyes you do not see yourself reflected as an equal . . ."'

A wave of emotion swept over her. In that instant she knew that she'd do anything, anything at all, to protect him.

'Easy, boy, you're safe now,' she said soothingly. 'You're safe. I won't let them hurt you, I promise.'

The men came running up, breaking the spell. Her father said: 'Well done, Casey. Very heroic of you. Poor beast. He was frightened out of his mind.'

'I'm not sure heroic's the right word,' retorted the tallest of the three men, a bald man with fingers as thick as sausages and stained blue overalls, speckled with blood. He smelled of boiled bones, death and disinfectant. 'Crazy's more like it.'

He stepped forward and the horse scuttled back, throwing up his head in terror. 'Thanks, love, you saved the day. Wretched animal's insane. But we'll take over now.'

Casey clutched the rope tightly and moved so that her body shielded the horse. 'What's going on?' she demanded. 'Why was he screaming like that? What were you doing to him?'

A short, stumpy man with a burn mark across one cheek and similarly filthy overalls gave a snort. ''E's screaming because 'e knows what's coming. It's always the smart ones that give us the trouble, isn't it, Dave? The ones that know they're 'ere to meet the Grim Reaper. Well, this is a knacker's yard, isn't it? 'E knows 'e's here to be exited.'

'*Exited?*' Casey felt faint. A knacker's yard. She'd heard of such places, but had chosen to believe that they were an evil prevalent in medieval times or Victorian England, long since consigned to history. 'You're planning to . . . ?' She lowered her voice. 'You're planning to slaughter him?'

'Put him out of his misery more like,' roared Dave, who was growing impatient. 'Our instructions were very clear on that, weren't they, Midge?'

The stumpy man scratched the stubble on his chin. 'Sure were. The man who brung 'im told me 'is father's obsession with it had destroyed their lives; cost them almost everything, which, I gathered, was a lot.'

'How does a horse manage that?' asked Roland. 'Especially a mangy animal like him.'

'Wasn't always this way, so the son claimed,' responded Midge. 'Had some cock and bull story about 'ow 'is dad spotted this horse going berserk at a circus in Lithuania or Ukrainia or one of them old Soviet places – 'e was foreign himself, the dad – and became convinced it could be the greatest racehorse the world had ever seen. Brought it to England and spent a fortune training and pampering it. Off the racetrack, it clocked up record times, the son said. Silver Cyclone, they called it, on account of its colour, not that you can see much of that now. Fur like a mule.'

'A load of garbage, if you ask me,' barked Dave impatiently. 'Silver Cyclone! As if a thing like that could win an egg and spoon race.'

'What happened?' Roland wanted to know. 'Did Silver Cyclone win any races? Very hard to believe, looking at him now.'

'Not one. Dud on the racetrack, 'e was. Wouldn't even leave the start box. Afraid of 'is own shadow. Years this went on. The family begged the old man to get rid of it, but 'e was a fanatic. It was only when it threatened to bankrupt 'im that 'e took against it. So 'e brought it to be turned into dog food, to have done with it once and for all.'

'And if you're done jawing, that's what we're going to do now,' said the third man, a gaunt figure with skin the colour of molten candle wax. 'Kill him.'

'That we are,' agreed Dave. 'Young lady, I know it's harsh but you're going to have to accept the inevitable.'

'No!' cried Casey.

Dave made a grab for the rope just as the ghostly man closed in on the horse's quarters. There was a hideous crack, like a tree branch breaking, and the man was on the ground, writhing in agony. ''E's broken me leg,' he shrieked incredulously. 'The nutter's broken me leg. Midge, call an ambulance.'

'This is your fault,' Dave yelled at Midge, who was on his mobile, dialling 999. 'You and your big mouth.'

The horse's eyes were wide with panic and rage. The blood from a cut on his side was staining the snow pink and he was trembling. White flakes settled like confetti in his tangled mane. Casey was petrified that he was going to die of cold and shock where he stood.

'Give him to me,' she said. 'Give him to me and you won't have to deal with him any more. We'll walk away and you'll never see any of us ever again.'

'Casey!' cried her father, alarmed. 'Think about what you're saying. What would we do with him? He can hardly live at No. 414.'

Dave chuckled rudely. 'You're having a laugh you are, girl. Where are you going to take him? Set him free in Victoria Park? This is life, not a movie.'

Midge squatted on the snowy ground, reassuring his friend that an ambulance was on its way. The man's jeans were torn and something that looked suspiciously like a bone was poking through.

'I'm serious,' Casey said. 'Give him to me and he's off your hands. No more problems.'

'Can't do that. Well it's the law, isn't it? Money has

to exchange hands otherwise it's not legal. I could sell him to you but not give him away. Plus I got a broken gate and one of me best men down. There's compensation to think about.'

'Casey, please,' implored her father. 'I feel for the horse as much as you do, but there must be some other way. Why don't we go home and call one of those horse rescue charities?'

'I have a piggy bank,' Casey told Dave. 'It has about fifty-five pounds in it. I can run home and get it and be back in under an hour.'

'And what are we supposed to do with him in the meanwhile?' Dave demanded. 'Stand around whistling while he kicks holes in every man in our yard? Thanks, but no thanks. Hand him over and he'll be dead in ten minutes, of that I can assure you. Give him to me.'

He wrenched the rope from Casey's hands before she could stop him. The horse came to life again. His ears flattened, his neck snaked and he sank his teeth into the man's arm, drawing blood. Dave lashed out with his good arm, intending to punch the horse on the nose, but Roland Blue beat him to it. A champion boxer in his youth, he blocked Dave's fist with a grip of iron.

'There'll be none of that. I'll not tolerate anyone harming an animal in my presence. If he's bitten you, it's no more than you deserve. My daughter's offered you a solution, which you won't accept. What will it take for you to part with the horse?'

'What's in your wallet?' snarled the man, sucking at

his wound. 'Give me everything in it, we'll sign the transfer of ownership documents and be done with it. Why you want to saddle yourself with such a monstrous beast is beyond me, but that's your business.'

Roland Blue reached for his wallet, although he already knew what was in it. Nothing. By Saturday he'd usually spent the pitiful sum the government called Jobseeker's Allowance on food, bills and incidentals, and the seventeen pounds and twenty pence he'd kept aside for his night out with the boys was sitting on his dresser at home.

He turned apologetically to his daughter. She looked stricken. 'I'm sorry, Casey. The gas and electricity bill swallowed up nearly everything this week.'

'Right,' said Midge, abandoning the patient, who was prone on the ground making puppyish moans. 'Game over. We're taking the horse.'

'Wait!' cried Casey. 'The dollar. Give him the dollar, Dad.'

'A US dollar?' Dave took the note and tapped it as it lay across his palm, leaving a bloody fingerprint on George Washington's cheek. 'This takes the biscuit. You're not in the real world at all, are you? What am I supposed to do with this?'

'It's legal tender,' said Roland Blue. 'Not in this country, perhaps, but it should be sufficient proof of payment for any document you want me to sign.'

Dave looked from him to the pale, thin girl who was regarding him from under her long lashes with a disturbing stare. It was as if she'd seen into his very soul and didn't like what she found there. It made him as uncomfortable as he'd been two hours earlier when he'd taken delivery of the horse. It had sprung off the ramp of the horsebox and surveyed the gathered men with a hatred that had sent an icy shiver up his spine. In all his years of slaughtering animals, he'd never met another quite like it. Truth be told, he was desperate to be shot of it, but what remained of his conscience made him reluctant to palm off such a dangerous brute on two clueless innocents.

'I'll give you one last chance. He's yours if you want him, but I'd advise you to think long and hard about what you're taking on.'

'We already have and we're quite certain,' Roland Blue told him, but as he turned away he said under his breath: 'Casey, what are we going to do with him when we leave here? We can barely feed ourselves, let alone a horse.'

'I'll take him to Hopeless Lane and worry about what happens next when I get there.'

'But what will Mrs Ridgeley say?'

'I don't know and I don't care,' said Casey. 'All I care about is getting him away from here and getting him help. He's totally traumatised.'

The wail of the ambulance siren was getting louder. Midge gave another snort. 'How are you going to get him there? Stroll him through the traffic? Good luck with that. It'll be headline news tomorrow. Girl and horse crushed under ten-ton lorry.'

Casey's chin lifted. The prospect of leading a crazed horse through the manic streets of Saturday afternoon Hackney was beyond terrifying, but she wasn't about to show she was scared to anyone, not even her father. 'We'll be fine. I'm going to blindfold him with my sweatshirt to avoid frightening him any more than he already has been, and we'll be perfectly okay.'

Dave stared at her in wonder. 'Well, that's it then. On *your* head be it. One deranged skeleton of a horse sold to a couple of lunatics for a dollar.'

4

M RS RIDGELEY TOOK one look at the horse and said: 'I hope you've got money in that famous piggy bank of yours, Casey Blue. I'm calling the vet and we're having him put to sleep and you're going to be the one who pays for it.'

It was an ugly night, prematurely dark and viciously cold. Casey was not in the least bit surprised by Mrs Ridgeley's reaction, only by the severity of it. During the harrowing journey from the knacker's yard, a journey she'd insisted on doing alone, without her father's help, the horse had kicked over a stall of apples, come perilously close to dragging himself and Casey under a bus, and almost taken the head off a dog that nipped at his heels. On arrival at Hopeless Lane, wet, bloody and shivering, she was aware that the pair of them must have presented quite a spectacle. The entire yard had come to an open-mouthed halt.

Directed by Gillian, Casey had put the horse in the stable usually occupied by Arthur Moth's three donkeys, away overnight at a country fair. Then she'd prepared to face the music. Unfortunately, the horse, which had drained the water bucket Casey had given him and retreated glowering to the back of the stable, was now lying on the straw as if he'd lost the will to live.

Mrs Ridgeley squinted into the shadows. 'Poor desperate creature. Whoever's done this to you should be locked away for life. Casey, I understand that you rescued him with the best of intentions, but the road to hell is paved with them. The fact of the matter is that you're now going to have to be cruel to be kind. Surely you can see he's suffering. He needs to be put out of his misery. It's the right thing to do. The *humane* thing to do. I'm phoning the vet and I'll not hear another word about it. If money's an issue, I can settle up now and you can pay me back later.'

'No!" Casey barred her way. 'I made a promise. I promised him that I'd take care of him and keep him safe, and I have no intention of breaking my word. He's been betrayed by humans all his life and I'm not going to be one of them. If you call the vet, we'll be gone by the time you get back.'

Mrs Ridgeley stared at her as if she'd taken complete leave of her senses. 'And where will you go? Out into the heaving streets of Hackney? Sleep under a bush, will you? You'll die of hypothermia before the night is through.'

Casey wasn't confident she wouldn't die of hypothermia anyway. Her coat had been lost during the bus incident and her sweatshirt was no defence against sub-zero temperatures. Still she remained defiant. In a situation in which he'd wanted to attack any man who came near him, the horse had trusted her enough to allow her to stop him, hold him and, admittedly with some difficulty, blindfold him. On the journey to Hopeless Lane, when the reality of what she'd taken on had begun to sink in, the line from Mrs Smith's cross-stitch picture had gone through her head over and over. The horse had looked into her eyes and seen an equal, of that she was sure.

'What's it going to be, Casey?' demanded Mrs Ridgeley. 'Will you let me call the vet? I've warned you before about being too sentimental about animals. It's important that we care about them and try to understand them, but they're not in the same league as people. Not at all.'

No, they're a million times better than us.

Casey's heart contracted as she glanced at the horse. She came to a decision. 'Give me twenty-four hours. I'll nurse him as best as I can. If he's no better or if he's worse, I'll call the vet and have him put to sleep if the vet says there's no option. But what happens if he makes a miraculous recovery? What then?'

'He won't, trust me. I know a dying horse when I see one.'

'But let's say he does. Is there any chance you would let me keep him here?'

'Night, Mrs Ridgeley; good luck, Case,' called Gillian, squinting into the stable and raising her eyebrows as she left. Out in the yard it was silent. Everyone but Casey and Hopeless Lane's owner had departed for the evening.

'No you cannot. Every stable is full and I can't afford another mouth to feed. Even if he does recover, he's hardly likely to be riding school material – a wild bag of bones like him.'

'First,' Casey said, 'it wouldn't cost you a penny. I'll pay for all his food and vet bills myself.'

Mrs Ridgeley laughed so loudly the horse momentarily roused himself before his eyes slid shut again. 'What, with your Saturday wage from the Tea Garden? Give me a break. Have you any idea what it costs to keep a horse? Hundreds of pounds every month and that's only if they're well. If they get sick or injured, you need a bottomless bank account.'

'My dad has a great new job,' said Casey with more confidence than she felt. It remained to be seen whether or not Mr Singh would actually honour his agreement to hire an ex-con. Whatever happened, they'd be struggling to get by on the little her father brought home and she had no intention of asking him to make more sacrifices than he already did for the sake of a horse she'd chosen to rescue. Not that she was about to admit that to Mrs Ridgeley. 'Between us, Dad and I will look after him,' she lied.

She got a glare in response. 'Where exactly are you planning to keep him, Casey? Every stable is full and Arthur Moth will be back tomorrow afternoon with his donkeys.'

'How about the old storeroom? You've been saying for ages that you'd like someone to clear it out for you. I'll do it and he can live in there.'

Mrs Ridgeley checked her watch. She had people arriving for dinner in less than an hour and she hadn't even begun to cook. Her blood pressure mounted. She cared for Casey a great deal and frequently fretted about her, but as a volunteer she sometimes wondered if the girl was more trouble than she was worth. Only Casey could pick up some half-dead horse off the street and imagine it could be saved at no other cost than a lot of TLC.

'Twenty-four hours,' she said. 'Twenty-four hours is all I'm giving you. If the horse is not on his feet and bright-eyed and bushy-tailed by then, I'm calling the vet to put an end to his suffering, and, yes, you'll be paying for it.'

Casey threw her arms around the sturdy little woman. 'Thank you, Mrs Ridgeley. Oh, thank you so much. You won't regret it.'

But as Mrs Ridgeley's footsteps faded into the night Casey's shoulders slumped. The horse's breathing was so shallow that she feared he wouldn't make it until morning. And if he did, what then? Casey did not have the faintest idea. She refused to worry about it. Once she'd had a chance to think, she'd make a plan.

5

CASEY RARELY SWORE but catching sight of the
stable clock she did so now. It was 10.16 p.m.,
meaning that she was six hours and sixteen minutes
late for tea with Mrs Smith – a date that she had until
this moment completely forgotten about. Ideally, she'd
have called but Mrs Smith didn't have a phone.
Couldn't see the point, she'd told Casey, when her only
family were her few friends – the kind of people one
could drop in on any time, and the stray cats who used
her pocket-sized Victorian apartment 'like a hotel'.

If it were anyone else, Casey would not have
considered leaving the horse alone, but quite apart
from the fact that she was in real danger of catching
her death of cold she couldn't bear the thought that
she'd let down one of the kindest people she'd ever
known. For that reason, she crept closer to the

unconscious horse, bent down and kissed him goodbye on his rough cheek. He didn't stir. She stayed looking at him for another half hour, terrified that he'd be dead by the time she returned.

'You're not allowed to die,' she told him. 'I know we've only just met but it would break my heart. Stay alive and let me show you what it's like to be loved. Keep on fighting and let me show you what it's like to be happy.'

The horse didn't move a muscle. She shut the stable door with great reluctance and set off at a jog through the snow to beg forgiveness from Mrs Smith.

Casey's classmates would have found yet another reason to jeer at her had they known that her best friend was a sixty-two-year-old cat-obsessed spinster and not someone cooler and closer to her own age. But that was only because they didn't know and couldn't appreciate that Mrs Smith was way cooler, smarter and more generous-spirited than any teenager Casey knew. More importantly, she took Casey for who she was, without judging.

Casey had always found it hard to make friends. She was extremely shy, which didn't help, but she also had the sense that she was *too* something. Too plain, too ordinary, too intense, too clever, not clever enough, too studious, too boring, too tame and not on Facebook. Yet prior to her dad being jailed, she had been reasonably well liked, if always something of an outsider.

That all changed when her father was arrested and charged with breaking and entering. By coincidence, one of the most popular girls in school had had her house burgled on the same evening. The crimes were not connected, but once a link had been made most people in the school were convinced they were.

Overnight, Casey became a pariah. There were kids in the school whose fathers battered their mothers or vice versa; kids who came from families where nobody had worked for three or four generations; who had mums and dads who all but lived at the bookmakers or the pub; or single parents who discouraged achievement and encouraged truancy. There were plenty of teenagers at her school who shoplifted sweets almost every day after class, and some who were in gangs that roamed the streets randomly terrorising law-abiding citizens or spraying graffiti on buildings. And yet these things were as nothing when stacked up against a father who was a burglar.

'Is that your watch, or did your father steal it?' she was routinely asked. 'Is that your lunch money, or did Daddy have to mug somebody?' 'Hey, Casey, I'm going to a fancy dress party. Mind asking your dad if I could borrow his stripy burglar suit?'

Some days Casey felt as if she was wearing a Scarlet Letter, as if it were branded on her skin: 'My Dad is a Thief. What's More, He's a Bad Thief. He Got Caught.' At those times she wanted to run home and scream: 'Why did you do it, Dad? How could you?'

But it was no use because she already knew why he'd done it. He'd explained himself as many times as he'd said sorry. After years of failed ventures, of debt, of struggle, he'd just wanted a break. He'd fallen in with a bad crowd and they'd convinced him that it was his due. 'We'd never have taken sentimental things,' he'd told her. 'We were only after the money in his safe. A few thousand. He's a multi-millionaire. He'd hardly have missed it. I did it because I wanted to give you some of the things I've always wanted to, fool that I am.'

And so his guilt became her guilt.

If Hopeless Lane was her sanctuary, Mrs Smith's friendship was her salvation. They'd started chatting one Saturday when Casey was waiting tables at the Tea Garden and had discovered a mutual love of horses. A couple of weeks later Mrs Smith had invited Casey home for afternoon tea and their relationship had blossomed.

Unlike Casey, who often felt invisible so rarely did anyone appear to notice her, Angelica Smith was the kind of person to whom all eyes swivelled when she walked into the Tea Garden. Frustratingly, she was vague about her riding past. That she'd had a 'few ponies' and 'won a few rosettes' was as much as Casey could get out of her. She'd been prepared to go into much more detail about her wastrel ex-husband, Robert, who had, she claimed, blown her fortune on wine, women and roulette.

'But,' she told Casey with a laugh, 'he didn't get everything. I made sure of that.'

Casey took many of these stories with a large pinch of salt. If Mrs Smith had money under her mattress it certainly didn't show. Apart from keeping an epic number of neighbourhood strays in cat food and enjoying a weekly lunch at the Tea Garden, she lived frugally. Her one-bedroom apartment was spotlessly clean but sparsely furnished. The cross-stitch aside, few pictures adorned the walls.

In spite of her reduced circumstances, Mrs Smith had an elegance and refinement that was unmistakable. To Casey, she was also ageless. She had long, silver-streaked fair hair, which usually hung in a plait down her back. She wore clothes bought from charity shops with a style that made them look almost fashionable. However, it was not those things that attracted attention. It was something she radiated. A warm, vital energy.

As Casey had got to know her, though, she'd observed something else about Mrs Smith. A restlessness. She had the sense that Mrs Smith was waiting for something, and not in the way of many of the old biddies in the Tea Garden who liked to joke that they were in 'God's Waiting Room'.

When Roland Blue was outed as a failed burglar it had caused a sensation among the gossips at the cafe, but Mrs Smith had hardly batted an eyelid. 'Oh, my dear, I feel for you, but try not to take it to heart. It's your dad's mistake, Casey, not yours. Doesn't make him a bad man. Doesn't even make him a bad father. It makes him an idiot who did something wrong and stupid once. Hopefully he'll learn from this and move forward. It might even be the making of him.'

She took a sip of tea. 'Don't get me wrong, I'm not condoning burglary, but his biggest mistake was being poor and not being able to afford a decent lawyer. There are plenty of people wandering the streets who should be in jail but aren't. Ask my ex-husband. He's one of them. White-collar criminals they're called. Steal a billion dollars from an investment bank and you're practically a hero. They put you in an open prison and let you out a few weeks later for good behaviour. Newspapers buy your story. Publishers pay six-figure sums for you to write a bestseller about how you did it. Blue-collar crime is a whole other matter. If you're a single mother who steals ten pounds because you can't afford a tin of baby milk or to pay your TV licence, they lock you up and throw away the key. That's modern justice for you.'

Despite this apparent show of support, Casey had fully expected Mrs Smith to find some excuse not to invite her round. But the teas had continued as before. If anything, Roland Blue's prison sentence had brought the pair closer because it had shown Casey that Mrs Smith was a true friend.

And now she'd let her down.

She knocked for a third time. The door creaked open a fraction before snagging on its chain. Mrs Smith made no move to release it. Her eyes ran over Casey, taking in her bedraggled appearance. 'It's late, Casey. I'm afraid I don't have the energy to receive visitors now. Let's talk some other day.'

A ginger cat shoved its nose through the gap and let out a high-pitched meow. It looked equally displeased.

Casey was distraught. 'I'm so, so sorry, Mrs Smith. If you let me in I can explain.'

'No explanation necessary, but I would have appreciated it if you'd tried to get a message to me. When you didn't show up, I was so worried I went to the café. One of the girls told me that a nightclub was opening in Hackney tonight and that you and the rest of the staff would be there. That's okay. You're young, you want to have fun. No hard feelings.'

'A *nightclub*? Look, I'm incredibly sorry I didn't show up. I feel awful, but it's definitely not because of any club. There was a crisis with a horse. I was utterly preoccupied with saving him and everything went out of my head.'

There was a silence. Mrs Smith said through the gap: 'Patchwork?'

'No, not Patchwork. A wild, starving horse my dad and I saved from the knacker's yard this afternoon.'

The chain was removed and the door flew open. 'Come in,' said Mrs Smith, 'and tell me everything. Leave no detail out. You might want to text your father and tell him that you're with me and likely to be back very late, but that I'll see you home safely in a taxi. Now, you look as if you're about to faint on your feet. Can I offer you a spinach and mushroom pie?'

That's how Casey came to be at Hopeless Lane just after midnight, watching Mrs Smith apply a paste to the cut on the horse's flank. She'd already made him swallow, not in the least willingly, a brown liquid that she'd collected from a friend on their way to the stables.

'Based on the symptoms you're describing – fever, malnutrition, trembling, weakness – he doesn't need a vet, he needs one of Janet's potions,' she'd told Casey. 'A bit of food, warmth and kindness and it wouldn't surprise me if he makes a complete recovery.'

'What's in the potions?' Casey had asked worriedly when Mrs Smith had emerged from a crumbling mansion in one of the worst areas of Dalston with a lunchbox oozing white paste and three big soft drink bottles filled with a liquid that looked like an algae smoothie.

'Haven't the foggiest,' was Mrs Smith's response. 'Don't fret. I don't know anyone who's died from one of Janet's concoctions and I know plenty who've been cured.'

'But does she know anything about horses?'

Mrs Smith hadn't replied and hadn't been prepared to wait for the morning either, when a vet could be consulted. 'You don't want to lose him, do you?' she'd said flatly before kneeling down and preparing to cover the horse with a thick tartan blanket she'd taken off her own bed. 'Nor do you want to pay a fortune to some quack. No need with people like Janet about.'

Casey had been too exhausted to respond. It was a relief that someone had taken over and that that someone was Mrs Smith, who not only believed that Casey had done the right thing by rescuing the horse, but seemed confident that he would live.

Mrs Smith stood up. The horse had struggled feebly when he was made to ingest the foul-smelling liquid, but had slumped back down again. 'Okay, horse, let me look at you.'

She took the torch from Casey and moved it slowly over his unconscious form. Her hand went to her mouth. 'Oh my goodness. Oh my goodness.'

'What?' cried Casey. 'What?'

'Look at his head. See the shape of it and the fine bones. Not so impressive now because his eyes are sunken and he's horribly malnourished, but he's a class horse if I ever saw one.'

Casey leaned forward. 'You're joking?'

'Never been more serious in my life. His knees only appear knobbly because he's so thin. If you look closely you'll see that he has beautiful straight legs, nicely sloping quarters and short cannon bones – that's a good thing. His back is the perfect length, not too long and not too short. Personally, I like the angle of the pastern and hoof to match, and his pasterns are textbook.'

She laughed. 'I could go on. The breadth of his chest alone shows his pedigree. He'll have a huge heart in there; massive lungs. Built for speed and endurance, no doubt about it. No flesh on him now, let alone muscle, but he'll have been a powerhouse once, you can be sure of it. If he's raced I'm guessing he's a thoroughbred, but it could be that there's a touch of something heavier in there. Or maybe it's just Darley Arabian, one of the great ancestral sires, exerting his genes.'

Casey couldn't believe her ears. 'Are you sure? He seems so . . .'

'Broken? Pathetic? Absolutely. In his current state, he's not worth the dollar you paid for him. He's the world's poorest excuse for a horse. He's barely worth the cost of turning him into dog food. But, Casey, we can change that. I studied his teeth when I was giving him Janet's potion. He's a young horse – barely eight years old if I'm not mistaken. If he survives the night, and that's by no means guaranteed, he'll have his whole life ahead of him.'

She knelt down again. Tenderly, she stroked the horse's neck. 'You've been bred to be something very special, haven't you? And you will be again. You will be again.'

6

W HEN CASEY ARRIVED bleary-eyed at Hopeless
Lane the following morning, the first thing she
noticed was that, in every stable bar one, a horse's
head was framed in the doorway.

Tears sprang into her eyes. During a night of fitful
sleep and fragmented dreams, she'd convinced herself
that the horse would live and she'd have a pony of her
own, a friend. How she was going to afford this friend
she hadn't a clue, and she'd tiptoed out of No. 414
before her father woke up and asked her. She only
knew that she'd do her utmost to love him and nurse
him back to full strength. But if he was still lying down,
it was the worst possible sign. Either he was dead or
he wasn't far from it.

She broke into a run, cursing Mrs Smith for giving
him Janet's dodgy mixture and herself for leaving him

at all. Mrs Smith had put her in a taxi driven by a woman they knew well from the cafe at around 1.30 a.m. after persuading Casey that she'd be no help to the horse if she caught pneumonia. Casey, whose limbs by then felt like frozen legs of lamb, had been inclined to agree, especially since Mrs Smith had promised to watch over him until morning.

'But what about you?' Casey had fretted. 'You must be exhausted. And I'll be worried that you'll freeze to death.'

'Freeze? Not a chance. This coat would have seen Shackleton across Antarctica. As for sleep, there'll be time enough for that when I'm dead.'

And so Casey had gone home and left the horse to his fate. As she drew nearer to his stable door, she stopped, unable to find the courage to approach it.

There was laughter and Mrs Smith appeared out of the tack room with Mrs Ridgeley close behind.

'I take it those are happy tears, Casey,' Mrs Smith teased. 'Have you said good morning to him yet?'

'I ... No. I thought ... I mean ... Well, I was scared ...'

Mrs Smith smiled. 'I know what you thought. Why don't you put your head over his door and see for yourself how he is?'

Casey hesitated.

'Don't blame you,' said Mrs Ridgeley. 'When I came in at six I fully expected him to have gone to the Great Paddock in the Sky. Almost had a coronary when he moved. Go on, take a look.'

Casey moved towards the stable door on legs as heavy as moon boots. It took a couple of seconds for her eyes to adjust to the dim light of the stable and in that time she heard a hrrmph so soft that she wasn't sure if she'd imagined it. Then she saw him. He was standing in the shadows with his ears pricked and head raised. She had a momentary insight into the magnificent creature he must once have been, then the ghostly image fled and he was once more the starveling she'd rescued. However, he was on his feet and the light had returned to his eyes. He was still very fragile, but he'd taken several paces back from death's door.

His nostrils fluttered again and her heart skipped. He was pleased to see her. The horse who, just hours ago, had wanted to kill anyone who approached him, was pleased to see her.

'Oh, thank you, Mrs Smith! Thank you for saving him,' she cried, afraid to look away from the horse in case he vanished, like a mirage.

Mrs Smith laughed. '*You* saved him, Casey. I can't take any credit. You and Janet's miracle drink. The pony nuts did the rest. Course I virtually had to get down on my knees and beg a handful from this old scrooge here.'

Casey was horrified. In the year and a half she'd been volunteering at the riding school, nobody, let alone a virtual stranger, had ever dared talk to Mrs Ridgeley in such a disrespectful manner.

To her astonishment, Mrs Ridgeley had a twinkle in

her eye as she retorted: 'With an attitude like that, it's no wonder you were always being marked down in the dressage, Angelica.' Seeing Casey's bemused expression, she explained: 'Turns out that your Mrs Smith and I rode in some of the same shows way back when. Never knew each other, but our paths crossed from time to time. Ran into some of the same people, had the misfortune of riding in front of some of the same judges. Do you remember that imbecile Charles Smedley-Wallington? He was a piece of work.'

'Do I ever,' said Mrs Smith. 'Didn't know a piaffe from Edith Piaf.' And they burst into laughter again.

Casey had no idea what they were going on about, but she was startled to learn that her friend had been a dressage competitor. It was the first time she'd ever mentioned it.

'Well, I must be getting on,' said Mrs Ridgeley. 'Can't stand around indulging in idle chatter all day. About what we discussed last night, Casey: I'm prepared to let you keep your horse here on a month-by-month trial basis, on condition that you take sole responsibility for him. *You* groom him, *you* feed him, *you* pay for him. The minute he disrupts my school, costs me money or becomes a problem in any way, you're both out of here. Understood?'

Casey tried to be serious, but her grin stretched from ear to ear. 'Understood.'

'Don't look so pleased with yourself. Yes, you were right about him and I was wrong, but there's no need to be smug about it. You have until three p.m. when

Moth returns with his donkeys to shift about a decade's worth of junk out of the storeroom. I dread to think how many rats and spiders have taken up residence in there.'

'Thanks, Mrs Ridgeley. I owe you.'

'Don't make me regret it,' Mrs Ridgeley cautioned. 'And Casey . . .'

'Yes, Mrs Ridgeley?'

'I'm glad to see that you have someone sensible fighting your corner for a change.' She winked at Mrs Smith. 'Long may it continue. Now don't forget to order me some of your Janet's magic bottles, Angelica. I might start drinking the stuff myself.'

She walked away, chuckling. 'Charlie Smedley-Wallington. What a moron.'

'Good woman,' Mrs Smith mused when they were alone. 'No nonsense. Cuts straight to the chase. I like her.' She unbolted the stable door. 'I'm afraid I haven't yet attempted to put a headcollar on him, Casey, but I think we need to get him used to being handled as soon as possible.'

'Dressage?' Casey said wonderingly. 'Why did you never say anything?'

Mrs Smith handed her the headcollar. 'Nothing to say. I dabbled in it but did nothing worth speaking of. Now, are you going to put this on him, or shall I?'

For some reason, Casey was a thousand times more

nervous than she had been the previous day when the horse was filled with rage and madness and nobody would have blamed her if she'd run screaming in the opposite direction. She approached him tentatively. When he saw the headcollar, his ears flattened and he sidled away with an angry toss of his mane. Butterflies intensifying, she inched closer. He showed the whites of his eyes and made as if to bite her. She tried a third time and he shifted his quarters menacingly towards her.

Casey backed away. She had a flashback to the previous day – the knacker's yard man clutching his smashed leg in agony.

'I've always found that reading helps in these situations,' remarked Mrs Smith. 'Is there a book in the vicinity? Something good and absorbing.'

'Excuse me?' Casey was incredulous that Mrs Smith could think of reading at a time like this.

'A book. Would you be kind enough to find me a novel of some kind?'

If it had been anyone else Casey would have flatly refused, but Mrs Smith had just spent one of the coldest nights of the year not only watching over the horse but, in all probability, saving his life. That entitled her to anything it was in Casey's power to deliver.

She went out to the stable-yard and returned with a dog-eared copy of *Dracula* lent to her by Gillian.

Mrs Smith raised an eyebrow. 'Excellent. Now I suggest that you sit in the corner of his stable and start reading.'

'*Reading?*'

'Pretty soon he'll become inquisitive. He'll cock an ear in your direction and maybe take a step towards you. You do the opposite. If he moves towards you, move away from him. Think of it as a sort of dance. Leave the stable door open so that he doesn't feel boxed in. Now I'm off to have a well-earned cup of tea.'

'But . . .' Words failed Casey.

'One more thing. Don't make direct eye contact with him. Not immediately. Keep your eyes lowered for hours or even days. He's been tormented and abused possibly for years and yesterday he was driven to a slaughterhouse to be killed. It's crucial that we make him feel safe and that you, as his carer, approach him with humility and as a friend.'

Then she was gone and Casey was alone with the horse and the gusting winter wind. At a loss to know what else to do, she sat cross-legged on the stable floor, as far from the horse as possible. She opened the book with an apology to him. 'Sorry about this. I'm sure that after the night you've had and the life you've lived, it's the last thing you want to hear. It'll probably confirm all your worst suspicions about human beings. But it was the only book I could find. To be honest with you, it is pretty gripping. Here, I'll read you a bit . . .'

When Mrs Smith returned, Casey was leaning against the stable door, reading out loud. '*He bowed in a courtly way as he replied, "I am Dracula, and I bid you welcome, Mr Harker, to my house. Come in, the night air is chill, and you must need to eat and rest." '* The horse was not near her but he was facing her, ears pricked. Over the past hour he'd taken several steps in her direction and each time she'd moved away.

'It worked,' Casey said, unable to keep the excitement out of her voice. 'It happened exactly as you predicted. Each time I moved away, his ears would flicker uncertainly for a while and in the end he couldn't help himself. He had to know what I was up to. What do we do now? Should I try again with the headcollar?'

Mrs Smith smiled. 'If you want my advice, no, you shouldn't. Not right now. Leave him wanting more; leave him feeling safe. Go clean the storeroom, as Mrs Ridgeley suggested, and come and see him later. You may have to spend days reading and withdrawing and let him grow ever more confident. Only attempt to put the headcollar on when you're certain he's ready for it. Don't allow anyone to hurry you. If the worst comes to the worst Mr Moth's donkeys will have to sleep in the storeroom for a few nights. I'm sure they'll get over it.'

She reached into her pocket. 'Here's a roll of Polo mints. Why don't you offer them to him as a thank you for work well done.'

The elation Casey felt when, after some hesitation, the horse stretched out his rough, scrawny neck and delicately lipped the sweets from her palm, was huge. It was like winning the lottery.

'Does he have a name?' Mrs Smith asked, coming into the stable.

'Silver Cyclone,' Casey told her. 'But apart from the fact that it doesn't suit him, I feel he should have a new one. His name belonged to his awful past and as far as I'm concerned it should stay there.'

'Quite right. Ridiculous name, Silver Cyclone. You'd probably find that he refused to race on principle. What would you like to replace it with? I'm a big believer in the importance of names. The right name can change a person or an animal's destiny. Give him one that he can be proud of.'

Casey shrugged. 'I've been racking my brains, but I can't think of anything. All the names I've come up with have either been too lame or too fancy.'

'Yesterday, when you were describing him, he sounded to me like a force of nature,' said Mrs Smith. 'I suspect that when he's back to his old self, he will be again.' She reached out a hand and stroked the horse's flank. His ears flattened and he shifted uncomfortably but he didn't move away. 'Let me show you something interesting. I noticed it last night when I was tending to his wound.'

Casey watched as she parted the horse's dull grey-beige hair. Beneath it was a layer of dark silver.

'The thing that struck me,' Mrs Smith went on, 'is that, although his true colour is a more thundery shade of grey than your eyes, it has the same quality about it. As they say on the weather forecast, it's as if a front is moving in.'

Casey grinned. 'Like a storm warning?'

As soon as it was out of her mouth she knew she'd hit on it.

Mrs Smith clapped her hands together. 'That's it exactly.'

So Storm Warning it was, and the instant the words were spoken aloud they became real. It was as if the destiny to which Mrs Smith had referred had moved in and was swirling around the stable, engulfing them and the horse they'd named. The past was obliterated. The future lay before them, unmapped and uncertain.

7

THE SPRING WILDFLOWERS that somehow thrived on the toxic wasteland were in bloom before Casey made any attempt to ride Storm, as he'd become known. For a long time she hadn't even considered it. She'd been too intent on healing him. Physically, it was going well. Nothing was more rewarding than watching the flesh return millimetre by millimetre to his gaunt frame. But the process of gaining his trust had been tortuously slow. For every step forward, they had taken several back.

Casey herself was not the problem. For the past three months, she'd groomed, fed and exercised him in hand in the yard every day before and after school. Not one thing had been a chore. Every minute with him was a pleasure. All her life Casey had yearned to have a horse of her own, without the least expectation that that wish would ever be granted. Now she had a horse who watched her with wary but increasingly kind eyes. A horse whose shabby, almost ugly exterior hid an indomitable spirit. A horse with a mind of his own who needed and depended on her utterly.

This last part was also scary. The hard-earned contents of her piggy bank, along with her tiny Saturday wage from the Tea Garden, had kept Storm in pony nuts and a weekly dose of Janet's vitamin potion, but there was not a penny left over for emergencies. And with a horse like Storm Warning, there was the potential for plenty of those.

Right from the start there'd been worrying incidents. Loud noises sent him into a frenzy. Early on, he'd broken a gate when a police car had screamed up Hope Lane. Casey had been forced to appeal to every staff member and half the clients of the riding school to keep Mrs Ridgeley away from the gate until Roland Blue finished work at 5.30 p.m. and could come and fix it.

Storm's tendency to explode without warning was one thing. Much more concerning was his loathing of people. With the exception of Casey and Mrs Smith, with whom he was quite gentlemanly, he tolerated very few. Gillian and Hermione were wonderful with horses but it was six weeks before Storm would put up with them patting him if they went by, and then only with bad grace. He treated Andrew, who Casey suspected was secretly scared of horses, with an indifference that was almost human. That was as far as his good will extended. The riders of Hopeless Lane knew to give him a wide berth because his ears went back or he snapped at them or showed the whites of his eyes if they approached the door to the storeroom, his new stable.

Once, when Casey was hosing him down, Jin, a sixteen-year-old Chinese girl in her first week of volunteering, made the mistake of looming suddenly out of the darkness and patting him on the rump. He'd kicked her halfway across the stable-block. By sheer chance, his hooves had struck the pocket of her coat, in which she had gloves and a pony magazine. The padding protected her from the worst of the blow, but she'd limped for several weeks afterwards.

Fortunately, Jin, a skinny girl with milk-bottle glasses, braces and a ponytail, was as horse-obsessed as Casey and more inclined to blame herself than Storm, and thus didn't complain to Mrs Ridgeley. But Casey knew it could have been very serious.

When Storm had first arrived his feet had been in a criminally poor state, and he'd refused to let Casey anywhere near them. It was Mrs Smith who'd shown her how to use a feather duster to get him accustomed to having his legs touched. Within days, he was sweetly picking up his feet if Casey so much as ran a fingertip over his fetlocks.

Sadly, when the farrier came to attend to the school horses, Storm behaved like a wild mustang. The man refused to shoe him.

'But surely you must have methods for dealing with difficult horses,' Casey protested.

'Sure I do. I avoid 'em.'

It had taken much pleading and begging for Casey to persuade him to give her instructions from the safety of the door while she clipped and filed Storm's feet herself. Shoeing him was obviously impossible.

None of these things made even the tiniest dent in her feelings for Storm. Within hours of saving him from the knacker's yard, she'd fallen hopelessly, irrevocably and head over heels in love with him. Nothing had happened since to change that. Quite the reverse. The proud spirit that continued to burn in Storm, despite all that had been done to crush him, was the thing she adored most about him.

Her initial thoughts of riding him came not out of a selfish desire, but because Mrs Smith had observed that, cooped up in his stable all day, he needed a lot more exercise than Casey could give him, no matter how many times she trotted him in hand around the school.

'He's like a freshly lit stick of dynamite,' she told Casey. 'If you don't direct that energy into something positive, it'll manifest itself as something negative. He's plenty strong enough to carry you now and it'll give him a boost emotionally if he gets to work through his paces each day.'

Not for the first time Casey wondered how a woman who'd done 'nothing to speak of' in dressage knew so much about how horses think.

'Any advice?' asked Casey as she led Storm to the mounting block one evening. The last client had left for the day and Hopeless Lane was quiet. An apricot sunset showed over the uneven roof of the ramshackle stable-block.

It was the first Saturday of the Easter holidays. Casey's afternoon teas with Mrs Smith had, by mutual agreement, been relocated to the riding school. Once a week they would picnic on a rug in Storm's stable, drinking coffee from a flask, eating shortbread, and sharing sugar cubes with the horse. It gave Casey a chance to show off his progress. What Mrs Smith got out of it, she wasn't sure, except that the older woman rarely looked happier than when she was around horses.

On a couple of occasions they'd been joined by Jin, Casey's volunteer friend. The Chinese girl was a big fan of Storm and one of the few people the horse had come to tolerate. Like Casey, she was intensely shy and said little, but it was plain she doted on Storm. That was more than enough to endear her to Casey. Mrs Smith aside, Jin was the only person she'd have trusted to groom Storm in her absence. She also found it amusing to listen to Jin and Mrs Smith exchange mystical notes on herbs and Zen Buddhism, all discussed in a sort of verbal shorthand.

'Soft hands, calm thoughts,' Mrs Smith told her now.

61

'If he gets hot and bothered, don't add to the adrenalin. Think leisurely walks in whispering pine forests, bubbling brooks, feathers floating to earth.'

Casey gathered the reins. 'Storm, are you listening? No explosions. Only whispering pine forest-type performances allowed.'

Her tone was light-hearted but her palms were sweating. The previous night she hadn't slept at all. She'd had visions of Storm going berserk. Of being smashed to the earth and leaving Hopeless Lane in an ambulance.

Cautiously, she placed her foot in the stirrup. Storm's ears went back and he shifted away, but on the third try she was able to mount without too much of a struggle. As soon as he felt her weight in the saddle, he began to dance and tug at the bit. Unlike Patchwork, he was keen. Eager to be moving. Alive. From his 16.3 hh back, the ground seemed a long way down. Mrs Smith opened the gate and horse and rider proceeded into the school at a respectable pace, as if they'd been doing it all their lives.

'It's paid off,' thought Casey. She'd spent weeks preparing for this moment, first tying a loose bandage around Storm to remind him of the feel of a girth, then attempting a saddlecloth and surcingle. Finally she'd progressed to an old riding school bridle and saddle. 'The time we've spent, the love, the patience: it's all paid off.'

Her nerves subsided and her smile stretched wider and wider.

'Probably best not to go faster than a trot,' cautioned Mrs Smith. 'Test the water.'

But Casey's head was in the clouds. She was sitting on *her* horse. Her very own horse. Nobody could tell her what to do.

That first ride on Storm was unforgettable. It was like being strapped to a rocket launcher. His ears were pricked and his scruffy neck was arched. He was bony and unfit but he carried himself with pride. When they began to trot, he bucked a couple of times and for the first time she had an inkling of the latent power in him. To Casey, who'd had a sum total of ten riding lessons in her life – not counting the odd tip cadged from Gillian, Hermione and Andrew – it was pure bliss to ride a horse that felt charged. That wasn't wooden and resentful like many of the school ponies.

'Moves well,' commented Mrs Smith, 'but he has zero muscle tone. Hardly surprising, but there you go. Lop-sided and lazy. Bit of a belly on him too.'

'*Lazy!*' Casey was insulted on Storm's behalf. 'If I gave him his head he'd be halfway to Victoria Park by now.'

'There's more than one way to be idle,' said Mrs Smith, perching like a cowgirl on the top rail of the paddock fencing. 'He's all on the forehand, quarters forgotten. No doubt he's become accustomed to not thinking and is mentally lazy as well. That's okay. All you want to do for the moment is stretch his legs and get him used to being ridden again.'

But Casey wasn't listening. She wanted to prove that Storm was the opposite of idle. To give in to her own love of speed. Forgetting that he was an ex-racehorse, she gave him a kick.

He leapt forward into a flat-out gallop. They flew around the school, getting faster and faster with every circuit. Mrs Smith and the silhouetted heads of the other horses, framed in their doorways, became a blur. Casey tried thinking: *Soft hands, bubbling brooks, floating feathers*. When that didn't work, she hauled desperately on the reins. Mrs Smith was shouting something, but the wind was whistling in her ears and she couldn't hear a word.

It's hard to know what would have happened had the fire alarm not gone off in Mrs Ridgeley's apartment over the office. Perhaps Casey would have gradually brought Storm back under control and would, over the months, have turned him into a safe, fun horse. They might have spent many happy hours doing flatwork at Hopeless Lane and hopping over the occasional pole. They could have grown old together, a much-loved horse and a rider who meditated on pine forests and mountain streams.

Instead, Casey hit the ground face-first and lay winded and gasping. She had a worm's-eye view of Storm sweeping at breakneck speed towards the section of railings nearest to him – one preceded by an untidy stack of jumping paraphernalia. On the opposite side of the fence was a wide concrete water trough.

'No!' yelled Casey, but no sound came out.

In the purple twilight, Storm was almost black. His long mane flew. Ears pricked, he launched himself into the air, arching high over the railings and trough. Landing easily, he swerved towards the stable-yard.

Mrs Smith came rushing over. 'Casey! Oh, my dear, are you all right?'

Casey climbed dazed to her feet, the vision of Storm's leap still imprinted on her retinas. 'I-I'm fine. In fact, I'm a million times better than fine. Oh, Mrs Smith, did you see Storm fly? Wasn't he amazing? He was like a horse of fire; a horse with wings. A horse like that could take on any jump in the world. A horse like that could win Badminton.'

8

'N O,' SAID MRS Smith. 'N.O. Been there, done that and have no desire to wear the top hat and tails ever again. Ask Penelope Ridgeley or one of the girls. That Gillian seems a pretty capable horsewoman. Besides, what I know about eventing would fit on the back of a postage stamp.'

'But you know about dressage,' persisted Casey. 'Eventing is a sport of three disciplines. If I can't impress the judges in the dressage, it won't matter how good Storm is on the cross-country or show jumping. Anyway, I can't afford lessons from Gillian or Mrs Ridgeley.'

Mrs Smith said teasingly: 'Oh, so you're wanting me to teach you for free?' She began unwrapping the fish and chips they'd bought for their Saturday dinner after deciding that the afternoon's excitement had given them an appetite shortbread alone wouldn't satisfy.

Casey blushed. 'Not for free. I'll give you a share of my winnings.'

'What, in five, six or seven years' time? That's how long it can take to prepare a horse and rider for top-level eventing. Not to mention the cost. And if you're serious about Badminton you have to have the right horse, not just any horse.'

Casey reached past Mrs Smith and stole a salt-and-vinegar-drenched chip. 'Storm *is* the right horse. You know he is.'

'I know he's a horse who's been traumatised in ways we can't begin to imagine. I know that three months ago he was practically feral and that, although you've made remarkable progress handling him, he's an unknown and, judging by today's performance, potentially dangerous quantity as a mount. I also know that horses are flight animals and a lame Shetland pony might clear an army tank if it were trying to escape from something that had frightened it. Storm was only doing what comes naturally.'

'Maybe, but he was brilliant,' Casey said stubbornly. 'If he can jump a metre-and-a-half-high fence when he's unfit, untrained and nowhere near full strength, imagine what he could do if he was well-schooled and fighting fit.'

Mrs Smith handed her a plate with a smile. 'I'll leave the imagining to you, Casey. Now let's say no more about it. How about we watch an old movie with our dinner?'

All of the frustrations of the past year, all of the rejections and the hurt, came brimming to the surface at once. Casey banged her plate down on the counter. 'That's it? No explanation? If you don't want to teach me, fine. I totally respect that. But at least tell me why. You and Dad are always saying that I should follow my dreams and not settle for a life of drudgery in a job I hate, and yet when an opportunity comes along for you to help me do exactly that, you turn your back.'

'Casey, it's not that simple.'

'Why isn't it that simple?' Casey demanded emotionally. 'I thought we were friends. Why is your past with horses such a secret? What's the big mystery? Did you have a bad fall and lose your nerve? Is that it? Did you try to make the grade in dressage, fail and quit and now you're bitter? Or are the fancy ponies and rosettes just some fantasy you've made up to entertain me? Did it never really happen?'

Mrs Smith put her own plate carefully on the counter. Everyone always said that the eyes are the windows of the soul and what Casey loved about her friend's was their inner light and life, a kind of mischievousness. But they were not like that now. They were haunted.

Casey was mortified. Why had she said such hateful things? She'd have done anything to take back her thoughtless words. But the accusation hung in the air, irretrievable. *Did it never really happen?*

'Not in those ways it didn't, no,' Mrs Smith answered quietly. 'You're wrong on every count. It saddens me that you could think that way, but I've kept you in the dark and have only myself to blame. I should never have allowed myself to be drawn into trying to save Storm. It rekindled something in me, stirred up memories I've spent decades trying to forget.'

She took a deep breath. 'But you are right about one thing: I owe you an explanation. It's a long story so before I start I'm afraid I'm going to insist that we eat our lovely supper. I can't abide waste.'

Casey was bursting at the seams with fish and chips and the best homemade apple crumble and custard she'd ever eaten before Mrs Smith would consent to unlock the wooden chest that served as a coffee table. Its contents would, she said, explain everything.

As soon as the first item, a photograph, was removed from the chest, Casey knew that for every answer she'd have six more questions. It showed a young and very beautiful Mrs Smith seated on a magnificent dark bay stallion. She was immaculately turned out in a top hat, tails and white breeches, and was smiling broadly as she reached down to shake the hand of a member of the Royal Family.

Casey gasped. 'You finished second at the European Championships. That's incredible.'

Mrs Smith didn't respond. She was unpacking several large trophies, their silver dull with age. These were followed by a clutch of rosettes and certificates, and a photo album showing her competing on the bay stallion in a variety of arenas before spellbound crowds.

Casey was stunned. 'I don't understand. How could you not have told me about any of this? If I'd achieved what you have, I'd be shouting it from the rooftops.'

Mrs Smith stopped rummaging in the chest and ran a weary, dust-streaked hand across her brow. 'That's because all you can see is the glory. That's because you don't know how the story ends.'

Casey said nothing. She could hardly deny it. In the time they'd been friends, all she'd gleaned about Mrs Smith's history were selective fragments from the beginning and middle. The final chapters had been shrouded with obscure references and sketchy details, many of which Casey had dismissed as owing a great deal to creative licence.

What she did know was that Mrs Smith's mother had died in childbirth and that, like Casey, she'd been brought up by a father she adored. She too had lived, breathed and slept horses. But there the similarity ended.

Unlike Casey, Mrs Smith had been born with the shiniest of silver spoons in her mouth. Her wealthy father had owned a Gloucestershire estate with its own forest. Her childhood had been one of privilege, of skiing holidays, garden parties attended by the great and good, and a stable full of fine ponies. About these horses Mrs Smith had been evasive, only saying that she'd been given far too much, far too young.

'Never a good thing, my dear,' she'd confided.

When she was twenty-five, her father had died and left her his entire estate. It was, it transpired, a poisoned chalice. Behind the glossy façade lay years of foolhardy investments. Debts and death duties forced the immediate sale of both property and horses, with barely enough over for Mrs Smith to buy a modest cottage nearby. It was there she lived until the dashing Robert had swept her off her feet a year later.

Mrs Smith closed the lid of the chest and came to sit beside Casey on the sofa. Her hands were clasped tightly together, as if she were praying. 'What I didn't tell you is that when the estate was sold I kept the nine-year-old dressage horse I'd been training for five years. You've heard the phrase "poetry in motion"? Well, Carefree Boy defined it. He was a Hanoverian stallion and he was, and remains, the love of my life.'

She gave a dry laugh. 'A bit like Storm, he was famously difficult. I first saw him when he was a four-year-old at auction. For no obvious reason, he went crazy and threw the rider who was demonstrating his paces. My father was extremely reluctant to buy such a horse for me, but I was already besotted with him. His untamed spirit appealed to me. And I was very strong-willed in those days—'

'*Those* days?' Casey said meaningfully.

Mrs Smith smiled. 'Okay, I admit it. I still am. At any rate, from the day Carefree Boy arrived, he and I clicked. You could say that we were soul-mates. Throughout his life he was challenging and almost violently unpredictable with strangers and grooms he didn't know, but with me and with my German coach, Nikolaus, the horse whisperer of the dressage world, he was as gentle as a kitten. We were a partnership. Most importantly, we were friends. At dressage championships, we proved a lethal combination. Carefree Boy loved to show off. The larger the crowd, the more he rose to the occasion. Riding him at his best was like riding a creature of myth. I was young and ambitious. I saw no limits to what we could achieve.'

She looked down. 'It was that tunnel vision that brought about my ruin.'

Casey was on the edge of her seat. 'What happened? What went wrong?'

'With all the competing and travelling, I'd left my affairs in the hands of my husband, Robert. There'd been rumours about his gambling, drinking and womanising ways before I married him but I'd chosen to ignore them. By the time I woke up, it was too late. Carefree Boy and I had been selected to compete for Great Britain at the Olympic Games and I was focused on that to the exclusion of all else.'

'You ...? You were in ...? Wow! WOW!' Casey stared at her friend in open-mouthed admiration.

'I didn't say I took part in the Olympics, I said I was invited to. There's a big difference.'

'But ...'

There was a pause and when Mrs Smith spoke again there was a catch in her voice. 'A month before the British equestrian team was due to leave for the Games, Robert came to me with a confession.

72

Unbeknownst to me, he'd put up both the cottage and Carefree Boy as collateral for his gambling debts. He'd risked everything on one last throw of the dice. And lost. I'd given him power of attorney over my finances so that he could handle my business interests while I was away. There was not a thing I could do.'

Casey was aghast. 'Carefree Boy was snatched away from you?'

'On one memorably awful day, I lost my home, the horse I loved more than anything on earth, and my dream of going to the Olympics. I lost my husband, too, but that was just as well. If he hadn't gone to ground, I might have shot him. To crown it all, Carefree Boy was sold to my arch rival, a man with a reputation for using brutal methods to achieve his aims with horses.'

'Was there no way you could persuade him to sell your horse back to you?'

'Believe me, I tried everything. Unfortunately, Robert had virtually bankrupted me. Nikolaus offered to loan me the money but this man refused to part with Carefree Boy for any sum. He was well aware of the stallion's potential for greatness. Unfortunately, his grooms were not so astute. A month after Carefree Boy moved to their yard, he contracted colic. He died in agony.

'For a time, I felt that life was not worth living. Oh, there were lots of kindnesses. Loyal sponsors stuck by me; well-intentioned friends lined up to offer me places in other yards or wonderful horses to ride. But for me it was over. I walked away from the only world I knew with nothing but a suitcase. My mother had been born in the East End of London so I chose to come here. Back then, it was dirt cheap and anonymous, which suited me fine.'

She rubbed the cheek of the ginger cat dozing on the back of the sofa. 'Plus it turned out that there were plenty of strays in need of rescue.'

Tears were pouring down Casey's cheeks. She wiped them away with her sleeve. Mrs Smith handed her a tissue.

After a while, Casey said: 'So Storm is the first horse you've been close to in more than thirty years?'

Mrs Smith glanced sideways at her. 'I like my life, Casey. I enjoy visiting Storm and having tea with you on a Saturday afternoon, but my equestrian days are over. I came to terms with that decades ago.'

Casey took her hand. 'But they don't have to be. You, me and Storm, we could do something amazing together.'

Mrs Smith pulled away. 'No, Casey, we can't. Surely you can understand why.'

Casey gazed at the photographs, rosettes and trophies still scattered on the threadbare living room carpet. The sight of Carefree Boy brought fresh tears to her eyes. 'Yes. I can. If someone stole Storm from me I'd feel exactly the same way. I'm sorry that by asking you to teach me I brought back so many painful memories for you. I give you my word that I'll never ask again.'

It was close to 10 p.m. when Mrs Smith walked with Casey to Redwing Tower. Casey had tried to dissuade her, but Mrs Smith had insisted she needed both the air and the exercise. The Saturday night streets thronged with hyperactive clubbers, downcast weekend workers and the type of men who wear sunglasses at night. Chest-thumping bass issued from the windows of impatient cars. Drivers leaned on horns.

Casey saw none of it. She was talking animatedly about her father. 'I think he's discovered his true vocation, I really do. I've never seen him so happy. He's tried a lot of jobs and had a zillion business plans over the years, but mostly they haven't worked out. Some have been plain disastrous. But the Half Moon Tailor Shop is different. He practically skips out of the door on a Monday, he's so keen to get there.'

Mrs Smith laughed. 'He likes his boss?'

'Are you kidding? It's as if they've been best buddies all their lives. Dad says Ravi Singh is the most decent man he's ever known, and Ravi thinks Dad is a real find. He believes he has a natural gift for sewing and design. He told Dad—'

She stopped so suddenly that Mrs Smith ran into her. They were passing the Gunpowder Plot pub, one and a half blocks from Redwing Tower.

'What is it? You look as if you've seen a ghost.'

'I, umm . . .' Casey struggled to control her emotions. 'Sorry, what were you saying?'

'Casey, what just happened?'

'Nothing. Nothing happened. I'm tired, that's all. I think I'd like to walk home alone from here if that's okay. Thanks again for this evening.'

'Not so fast.' Mrs Smith grabbed her arm and all but marched her back to the window of the pub. 'You glanced in and saw something you didn't like. Now what was it?'

She squinted into the dimly lit interior. 'Your father! What's he doing here? I thought the Tin Drum was his usual Saturday night haunt? And who are those men? I wouldn't want to meet that tall, bald one in a dark alley.'

'It doesn't matter.' Casey tugged free of Mrs Smith's grasp. 'Goodbye and goodnight.'

Mrs Smith rushed to catch up with her. 'Clearly it does matter. The men he's with, I take it they're associates – friends – of whom you don't approve?'

Casey nodded miserably. It was no use trying to hide anything from Mrs Smith. She had X-ray vision where thoughts were concerned.

'They're the so-called mates he took the rap for,' she burst out. 'They're the reason he went to prison. They sat in court and let him go down without saying a word to stop it. I saw them laughing in the car park afterwards.'

'If it's any consolation, he didn't look as if he wanted

to talk to them. He was shaking his head and his body language was defensive.'

But Casey was beyond caring. They'd reached the steps of Redwing Tower. All she wanted to do was creep up to No. 414, crawl into bed and put her head under the covers.

'Don't worry about it. It's not important. I may as well get used to the fact that I'll never escape my destiny. Places like Redwing, they're like superglue. We're stuck here. There's a boomerang effect. People – Dad, for instance – try to get away, but it keeps dragging them back. The most I can hope for is that Mrs Ridgeley will take me on as an assistant instructor next year and allow Storm to stay at Hopeless Lane. But that all depends on whether or not Dad stays out of jail. Don't get me wrong. I'm not feeling sorry for myself. I'm being realistic. Going to Badminton was a pathetic dream, anyway. As if a teenager who can barely ride could compete in a three day event on a one-dollar horse from a knacker's—'

'Stop!' cried Mrs Smith. 'Just stop. I can't bear to hear you talking like this. You're better than that and so is Storm. All right, I'll teach you, but you'll have to accept that becoming a champion eventer could take at least five years and that's only if Storm stays sound and proves physically and temperamentally suitable.'

Casey stared at her, scared to hope she might be serious. 'I don't have five years. I have two at most. If I haven't made it as a professional rider by the time I turn eighteen, I'll have to get a proper job. *Any* job.'

'Impossible. Only a couple of riders in history have done it and they've had every conceivable advantage.' Mrs Smith gestured towards Redwing Tower, its prison-grey façade, peeling burglar bars and banks of CCTV cameras, forbidding in the moonlight. 'And, as you pointed out, you have none.'

Casey's jaw was set in determination. 'I *can* do it if you coach me. I *can* do it if you help me train Storm to be as good as Carefree Boy.'

A gang of giggling girls spilled from the foyer. Cigarette smoke hung like dragon's breath in their wake.

Mrs Smith didn't notice them. She was too busy thinking: 'Angelica, you're certifiable. You were done with this madness years ago. Walk away now. Walk away while you still can.'

Infuriatingly, her feet refused to cooperate. She heard herself say: 'I'll teach you on one condition. That you do what I say and don't – within reason – question it.'

Casey squealed and hugged her. 'I promise faithfully. Oh, thank you, Mrs Smith. Thank you, thank you, thank you.'

Mrs Smith extricated herself and straightened her clothes. She felt strangely exhilarated. It was done and there was no turning back. At sixty-two she was entering the second phase of her equestrian life. 'What time does the first client arrive at Hopeless Lane on a Sunday?'

'Around nine.'

'Right, I'll see you there at five a.m.'

'Five a.m.? On a *Sunday*?'

'What did I say?'

Casey grinned. 'Just testing. Five a.m. it is.'

9

'I'M DISAPPOINTED IN you, Angelica, I refuse to pretend I'm not,' said Mrs Ridgeley, her stocky frame bristling with indignation. 'I was counting on you to be a restraining influence on that girl, but I fear you've made her a thousand times worse. Please tell me it's nothing more than a rumour designed to provoke me that you and she are planning to enter that flighty animal in the Brigstock International Horse Trials in two months' time?'

'Indeed we are,' responded Mrs Smith. She was reclining in an ancient faux leather armchair in the sunshine, sipping jasmine tea. The springs were broken and the seat sagged so close to the ground that she was barely visible. 'Casey and Storm Warning will be competing as novices. It'll be Storm's first event, so our expectations are on the low side, but I'm sure they'll do very well.'

'And how are the three of you planning to get all the way to Northamptonshire? Take a train?' Mrs Ridgeley's voice rose to a sudden roar: 'MANDY PHILPOTT! HOW MANY TIMES HAVE I TOLD YOU THAT YOU ARE BANNED FROM ENTERING MY STABLE-YARD WITHOUT A HAT!'

Mrs Smith removed her hands from her ears. 'Arthur Moth. Arthur has kindly agreed to drive us to Northamptonshire in his donkey van. We'll give him the petrol money, of course.'

'Well, I suggest you take out some very good public liability insurance before you go. That beast is enough of a menace around the yard. Goodness knows what he'll be like at a show. You'll be sued for everything you possess by the daddy of some rich kid he's kicked to bits.'

The subject of their conversation crossed their field of vision. Casey was on her way to give Storm his second walking session of the day.

Mrs Ridgeley scowled her disapproval. 'Where exactly are you going with all of this, Angelica?'

'I'm giving a girl who doesn't have a whole lot of light in her life a reason to smile. Isn't that something of a speciality here at Hopele— at Hope Lane?'

'Yes, but we don't deal in false hope.'

Mrs Smith's smile was enigmatic. 'Neither do I, Penelope. Neither do I.'

Casey did not share her confidence. Two weeks into their preparation for the Brigstock event, she was already beginning to question Mrs Smith's judgement.

For the past fortnight she and Storm had done nothing but walk. Mrs Smith had them on a strict schedule. At 6 a.m., after Storm had been groomed and fed, Casey walked him in hand for forty-five minutes. Next, he returned to his stable for two hours to relax and eat hay while Casey did thirty minutes of balance, stretch and strengthening exercises in the office at Hopeless Lane (under Mrs Smith's tutelage) with a Swiss ball and five-kilogram dumbbells they'd picked up at a charity shop. Every second day, she had to jog several times around the block.

'A fit horse needs a fit rider,' Mrs Smith told Casey when she protested.

After a breakfast of instant oats and mashed bananas, another innovation of her new coach, Casey rode Storm no faster than a walk for another three-quarters of an hour. She then turned him out in the small field behind the stables. In the evening, when the last client had left, she led Storm briskly around the school for a final forty-five minutes. The most exciting thing that happened during these sessions was the occasional halt.

Casey could not deny that Storm was significantly less explosive, but other than that she could not see the point. Days were going by with no gain except pain – her own. Her muscles screamed at the slightest movement. At Brigstock she and Storm would be expected to do a dressage test, showjump and complete a small but tough cross-country course. With under six weeks to go, neither of them was remotely equipped to do any of those things, as Andrew took great delight in pointing out to her.

'Hey Case, you do know it's the horse that's supposed to gallop the cross-country course, not the rider?' he mocked one morning when he came across Casey nursing a stitch after her pre-breakfast run.

'Watch and learn,' Casey panted loyally. 'We know what we're doing. Mrs Smith is an expert.'

He pushed his greasy brown fringe out of his eyes. 'Yes, but what is she an expert on? Knitting socks? Meals on wheels? On current form, Storm makes Patchwork look like Seabiscuit.'

'Hadn't you better check on Hermione?' said Casey. 'I saw her talking to that cute Lithuanian boy who—'

He was gone before she could finish the sentence.

But by the end of the next week, Casey was beginning to have more than a few doubts herself.

'Why the long face?' Mrs Smith asked that evening, following her into Storm's stable after his third walk of the day and thinking, for the thousandth time, that there was no finer perfume in all the world than horse sweat, leather and hay.

Casey forced a smile. She took off Storm's bridle. 'No

long face. I'm good. Storm's good. It's all good.'

'I'm relieved to hear it,' Mrs Smith said cheerfully. 'Because it occurred to me you might be thinking that all this walking is a waste of time, just as it occurred to me that you might already have forgotten our goal.'

Stung, Casey retorted: 'You're the one who's forgotten our goal, not me. Our goal was to produce a horse that can do fancy dressage moves and clear a cross-country course against the clock. Our goal is the Brigstock International Horse Trials. In case it's slipped your memory, that takes place in hardly any time at all.'

Mrs Smith offered Storm a couple of mints. He lowered his head and allowed her to rub his ears. 'Oh. My mistake. I thought we were aiming for Badminton in two years time. Far more importantly, I thought your goal was to build a relationship with Storm in which his happiness is paramount. One in which you strive at all costs to avoid repeating the traumas of his past. One in which he is a partner and a friend, not merely a slave to your ambitions.'

'It is . . . I, uh . . .'

'If you ever decide you want to ride for the right reasons, get in touch with me. Until then, I'm terminating our agreement.'

Casey found Mrs Smith in the armchair in the darkened stable-yard, star-gazing. It was a cold, clear night and it was possible to see Orion's Belt, a sliver of moon and a dusting of Milky Way.

She put a mug of hot chocolate on the arm of the chair as a peace offering. Flopping down on the grass nearby, she hugged her knees awkwardly. 'Thank you,' she said.

Mrs Smith continued to look skyward. 'What are you thanking me for?'

'Oh, for nipping my egomania in the bud before it could really get going.'

'I wouldn't go that far.'

'I would. We're at the beginning of a journey that might take years and the first thing I've done is forget that you, Storm and Dad are more important to me than any trophy. It's scary. Is that how quickly it happens?'

A smile played around Mrs Smith's lips, but she kept her eyes on the stars. 'It is. Only most people take longer to realise it. Most never do.'

'I'm sorry. I was panicking; that's all I can say. There's so much to learn and so little time. '

'Yes, but think about this. A castle without foundations is as unstable as a shack. Rushing leads to injuries, falls, or problems of behaviour, muscle development and carriage that will come back to haunt you later on. If it's speed that you're after, slow down. The value of the simple walk in relaxing a horse and laying the foundations for power and greatness can never be underestimated.'

Casey was doubtful but she rested her chin on her knees. 'Go on.'

Mrs Smith took a sip of hot chocolate. 'That's a lesson you've yet to learn. You've been walking Storm for two weeks and you haven't done it right once.'

'You think I'm such a bad rider that I can't even manage a walk?'

'On the contrary, I think you're such a good rider, such an intuitive rider, that in years to come you'll understand that riding is an art form that takes a lifetime to master.'

She held up a hand as Casey opened her mouth to protest. 'Before you remind me that you don't have a lifetime, you only have a couple of years, let me say this: you're not going to win Badminton by having the fastest horse, the boldest jumper or because you can execute a flying change better than anyone else, although all of those things help. You're going to win it because you have a sound horse with good technique who'll try his heart out for you. A horse who trusts you with his life and who you trust with yours.'

She put her mug on the ground. 'Because that's what it boils down to, you know. Life and death. Love and courage. If you make it to Badminton, you'll be competing against the best riders on earth in one of the world's most high-risk arenas. The qualities you'll need to survive it can't be hurried. They have to be earned. Patience is the key. The best trainers know you have to be brave enough to stop, consider and go back to the beginning if necessary.'

Casey sighed. 'In other words, the faster I want to achieve my goals, the more I need to do the opposite.'

Mrs Smith put her hands behind her head and looked up at the stars again. They were alone in the darkness with only the shadows of the horses for company. 'The Chinese call it *Wu Wei*: effortless action. Followers of the *Tao – The Way*, a beautiful book of ancient wisdom – believe that what you don't do is as important as what you do. That what makes a piece of music exquisite is not the notes but the silence in between.

'The *Tao* teaches that while you can conquer others with power, it takes true strength to conquer yourself. It says: "Yield and be strong; bend and be straight."'

'I like that,' murmured Casey. 'Yield and be strong; bend and be straight.' She suddenly looked crestfallen. 'But who is going to teach me how to apply these things to riding?'

'Oh, I expect that if you hunt around the stable-yard, you'll find a crotchety old woman who might be persuaded to tell you what she knows, for what it's worth.'

'It's worth a lot. So can she?'

'Can she what?'

'Be persuaded.'

Mrs Smith laughed. She stood up and reached out a hand to Casey. 'Try stopping her. Oh, and Casey, I need you here half an hour early tomorrow morning because we'll be starting interval training and fast work. Trot for a minute, walk for a minute, trot for a minute, walk for a minute. In a week we'll move on to a canter and later to sprints. With a little jumping and "fancy dressage moves", as you call them, in between.'

'What happened to the value of the simple walk?'

'No point in going overboard.'

10

IN THE FINAL few hours of the journey to Northamptonshire Casey became increasingly queasy, and not just because of the fumes in Arthur Moth's donkey van. The night before she hadn't slept a wink. In the end she'd put the light on and tried to read but her eyes kept drifting to the magazine cuttings and posters on her bedroom wall. Most were of famous eventers. There were icons of the sport such as Mark Todd, Lucinda Green and Pippa Funnell, an idol of Casey's because she'd achieved the miraculous and won the Grand Slam, but Casey's heroine was a girl little more than a year older than herself and already tipped for global superstardom.

At sixteen and a half, Anna Sparks had won every event possible for her age group and she'd done it with style. The equestrian press was besotted with her. Journalists described her as the 'incredible Anna Sparks' or the 'hottest property in eventing', and used a lot of electrical metaphors to describe how she'd 'lit up' this event or 'caused sparks to fly' at that one with her 'dazzling performance on Rough Diamond'.

Anna was also blessed with film-star looks. Her heart-shaped face, long, pale gold hair and white smile appeared regularly on the covers of these magazines, as did her most famous horse, who was not a rough diamond at all, but a chestnut with a mile-long pedigree and a coat like a living flame. He seemed to glow from within, as if illuminated by Anna's electricity.

Casey had spent hours poring over Anna's eventing tips in magazines and, under normal circumstances, found her achievements inspiring. But as the night wore on she became painfully conscious of the Grand Canyon-sized void that lay between the world that riders like Anna inhabited and her own. And it wasn't just about money. Anna had at least ten years of experience in her favour. She'd been competing almost since she could walk.

Dawn dragged its heels. With the coming of morning, Casey's fears melted away and she was overcome with excitement at the prospect of competing in her first event. She ran into her father's room and bounced on his bed until he woke up, laughing and yawning.

'I'm guessing that this is my alarm call to cook you a champion's breakfast? What'll it be? Scrambled eggs and smoked salmon?'

'Sounds good,' Casey said with a grin. 'Will anything be missing?'

'Only the smoked salmon.'

'Fabulous. Can I order one of those, please?'

When Casey emerged from the shower in jeans and a sweatshirt, her scrambled eggs were ready. On the table beside the rack of toast was a brown paper package tied with a pink ribbon, a lunchbox filled with cheese and chutney sandwiches, and a tin containing a cake Roland Blue had baked in secret the day before.

'With real chocolate icing! The only thing missing is the baking powder. Oh, and the hundreds and thousands, but you can't have everything.'

Casey giggled and held up the package. 'It's not my birthday.'

He squeezed her shoulders. 'No, but it's a special occasion and I can't be with you so this is my way of being there in spirit. Ravi Singh gave me the idea. And the material, bless him.'

Casey untied the ribbon and gasped. Inside the paper were riding gloves made from leather so soft they felt like silk. She slipped them on. They fitted perfectly. They were the first she'd ever owned.

'Handmade by your old father,' Roland Blue said proudly. 'Ravi found the pattern for me but I cut them out and sewed every stitch.'

Casey was so moved she could hardly speak. Ever since she'd seen him with his thieving ex-friends at the Gunpowder Plot pub – a meeting he'd never mentioned – she'd been cool to him, had doubted him, when all the time he'd been working to do something amazing for her. 'Dad, I ...'

She stopped, choked up. She felt shame, relief and a wave of love for him all at once. Finally she managed: 'You're the best, Dad. The absolute best.'

He looked pleased enough to burst, but all he said was: 'It's nothing. Wait till you see the Badminton jacket I'm going to make for you when you qualify. Now, you'd better get going. It's seven a.m. Take care, Pumpkin. Here's some cash. It's not very much, I'm afraid, but it'll help towards fuel for Moth's van. Keep me posted by text.'

Casey had left the tower block suspended somewhere between happy anticipation and terror, and that was how she'd remained right up until Moth, as Arthur was nicknamed, pulled into a motorway service station shortly after lunch. While he was filling up, Mrs Smith bought a paper. In it they'd found a tiny story about the Brigstock International Horse Trials, announcing that 'celebrated young star' Anna Sparks would be competing on Rough Diamond.

The insecurities of the night came flooding back. Casey was again reminded that she was nothing and nobody and should not be attempting even a novice event on a one dollar horse. Mrs Smith, who knew her young pupil almost better than she knew herself, had immediately devised a series of silly competitions to get her and Moth laughing. It worked. By mid-afternoon they were pottering through postcard-pretty villages of thatched cottages adorned with climbing roses, and Casey was smiling again.

As they joined the column of cars and horseboxes heading into Fermyn Park, Casey wriggled through the back window of the van into the adjoining box to reassure Storm for the hundredth time. His ears were flicking back and forth like radio antennae. Bonnie, the donkey Moth had brought along to help ease Storm's nerves, chewed placidly, eyes half closed.

Storm's dark eyes locked on Casey's. There was anxiety in them but there was also the trust that shone there more brightly with every passing day. Throughout the journey, he'd looked to her as if she were a port in a tempest.

She put her arms around his neck and rested her young cheek against his rough one. 'This is going to be pretty nerve-racking for both of us, but hopefully it'll be lots of fun too. There'll be some proper jumps for you to fly over. Mrs Smith says that as long as we do our best, nothing else matters. And it doesn't. Even if we come last, you'll still be the most wonderful thing that ever happened to me. I'll still love you.'

The van rattled over a field and clanked to a stop. Mrs Smith tapped on the window. 'We've arrived.'

Peter Rhys, the seventeen-year-old son of a third-generation farrier, was bending over Rough Diamond's left front foot when, for no apparent reason, a cool tremor went through him, making the fine black hairs stand up on the back of his neck and goosebumps rise on his brown forearms. It wasn't so much a goose-across-your-grave feeling as like being splashed by a deliciously cold wave on a baking summer's day.

The feeling was so intense that he lowered the horse's leg carefully and scanned the buzzing lorry park to see what could have brought it on.

Initially, he saw nothing out of the ordinary. The Brigstock Horse Trials were open to everyone from novices to two-star qualifiers and the lorry park teemed with horses and riders of every stripe. Peter himself was a gifted horseman. Much to his father's frustration he'd never had the slightest interest in competing, but what he liked most about eventing was that it levelled people. Men and women, princesses, pilots and policemen, all were equals when it came to a ditching at the water jump.

The rigorous qualifying process also meant that giants of the sport were routinely pitted against amateurs as they sought to give their young horses experience and move them up the ranks.

Consequently, the lorry park, set amid idyllic rolling parkland, was crammed with horseboxes of varying degrees of smartness. The flashy ones belonging to the top riders were, in effect, horse hotels. These 'wagons' were so vast they could transport six horses in comfort, as well as provide luxury accommodation and bathroom facilities for their riders. They were plastered in vibrantly coloured sponsors' logos.

One had its side pulled open, revealing a compact living room with a flat-screen TV. Johnny Cash's 'Folsom Prison Blues' was playing louder than it should have been on the sound system. Beneath a canopy, three or four well-known riders were grilling burgers on a barbecue.

Grooms buzzed around these wagons like honeybees, hosing down showy, athletic horses or tacking them up in saddles, bridles and white numnahs worth more than Peter's annual wage. The amateur riders were almost as well turned out. Their horses and horseboxes may have been more modest, but their body language exuded confidence. They chattered excitedly in groups or trotted about on equally confident, fashionably clipped horses.

Having seen nothing that might explain the feeling that had rippled through him like a premonition, Peter was reaching for the horse's foot again when he noticed the girl. She was walking across the lorry park in his direction. She stood out, although it was not immediately apparent why. Her dark brown hair was windswept and tangled and her clothes did her no favours: cheap faded jeans with a rip in one knee and a sweatshirt at least a size too small.

And yet there was something about her that caught the eye and held it. Perhaps it was the curious mix of awkwardness and pride with which she carried her slender but gawky frame. Or the way that she gazed about her with a childlike wonder.

Suddenly aware that he was staring, Peter busied

himself with the horse. Rough Diamond had been shod by his father only ten days ago, but the Sparks' stable manager liked the horse to be double- or triple-checked before a show.

'Excuse me. I don't mean to bother you, but is that Rough Diamond?'

Peter knew from the way the hairs stood up on the back of his neck again that it was her. He took his time turning round because he didn't want to break the spell that had stolen over him as he'd watched her approach, and also because he was weirded out that such a plain, almost nondescript girl, seen from a distance, had caused his heart to pound as if he'd just sprinted the Olympic one hundred metres.

Then he glanced up and met a pair of serious grey eyes, the colour of which put him in mind of a squall at sea. They contrasted oddly but somehow fittingly with the striking innocence of her flushed, determined face and the shyness with which she pushed her brown fringe out of her eyes. He knew then that whatever she was, it wasn't ordinary.

Before he could respond, she'd answered her own question. 'Of course it is. He's a horse in a million. I've seen him in magazines and on TV, but those things don't do him justice. He's magnificent, isn't he?'

'Do you think so?' Peter said noncommittally. He had his own opinion on the horse, but wasn't about to share it.

'Would it be okay if I touched him?'

He smiled. 'Go ahead. I'm Peter, by the way.' He thrust out a hand.

She gripped it firmly but distractedly. 'Casey Blue.' Much to his relief, she didn't seem to notice his consternation. Her whole focus was on the horse. And who could blame her? In the afternoon sun, his coat shone like polished copper. The miniature diamond that had given him his name glowed on his brow like a star.

What Peter wanted more than anything was for Casey to go. Just vanish. The brief contact of their fingers had sent the blood fizzing through his veins and reduced his legs to ectoplasm. He worried they might give way beneath him. But what he wanted even more than her immediate and complete disappearance was for her to look at him, *really* look at him. Unfortunately, she was fixated on the horse.

Her brow creased. She was studying Rough Diamond's head and Peter knew, without knowing how he knew, that she'd reached the same conclusion he had. That the horse wasn't happy. That he was like an outwardly adored and indulged child who, behind closed doors, is stressed and depressed.

She frowned again. 'Do you think he ... ? I mean, it sounds odd, but he has the air of a horse with the weight of the world on his shoulders.'

Peter stared at her in surprise. She'd voiced his thoughts exactly. He was mustering a response when the volume in the field rose by several decibels. A bubble of autograph hunters bowled noisily across the lorry park, parting at last to reveal Anna Sparks and a sinewy groom with a hard, angular face.

After one final wave to her fans, Anna marched up to Peter. 'Are you done yet, or are you too busy chatting up girls?' She cast a black look at Casey.

The Sparks' horses were a big part of his father's business and Peter was accustomed to Anna treating him like the hired help. However, Casey, whose face had lit up at the sight of Anna, was not. She stammered: 'I'm so sorry. Please don't blame Peter. It's my fault. It's been my dream for years to meet you and to see Rough Diamond in real life. You're my heroes, you see.'

The effect was instantaneous. The pout was erased from Anna's face and replaced with a hundred-watt smile. If anything, she was more stunning in the flesh. The two dimensions of television did not convey the delicate rose of her skin and almost eerie perfection of her form. Over the years Peter had witnessed a number of people literally swoon at the sight of her. Casey didn't do that but she was obviously captivated.

'No problem, kid,' said Anna, as though Casey were half her age, when Peter doubted there was more than a year between them. 'Diamond and I, we like to make our fans happy. Do we meet your expectations?'

Halfway down the lorry park, a vehicle started with a grating roar. Peter saw Casey glance in its direction. Panic flashed across her face. 'I-I, yes, of course. It's amazing to meet you, Anna. And Rough Diamond. Thanks. Well, I'd better be going.'

'Anna, darling, wait till you see this!' A pretty, voluptuous redhead came rushing over in wildly impractical shoes. 'Edward's groom, Ricardo, has just told me that this motley crew has driven up from darkest Hackney in a donkey van, of all things.' She let out a peal of laughter. 'There it is now. Would you look at it? There's more rust on it than paint. Apparently the rider, this girl who's only been taking lessons for about five minutes, has brought her granny along as her coach. Ricardo says the horse has to be seen to be believed.'

The van trundled ponderously across the rutted field and groaned to a halt nearby, engulfing them in a pall of blue smoke.

Peter glanced at Casey. She was as motionless as a statue but she seemed to have shrunk, like a flower closing up to protect itself.

The doors of the van opened and out hopped a small, fit man with bristly grey hair, followed by an elegant woman in her late fifties or early sixties wearing khaki trousers and a loose, flowing shirt with an Indian print.

'You cannot be serious, V?' Anna said. 'Tell me that's not the coach! She looks as if she got lost on her way to the Taj Mahal.'

'It is! It is!' Vanessa squealed delightedly. 'Maybe she's hard of hearing and thought they did cross-stitch at Brigstock, not cross-country.'

They burst into laughter, only pausing when the van's ramp was lowered. Out came a chocolate-coloured donkey, followed by a grey-beige horse draped in an old tartan bed blanket, onto which someone had sewn a couple of green canvas straps. There were chunks of fur missing from the horse's quarters, revealing streaks of dark silver, almost as if someone had been practising with the clippers when they'd broken.

'It'll be the satnav's fault,' Anna said between giggles. 'Instead of leading them to the knackered old mule and donkey sale at the local county fair, they've ended up here. Someone should do them a kindness and tell them they're in the wrong place.'

Peter felt ill. He had an almost overwhelming urge to put his arms around Casey and protect her from the barbs of the vain, thoughtless girls. But before he could speak or move, the donkey van man caught sight of her.

'Hey, Case, give us a hand, will you?' he called. 'Did you find out Storm's stable number?'

Anna's laughter spluttered out. She had the grace to look embarrassed. 'OMG, you're with them, aren't you, kid? Sorry about that. We were only joking, V and I. You're not going to get upset, are you? Where's your sense of humour?'

At that, Casey came to life. Her gaze swung on Anna with the intensity of a lighthouse beam and her voice was calm and clear. 'Yes, I am with them. That's my friend, Moth and his donkey, Bonnie; the "Taj Mahal" lady is my coach, Mrs Smith; and the "knackered old mule" is my horse, Storm Warning. I'm every bit as proud of him as I'm sure you are of Rough Diamond, although I suspect I love him a whole lot more. We might seem like nothing to you right now, but that's going to change and when it does, we'll meet you at Badminton and the best rider will win. Good luck tomorrow.'

And with that she walked away, her stride long and proud.

'Good luck,' Anna called after her.

'You'll need it,' cried Vanessa, and she started giggling again. She prodded Anna with a manicured nail. 'Badminton! As if! What a fruitcake.'

'A class A nut,' agreed Anna. 'What a freak.'

Peter had another overwhelming urge – this time to shove their faces in a pile of steaming horse manure.

'What?' demanded Anna, seeing his expression. '*What?*'

'Would it kill you to be kind occasionally? You know, just once.'

She rolled her eyes. Snatching Rough Diamond's lead rope from him and tossing it to the groom, she snapped: 'Don't be a bore, Peter. Oh, I forgot, you can't help it.'

11

THE ENCOUNTER WITH Anna Sparks had a galvanising effect on Casey. Minutes before it happened, she'd been walking through the lorry park feeling as if she were an equestrian Cinderella. Part of her was enraptured because it was a dream come true to be at a real event with riders she'd only read about and real cross-country jumps. The other part became more convinced with every step that she didn't belong in this elite, monied world.

But when the girl Casey had put on a pedestal belittled her, sneering at her horse and her friends, the truth of Mrs Smith's counsel came home to her. What mattered in eventing and in life were the real things – love, courage, patience and building a relationship of mutual trust and respect with your horse. Everything else was superficial. Everything else was window dressing.

She'd said nothing to Mrs Smith about Anna's cutting remarks, but her friend had watched the exchange from a distance and drawn her own conclusions. Neither of them spoke about it until Storm was safely settled in the block of temporary stables – smart wooden ones with a marquee roof.

As Casey bolted the door, Mrs Smith remarked: 'That Rough Diamond, he's a good-looking horse.'

Casey pretended an interest in the label on a sack of feed. 'Yes, he is.'

'It's important to remember that those kind of horses, well, they're the notes in the music. The obvious things. They're all flash and dash. Horses like Storm Warning, they're the silence. They're the space in between that makes the music exquisite. Same goes for their riders.'

That simple thought gave Casey's spirits a boost. Laughing, she swung to go, slamming into the farrier's son. For an instant she was pressed against him and she had the sudden thought that it was the closest she'd ever been to a boy. She took a hurried step back, flushing.

'Can I help you?' she demanded, extreme shyness making her more abrupt than she meant to be.

He gave her a smile that would have charmed a bird out of a tree, but which for some reason annoyed her. 'Hi Casey. Umm, I hope you don't mind but I've come to ask a favour. I noticed earlier that your horse has a loose shoe . . .'

Casey spun to look at Storm and was appalled to see

that Peter was right. It must have happened on the journey. She'd been too worked up about Anna Sparks to notice it when she was grooming him, and Mrs Smith, who was usually very observant about such matters, had been rushing about since they arrived, familiarising herself with times, places and rules.

What made it worse was that Mrs Smith had been pestering her to get Storm reshod before they came, but Casey, desperately trying to save money, had insisted that the shoes the Hopeless Lane farrier had finally managed to put on Storm five weeks earlier – which they both knew were substandard – would do perfectly well for at least another fortnight.

For Peter to have been witness to Anna Sparks' mockery and now this was a humiliation too far. Casey was unable to keep the scowl off her face when she turned to him.

'Is there anything else that you'd like to criticise while you're at it? His tack? His condition?'

'Not at all. I was only wondering if you'd do me the favour of allowing me to shoe him for you? I'm an apprentice, you see.' He grinned. 'Scouting for future clients. I need all the experience I can get.'

Casey saw through the request at once. There was not a chance in the world that he'd have been working on Anna Sparks' horse unless he was very accomplished at what he did. He was only here because he felt sorry for her and if there was one thing she didn't need it was some boy with melty, dark eyes, black bed-head hair and unhurried, languorous movements, pitying her. 'Thanks, but we don't need charity.'

'On the contrary, we need all the charity we can get,' Mrs Smith interrupted. She smiled warmly and extended a hand. 'I'm Angelica Smith, and you are . . . ?'

'Apologies, ma'am. I'm Peter Rhys, the farrier's son.'

'Welsh, I take it?'

'Yes, ma'am. Born and bred on my grandfather's farm in Monmouthshire, near Hay-on-Wye.'

'Breathtaking spot. God's own country is how I think of it. Right, speaking for Casey and myself, we'd love you to tend to Storm's feet. I've been worrying for weeks about how we were going to fix studs in the current ones. I know there's a risk of tenderness but it's worth taking the chance. I'd like you to redo all four shoes if you'd be so kind.'

Casey stared at her in disbelief. 'Don't I get a say?'

'Yes and no. Yes, because he's your horse, but bear in mind the going will be very soft in places tomorrow and I'm sure you'll want to do all you can to prevent Storm from slipping or going lame. And, no, because you're in my care. If an opportunity to improve your safety or Storm's presents itself, I'm afraid I'm going to insist we take it.'

Casey looked at Peter. He shrugged as if to say, 'Work it out between yourselves. I'm not getting involved.'

She said ungraciously: 'Fine, shoe him if you want to. I warn you, though, he hates strangers. He went mad when the last farrier tried to touch him.'

Peter seemed amused. 'Like I said, I need the experience.'

After all that build-up it was galling that, far from behaving like a wild mustang, Storm was docile to the point of being half asleep with Peter. Casey knew that a lot of it had to do with the skill and gentleness with which the boy went about his job, not to mention his obvious love of horses. Faster than she'd ever have believed possible, Storm was back in his stable with four immaculately shod feet, munching on his dinner.

As if that wasn't bad enough, Peter had bonded with Mrs Smith almost instantly when he'd praised Storm's muscle tone. Mrs Smith was convinced it had a lot to do with her daily practice of 'strapping' the horse after he'd been washed and dried – slapping him with a dry cloth twenty times on three specific points of his body. It was an old-fashioned grooming technique, rarely used, but it turned out that Peter's dad was an enthusiast.

'He says that the horse's muscles contract and release during the process, which helps them stay sound. He swears by it. Says it's a terrific treat for them too. Our horses love it.'

After that, there was no stopping them. They'd raved on and on about some waterfall they'd both visited in Wales, and discussed Storm's conformation in terms so technical Casey felt she'd need a veterinary degree to understand them. What was apparent was that Peter knew enough about horses to see beyond Storm's shaggy coat and bony hips and understand that he had the potential to be something special. 'A genuine rough diamond,' he'd called him.

That should have made Casey pleased and proud, but she was still smarting from the Anna Sparks incident. Peter hadn't participated, but neither had he jumped to her defence. So the jury was still out on him. Consequently, everything he said or did rubbed Casey up the wrong way, even though he'd been brilliant with Storm and Mrs Smith was quite obviously charmed by him. She made an effort to smile and thank him as he left, but it was too little, too late. There was something downcast in the set of his shoulders as he departed, and she couldn't help feeling guilty.

By then, however, exhaustion had set in. Shortly afterwards, Mrs Smith departed for an uncomfortable night on the front seat of the donkey van, Moth set up his camp bed in the van's rear, and Casey snuggled into a sleeping bag on the floor of Storm's stable. Nothing could keep her from sleep.

That was how Peter found her when he returned to pick up a couple of tools he'd forgotten some time after 10 p.m. She was curled up on a bed of shavings, dead to the world, a shaft of moonlight falling across her face. The horse was standing over her, head drooping.

'He's watching over her,' Peter thought. Angelica Smith hadn't said a word about Storm's history and he hadn't wanted to ask, but he was prepared to bet that Casey had done her share of watching over him. In the short time he'd been around them, it was obvious the pair worshipped one another. The horse's gaze followed her every move.

Peter stayed watching the two for a few minutes longer and then abruptly walked away. Why this unlikely girl had got under his skin he didn't know, but he didn't like it. He definitely didn't appreciate feeling as if he were in some sort of emotional tumble dryer. What he needed to do was mentally rewind his life to the point before he'd met her – 4.30 that afternoon when he'd been inspecting Rough Diamond's left front foot, to be precise.

Tomorrow morning he'd wake up and his life would have returned to normal. He and his father would work side by side, and his friends would tease him about, among other things, his lack of interest in the pretty, sophisticated girls on the riding circuit. Perhaps he'd date one of those girls just to shut them up. It would be as if Casey Blue and her wounded warrior of a horse had never happened.

12

THE RIDING GLOVES her father had given her were the only new things Casey possessed. Everything else was old or borrowed, including the over-sized man's tweed jacket she'd found in a charity shop and would be wearing in the dressage, and Storm's Hopeless Lane-loaned jumping saddle, bridle and body protector. To Casey's astonishment, Mrs Ridgeley had lent her a dressage saddle from her competing days. It was not the best fit for Storm and, after a decade or so in the attic, smelled strongly of mildew despite extensive efforts by Jin to restore it to its former glory, but was no less appreciated for that.

Casey felt as if she were in a movie on Saturday morning when she went to the secretary's hut to pay her start fee and collect her number (324). It was a rush simply to see her name printed in the programme as owner and rider of Storm Warning. She'd listed her dad as co-owner so that he could feel part of her new life.

In the pocket of her breeches was something from her mum, a rose brooch. Her father had given it to her the previous Christmas and it was her most treasured possession. She carried it everywhere. 'Dorothy would have wanted you to have it, would have wanted to know that a little part of her was with you always,' was all he had said, and there was so much emotion in his voice that Casey was once again struck by the thought that her dad might have been a very different man – a stronger, more resourceful man – had Dorothy lived.

She supposed she'd have been very different too. Braver. More confident. But her mum was gone and never coming back. The rose brooch was all Casey had. As soon as Mrs Smith had entered her for Brigstock, she'd decided that it would be her good luck charm in eventing. Now the brooch would keep her and Storm safe.

At 3.30 that morning, Casey had been shocked awake by the crashing and banging of a clumsy groom. She'd opened her eyes to find Storm gazing down at her. His expression was soppily loving. Struggling upright, she kissed him on his velvet muzzle.

'You're a big softy, I don't care what anyone says,' she told him.

Her night on the stable floor had left her stiff and dishevelled, and a cursory wash under a freezing tap in the portable toilets didn't improve things. Storm fared rather better. Mrs Smith's dressage past meant that she did an immaculate turnout. Casey watched with awe as her horse, who thus far had defied all attempts to manage his dull, scruffy and unusually thick coat – something to do with him having been starved and rugless in previous winters was Mrs Smith's theory – was transformed with a neatly plaited mane and oiled feet. A dab of baby oil on his nose gave it a nice sheen. He was still shaggy; they didn't want to upset him by borrowing clippers at this late stage. But after some strenuous grooming Mrs Smith managed to make him look quite respectable.

'You'll be marked down for presentation, but don't let that bother you,' she told Casey. 'It's no bad thing if certain people underestimate Storm at this early stage of his career.'

Casey was tempted to say that there was not much danger of anyone overestimating him, but then she checked her watch and saw that it was time to warm up for her dressage test, and every other thought went from her head. With trembling hands, she pulled on her gloves.

Mrs Smith put a hand on her arm. 'Remember what I said – don't get ahead of yourself. If something goes wrong, correct it as quickly as you can and focus on your next move. Above all, enjoy yourself. Have fun.'

At first, Casey was decidedly not having fun. Her limbs were about as effective as limp spaghetti. Storm was equally jittery, spooking at signs and litterbins and whinnying hysterically. He bucked hard three or four times on the way to the warm-up area. Several riders glared at them as they came pounding in at a ragged trot as if to say, 'Don't you dare come over here and upset my horse.'

To make matters worse, Moth had ill-advisedly brought Bonnie along to watch. The donkey brayed mournfully from the sidelines until an apoplectic official moved them on.

For several minutes Casey prayed for a natural disaster – ideally, an earthquake – to tear up Fermyn Park and distract everyone. Then the sun stole out from beneath a cloud and she was suddenly reminded that this was what she'd wanted to do her whole life. She caught Mrs Smith's eye and grinned. Her friend mouthed something. Although Casey didn't catch it, she knew it would be along the lines of: 'Be calm, be open, be the space between the notes. Do nothing that interferes with Storm's flow.'

As she relaxed, so Storm quietened and became more responsive. Despite Casey's fears, he'd suffered no ill effects from being shod. Quite the reverse. He had a spring in his step. She regretted being so ungracious about accepting Peter's offer, but there was not a lot she could do about it The farrier's truck had gone in the night. She couldn't decide if she was relieved or sorry.

They were on their way to the dressage arena when Anna Sparks arrived on her novice mare,

Meridian, a skittish but exquisite bay. The hard-faced groom strode haughtily at her side. Unlike Casey, who was wearing her only pair of breeches, Anna could have stepped off the cover of *Horse & Hound*. She smiled at her fans as she entered the warm-up area, bathing everyone within a hundred-metre radius in the special Sparks glow.

Her groom, meanwhile, positioned himself at the entrance to the three dressage arenas. To anyone watching, he was merely taking a professional interest in the proceedings and it was sheer misfortune that he dropped his whip as Storm went by. No one but Mrs Smith saw him snatch it up and mischievously flick it at the belly of the departing horse.

Storm reacted as if he'd been scalded with a branding iron. He reared and spun round, quarters bunched to bolt. Casey was clinging to his neck, half out of the saddle, when the collecting ring steward called her name. It was testament to Mrs Smith's teaching that Casey managed to distract him with a series of half-halts and bring him under some semblance of control, but he entered the arena high-stepping like a circus horse. Things went downhill from there. At the end of the dressage phase, they were lying last with 49 points.

That set the tone for the day. In every discipline, something went disastrously wrong. In the show jumping, a spaniel slipped its lead and caused havoc in the practice jump area minutes before Casey's 11.15 a.m. start time. Not surprisingly, Storm knocked down the first four fences and rattled the fifth. Any further faults brought automatic elimination, but somehow the pair scraped through.

When they exited the arena Mrs Smith's mouth was set in a grim line, but it had nothing to do with Casey's performance. She'd caught sight of the spaniel's owner giggling with Anna Sparks' friend. After the whip incident (which she'd seen no reason to mention to Casey, remarking only that the downside of equestrian events was that they attracted vicious, biting insects), it seemed too much of a coincidence. Since Casey posed no possible threat to anyone, it was unlikely to be anything more than a coincidence or, at worst, a bit of mischief-making, but that didn't mean that the ridiculously nicknamed V shouldn't be shown that such behaviour wouldn't be tolerated.

As Mrs Smith stood debating the matter, a football hit her on the shin.

Vanessa was enjoying a chocolate chip ice-cream when a ten-year-old boy with a shock of strawberry-blond hair and a football tucked under one arm sauntered up to her. 'A lady told me to say that if you're wondering if your bum looks big in those jodhpurs, it does.'

Vanessa turned a mottled shade of puce. For a moment it seemed that she might use the cone as a weapon and attack him, but luckily common sense – not a quality with which V was abundantly blessed – prevailed. Hurling the ice-cream into a bin, she grabbed the boy by the shoulders. 'Which lady? Where is she?

Is she wearing skin-tight jeans and loads of gold jewellery?'

The boy wriggled out of her grip. 'Ow. You're hurting me. I don't think so. She's ancient – a granny.' He squinted into the sun. 'She was over there but she's gone. Anyway, she was nice. She gave me money for candy floss.'

'*Ancient?*' Vanessa turned a murderous glare on the crowd, but the donkey van girl's so-called coach was nowhere to be seen. 'Well, you can give that old witch a message from me ...'

Fortunately, Anna entered the collecting ring then so the boy was spared V's thoughts on elderly women who had the nerve to comment on her figure.

The object of her wrath was safely in the lorry park, preparing Storm for the cross-country and trying not to laugh whenever she pictured Vanessa's face. 'All things considered, Storm's doing remarkably,' Mrs Smith told Casey. 'Focus on the positive.'

Casey paused in the midst of pulling up Storm's girth. Mrs Smith looked especially radiant today, which was hard to understand when things were going so badly. 'What exactly was positive about the dressage? Name one thing.'

'I can name several but I'll concentrate on the rearing and high-stepping. It was nothing short of miraculous.'

'Miraculous? You mean, because I didn't fall off?'

'I *mean*,' continued Mrs Smith, 'because what he effectively did was a piaffe followed by what's known in dressage as the passage. These are two of the hardest movements to learn. Occasionally, a highly strung horse will do these things naturally if he's excited or afraid, but it was the way he did them that caught my eye. Somewhere along the line – perhaps in his circus days – he's had some advanced dressage training.'

Moth came round the back of the donkey van, tapping his watch. 'Casey, love, time to go.'

Casey had never forgotten the words of the knacker's yard man. *Dud on the racetrack 'e was. Wouldn't even leave the starting stall. Afraid of 'is own shadow.* In the recesses of her mind, the worry that those fears might revisit Storm in competition had never been far away. Now it became obvious they had. As the starter finished his countdown, 'One minute … thirty seconds … ten … five, four, three …', the horse stood rooted to the spot, quivering.

'Use your whip, deary,' a man called out from behind the ropes. 'That's what it's for.'

'Storm Warning it says here in the programme,' remarked his wife. 'More like Storm in a Teacup.'

'I'm not going to make him do anything he doesn't want to do,' Casey said, more to herself than them.

116

She stroked Storm's neck. 'It's all right, boy, there's nothing to be afraid of.'

She squeezed his sides. His ears went back but he didn't stir. Casey glanced at her stopwatch. The seconds were whirring round. Novice riders had four minutes and thirteen seconds to complete the course before time penalties kicked in, and she'd already used nearly a minute of that.

Out of the corner of her eye she could see Anna Sparks heading for the warm-up area on Meridian, a trail of admirers in their wake. Casey broke into a cold sweat. Somehow it seemed the most important thing in the world that Anna, who'd witnessed her dressage and showjumping debacles, did not see her further humiliated in the cross-country.

'What's it going to be?' asked the starter. 'Withdrawal?'

'Wait!' cried Casey. She'd spotted something shiny on the crossing path, glinting in Storm's eyes. A steward noticed it at the same time and rushed to snatch it up.

Nothing in Casey's experience or imagination prepared her for what came next. Before she could gather the reins, Storm bolted out of the start box at such speed that if she hadn't grabbed a handful of mane, she'd have been left in his dust.

At Hopeless Lane, they'd had no opportunity to practise anything even vaguely resembling a cross-country jump; Mrs Ridgeley had put paid to that. Instead, Mrs Smith had concentrated on teaching Casey technique and Storm 'boldness', encouraging him to leap low oxers draped with flapping bin bags or old, crackling newspapers.

Casey crouched low over the horse's neck, adrenalin pulsing through her veins. The warm-up fences – a sloping flowerbed, pheasant feeder and log double – might have been cavaletti, so easily did Storm fly over them, but the water jump was an unknown quantity. His eyes were out on stalks as they approached the shadowy dell, its swirling leaves casting spooky shapes.

'Come on, boy, you can do it,' Casey urged. He splashed through, snorting, bounded up the ramp and was soon galloping strongly again, ears pricked. As he grew in confidence, his speed increased dramatically. Casey tried to steady him, but he seized the bit and, blood boiling, burned up the track. Very quickly she realised she was no longer in charge.

They approached the garden trellis fence at reckless speed, clipping the top. For a heart-stopping instant it seemed certain they'd crash. Somehow Storm recovered, galloped a couple of strides and leapt dangerously off the bank. The trakehner flew beneath them, followed by the Elephant Trap. The steeplechase hurdle, Chicken House and palisade oxer – all were taken at Grand National pace.

Casey had totally lost control of Storm. Half terrified, half exhilarated, she clung on as he negotiated the Sunken Road combination at the speed of a downhill skier – over a log, down a step, round a corner, over a ditch and more steps. Most of the time, she was more out of the saddle than in it. Obstacles that had seemed manageable from ground level became monsters as he cleared them with half a metre to spare. After leaping a tree branch and the final fence as easily as if they'd been ground poles at Hopeless Lane, he swept at eye-watering speed towards the finish. They'd finished inside the optimum time with a second to spare.

Casey dismounted, collapsing into the arms of Moth and Mrs Smith. Her face was numb from the wind and she was shaking, but she couldn't stop smiling. 'That was the best three minutes and forty-two seconds of my life so far,' she told them between breaths.

Mrs Smith was white. 'Take a cross-country course at that speed again and you'll be lucky if you have a life. Plus you'll get time penalties for going too fast. First thing Monday morning, we're returning to the simple walk. And that's what we'll be doing until my nerves recover.'

Moth kept shaking his head. 'Blimey, Case, your old horse don't half fly.'

Energy expended, Storm did a very good imitation of being the meekest, sweetest horse at Brigstock. He munched on carrots, whickered and posed. His neck and legs were plastered in foam, but his ears were pricked and he kept shoving Casey with his nose in a proud way, as if to say, 'I know I nearly blew it but I made up for it, didn't I?'

And even though it was only a novice event and a hundred things had gone wrong and she and Storm had scraped through with the minimum number of points when the results were finally in – Anna Sparks, not surprisingly, was one of the top riders – Casey felt proud of her eccentric little team.

She texted her dad. *Thanks to Moth, Mrs Smith, your lucky gloves & Mum's rose brooch, Storm's gone clear in his first cross-country! It's not Badminton, but it's a start. Love ya. C xx*

There was no point in telling him how close they'd come to dying.

The horse and donkey were loaded and were waiting only for Mrs Smith, who was buying a fortifying greasy takeaway for the long drive home, when Casey noticed that the farrier's truck had returned. Perhaps it had only left briefly, to tend to horses at a nearby stud or refuel or something.

'Back in a sec,' she told Moth. 'There's something I need to do.'

Peter was hammering a molten-orange horseshoe into shape when Casey's shadow fell on him. 'Hello,' she said awkwardly.

He glanced up briefly before resuming his task. 'What can I do for you? Is there a problem with Storm's feet?'

'No, they're perfect. I'm here because I wanted to thank you. The shoes were one of the best things about our performance, actually. Probably saved it from being a lot worse.'

'Bad day, huh?' His voice was muffled and disinterested. Casey found herself riveted by his tanned forearms. She couldn't ever recall seeing such well-defined muscles on a teenager. His smooth chest, visible through the unbuttoned neck of his faded black polo shirt as he leaned forward, looked similarly buff.

Embarrassed, she glanced away. 'It was a disastrous day, to be honest. I feel a bit of a failure. Storm did his best, but my riding was at its worst. I totally lost control on the cross-country.'

He straightened and regarded her coolly. 'That's the way it goes sometimes. Is there anything else?'

Casey felt hot with shyness. She could have kicked herself for coming over. What had possessed her? 'No. I wanted to thank you, that's all.'

'Well, now you have.'

'Now I have,' she agreed, feeling unaccountably saddened, which was odd since she barely knew him. 'Goodbye.'

He banged the shoe with more force than was necessary. 'Bye.'

She was halfway to the donkey van when he came running up behind her.

'Casey?'

She halted in surprise. Now it was his turn to look awkward. He ran his fingers through his unruly black hair. 'I'm sorry. Look, it's hard to explain but it's been a strange couple of days. Can we start over?'

'Sure.' She smiled and put out her hand. 'I'm Casey Blue.'

He gripped it. 'And I'm Peter Rhys.'

She laughed. 'So I gathered.'

'What happened today ... you're not going to quit, are you?'

'Of course not. It's just the beginning.'

'Then you're not a failure. Dad says a person only fails if they quit. The true test of character is how you respond to losing.'

Across the lorry park, the donkey van spluttered to life, belching smoke. Casey took a step towards it. 'I'd better get used to it then. Something tells me I'm going to be making plenty of mistakes and doing a lot of growing.'

Peter said: 'About yesterday, when you stood up to Anna Sparks. That took guts. Not many people would have had the courage to do that. If you're serious about Badminton ...'

He wanted to warn her that Anna had a reputation for holding grudges. To say, 'Don't make an enemy of her. If you cross her, you'll have her father to reckon with.' But he didn't want to sound like someone from a B-movie thriller. And who knew when, or if, the girls' paths would cross again? Perhaps never.

'I am,' Casey responded. 'Serious about Badminton, I mean.'

She expected him to challenge her, but all he said was: 'In that case, Storm will want a good farrier. Any time you need me, I'll be there.'

Casey gave him a smile of such unalloyed delight

that Peter's heart did a pancake flip. 'Thanks. That means a lot. See you around.'

She was leaving and there was not a thing he could do about it.

'See you around,' he said casually.

13

I T WAS NOT often that Mrs Ridgeley was lost for words, but when Casey led a newly clipped Storm from his storeroom stable she was struck dumb for at least thirty seconds. She circled him several times, like a shark eyeing up a seal.

'Well,' she said. 'Well, well, well. It's not often I'm mistaken about horses, but I never saw this one coming. He's quite a looker, isn't he? Extraordinary colour. Dark silver, really, like a thundercloud illuminated by lightning. And he's filling out nicely. Hats off to you and Angelica for the work you've done. Keep it up and we'll be able to offer him as an advanced ride to some of the higher paying clients in the school. Course, Gillian will have to knock some of the nonsense out of him. Can't have him larking about the way he does with you—'

Casey was jolted out of the loving reverie she'd been in ever since her beloved horse had been transformed by Mrs Ridgeley's shiny new clippers. 'What? You're kidding. There's no way Storm's going to become a riding school hack. We're preparing him for Badminton.'

'If there's one thing I never joke about, it's money,' said Mrs Ridgeley. 'As you will recall, we had an agreement, young lady. I told you that you could keep Storm here as long as he didn't cost me money or disrupt my school. He's disrupted my school on many occasions but I've been prepared to overlook it because you're my best and most dedicated volunteer. But late payment I will not abide. Today is the seventh of June. You're a week overdue with Storm's feed bill.'

Casey went scarlet. Storm pranced restlessly and she put a hand on his silver neck to soothe him. It was like stroking velvet. 'I'm incredibly sorry, Mrs Ridgeley. It's been a tough month. You'll have the money tomorrow. I'll drop it round after I finish work at the Tea Garden.'

'And what happens next month or the one after that? What if you're ten days late or two weeks or don't pay at all? At what stage do I draw the line?'

'But I will pay,' Casey insisted. 'In the summer holidays, I'll be working full-time at the Tea Garden and doing dog walking and tons of other things. I'll be rolling in cash.'

'And in between you'll be competing' – it was on the tip of Mrs Ridgeley's tongue to say 'losing', but there was no point rubbing salt in the wound – 'at

Longleat and Brightling Park. How long do you think your wages will last then? You'll be haemorrhaging money on fuel, eventing grease and a million other things. Added to which, we need to talk about the wear and tear on my good saddle and bridle. It's high time you bought your own tack.'

With effort, she toned down the exasperation in her voice. 'Casey, why not make life easier for yourself? If you let me use Storm in the school five days a week, his livery will be free. No more feed bills. If he gets injured or sick, he'll be covered by our insurance. You can still ride him at weekends and you'll see him twice a day when you come in to groom and feed him. You'll need to make a big effort to socialise him so that he's nice to clients, but I'll say no more about the tack. It's a win-win situation. Your other option is to sell him. I know you adore him, but you could make yourself some money and save yourself a great deal of expense and heartbreak. Think about it.'

Casey did not need reminding about the status of her empty piggy bank. Or the looming impossibility of affording an eventing career on tips from a Hackney cafe. Night after night she lay awake sweating at the thought of having to give up her dream. She'd relived the Brigstock event a thousand times. In many ways it had been a disaster, but riding the cross-country had convinced her that there was no career she wanted more.

What really filled her with dread, though, was the idea of selling Storm. Quite apart from the fact that his loathing of most humans seemed as strong as ever, he retained a wild streak. Casey loved him for it but not every rider would be so accommodating. She had visions of some pony club brat 'knocking the nonsense out of him', as Mrs Ridgeley put it.

Nothing on earth will make me give him up, Casey told herself. We'll run away to the moors and live in a tent if we have to.

She said nothing to her teacher, but as usual she didn't have to. Not that Mrs Smith was much help. She'd taken to proffering clichés such as, 'If you watch the pennies, the pounds will take care of themselves,' as if Casey was in the habit of frequenting Selfridges luxury department store, blowing fortunes on handbags and designer jeans.

Casey couldn't know that it was agony for her friend to stand by and do nothing when the girl she loved like a daughter was struggling so much. At the same time Mrs Smith was aware she wouldn't be doing Casey any favours if she shielded her from reality. It was precisely that kind of cosseting that caused her, Angelica Mary Smith, to stumble out into the world wearing rose-tinted glasses, utterly ill-equipped to deal with a con artist like Robert, not to mention the monster who'd destroyed Carefree Boy.

Sneaking covert glances at his daughter's thin, pale

face over the dinner table each night, Roland Blue felt equally helpless. He knew the horse must be costing a small fortune.

'Talk to me, Pumpkin,' he said worriedly one night. 'You're too young to be shouldering all this responsibility on your own. I might not be a rich man but I will do my utmost to get you what you need for Storm, even if I have to take a second job.'

But Casey only made light of things and told him not to be an old fusspot. 'It's true that there've been days when his breakfast has been missing one or two ingredients, but Storm understands, like I do, that love makes up for a lot. Anyway, it'll all be fine when I get a sponsor,' she added, knowing full well that sponsors were not in the habit of doling out support to nobodies who came in last. 'Dad, this mushroom risotto is awesome. Anything missing?'

Her evasiveness was deliberate. Her father was earning high praise but not a lot of money from Ravi Singh's Half Moon Tailor Shop. As it was they were barely scraping by. She refused to burden him further. And at the back of her mind was the guilty fear that if Roland Blue had any inkling of how bad the situation was he might be tempted to make up the shortfall by teaming up with his criminal pals.

Mrs Smith watched with growing concern as the shadows under her pupil's eyes changed from mauve to violet. She, too, lay awake in the small hours of the morning, but for different reasons. Alone in the darkness, with the walls of her apartment closing in on her and memories hovering like spectres, raking up old hurts, she questioned both her judgement and her sanity. Was it wise to encourage an impetuous fifteen-year-old to pursue a wildly expensive sport, fraught with pitfalls, on such an unpredictable horse?

But in daylight her customary optimism came soaring back. Perched on the rickety fence at Hopeless Lane, the summer sun warm on her skin as she watched the girl and horse move like mercury across the school, her doubts evaporated. Casey and Storm, well, they were misfits. Both had energy and talent in spades, but it was woefully misdirected. Their best weapon was their unique bond.

Coaching them, Angelica felt like an alchemist. If she could only figure out the right formula, she could combine their gifts to explosive effect.

The formula she'd chosen to attempt was a traditional one, centuries old. Whether or not it would work on an event horse she hadn't a clue, but it had become abundantly clear that Storm needed a work model that would harness his fire without dampening his spirit. So, for that matter, did Casey.

'I've never heard of the Training Scale,' her young charge said. 'Sounds old-fashioned. A lot of the top riders now, their methods are cutting edge.'

Mrs Smith suppressed a twinge of irritation. At Brigstock, she'd caught a glimpse of Anna Sparks' groom schooling Rough Diamond in draw reins – which in the wrong hands created a whole catalogue of problems, in Mrs Smith's considered opinion – and had instantly resolved that whatever new-fangled training method he and Anna were using, she and Casey would be doing the opposite.

'Cutting edge is only useful if it's not shorthand for cutting corners,' she replied tartly. 'Don't forget that a lot of "new" methods were tried decades ago and rejected. Classical principles are classical for a reason.'

She ticked off the seven phases of the Training Scale on her fingers: 'Rhythm, Suppleness, Contact, Impulsion, Straightness, Collection and Letting the Aids Through. The German dressage trainer Klaus Balkenhol, a gold medal-winning Olympian and quite the best equestrian I've ever known, swears by it, and if it's good enough for him it's good enough for me. There are quicker techniques, but this is the gentlest and most natural. Of course, I'll throw in one or two of my own ideas along the way. Never have been one to follow any path blindly.'

'Gentle and natural with some Angelica Smith specials thrown in? You've sold me on it,' said Casey with a grin. 'How soon do we start?'

Mrs Smith checked her watch. 'We have one year, ten months and two weeks to get Storm ready for Badminton. How about right this minute?'

As soon as they started work on the Training Scale's first step, rhythm or *gracioso* (Spanish for graceful), Casey was a convert. It was a system that made perfect sense to her. There was a big emphasis on the relationship between horse and rider. Everything came down to trust.

'Horses are flight animals,' was the way Mrs Smith explained it. 'A horse without faith in his rider, or worse, a horse who fears his rider, is a tense horse. If the rider reacts by applying force, the horse resists by tensing further or trying to escape. If the rider's answer is to up the ante with auxiliary reins or brute strength, the problem quickly escalates.'

She nodded towards Storm, saddled and waiting impatiently for his ride. 'Rhythm produces suppleness, but that will only happen if Storm is relaxed, happy and enjoying his work. It's like an electrical circuit. There needs to be a continual, unbroken flow between your hands and his poll, neck and hind leg. Only then can you achieve good contact and what the Germans call *Losgelassenheit* – looseness.'

Combining these lessons with lunging, walking and what Mrs Smith called 'trust-building' sessions of massaging Storm and petting him, worked infinitesimally slowly. So slowly, in fact, that they got through only by the skin of their teeth at the Longleat International in the third week of June and the East Shore Classic in Devon in July.

'What does it matter where you finish in the field as long as you get the requisite points?' Mrs Smith said on the drive home from the East Shore Classic when Casey seemed particularly low. 'You're not only competing and gaining experience all the time, you're

131

moving up the points table. Have you any idea what an achievement that is?'

'It matters,' Casey told her, 'because there's a long way between bumping along on the bottom of a novice event and flying high at a four-star event. It's the difference between a battery-operated model plane and a rocket to the moon. Besides, no sponsor's going to look twice at us on present form.'

'Perhaps,' said Mrs Smith with a sly sideways glance, 'but at least Storm has nice feet.'

Storm did indeed have nice feet, thanks entirely to Peter, who insisted on checking his shoes prior to the start of any event where their schedules coincided. He changed them at the end if he thought it necessary. He continued to refuse to take a penny on the grounds that he was an apprentice.

'But you take money from other people,' Casey persisted. 'I've seen you.'

'Those are my father's clients. I'm merely helping out. You and Storm are *my* clients. I discovered you. But until I qualify I can't take money from you. Wouldn't feel right about it.'

Casey didn't believe a word of it. 'Will you let us pay then?'

Peter pretended to consider. 'I might have done, but now you're my friends. What kind of man charges his friends?'

'One who doesn't want to go bankrupt,' suggested Casey.

But Peter just laughed. He had the same slow smile

and husky laugh as his father, Evan, and the same olive skin that turned gypsy dark in the slightest ray of sun. But where Evan was short, stocky and had a bowling-ball paunch, Peter was tall and athletic.

'Takes after his mum in looks but fortunately not in temperament, or we'd be divorced too,' Evan had confided to Casey and Mrs Smith. Casey was shocked until she'd learned that Peter's mum had 'done a Shirley Valentine', meaning that like the woman in the movie, she'd gone off on an exotic holiday – in Mrs Rhys's case, to Tuscany on a painting course – and had fallen in love with a count. From what Casey could gather, she returned to the UK only rarely.

Not having a mother herself, Casey felt sorry for Peter until she learned that his mum hated horses and was trying, from afar, to push him into a career in banking. He so obviously enjoyed working outdoors and with his father, with whom he shared an easygoing relationship full of banter, that it was hard to think of the woman wanting to force him into a monkey suit and tear him away from the horses he loved as anything other than wicked. She decided, as Peter had, that he was better off without her.

At first, Mrs Smith worried that Peter would turn Casey's head. After a rocky start, they'd become such good friends so quickly and held each other in such high regard that she was sure a romance would soon blossom. Casey would lose focus and her eventing dreams would go out of the window. That would be the end of that. Added to which, her own experiences on the dressage circuit had left her cynical about men. She liked Peter very much but she was suspicious of his motives.

Her fears proved groundless.

'No boy is going to get in the way of Storm and me winning Badminton,' Casey announced one day, apropos of nothing. 'Not now. Not ever.'

She was not about to tell her friend that she'd interrupted Peter changing his T-shirt behind the farrier's truck and that the sight of his taut brown stomach above his jeans had made her own feel as if it was plummeting thirty-four floors down a lift shaft. At that moment Casey had vowed to herself that she would never, ever fall in love with him. From then on, she'd purposely treated him like a brother. Most of the time she hardly seemed to notice him, so absorbed was she in her horse.

It was clear to Mrs Smith that Peter did have feelings for Casey, but he hid them so well that she doubted the girl was aware of them. What really won Mrs Smith over was that he cared for Casey in a way that was wholly unselfish. He wanted the best for her and Storm, regardless of what it meant for him.

The farrier and his son were among the few who didn't think of the donkey van crew as an enjoyable joke. Some of the greatest eventers, Mary King included, came from humble circumstances and even those who didn't tended to be equalised by the sport, but that didn't mean that there weren't plenty who didn't find comic value in the less fortunate competitors.

Grooms took bets on whether Casey would appear in the same hideous tweed jacket and pair of stretched breeches she'd worn since May, or whether the donkey van would break down and have to be pushed out of the lorry park again as had caused so much merriment in Sussex. They speculated about whether or not Mrs Smith, who liked Indian cottons, would show up in a sarong.

Outside of the Sparks' camp, nobody made fun of Storm any longer, although there were some who muttered that he wasn't a bad-looking horse and it was a damn shame he was in the hands of those half-baked Londoners.

They were more aggrieved still when Casey and Storm stunned everyone by finishing sixth at Larksong Manor after a double clear, beating several big names and qualifying for the Intermediate class at Gatcombe in September. When Peter and his dad discovered that, on top of this success, it was Mrs Smith's sixty-third birthday, they immediately organised a celebratory barbecue in the lorry park.

It was a gorgeous late summer afternoon. As rider after rider came over to congratulate her, Casey had to pinch herself. To have a top ten finish and know that in a month's time she'd be riding at Gatcombe, the historic home of eventing royalty Princess Anne and Captain Mark Phillips, parents of gifted eventer Zara Phillips, was a dream come true. Standing in the lorry park with her little circle of friends, Casey felt a sense of belonging for the first time in her life. She was part of something – part of a community.

On top of everything, she was wearing the new riding hat her father had bought her for her birthday, and respectable breeches. Overnight, some kindly (or patronising) soul had left second-hand ones in her size in a bag with her name on it on a hook outside Storm's stable. Casey wasn't sure whether to be happy or humiliated. But when they fitted perfectly, her overriding emotion was gratitude.

She'd not seen Anna Sparks since Brigstock. The young star had been too busy blazing a trail through various starred events, both in the UK and abroad, on Rough Diamond. The sour groom, Raoul, and the Sparks' top stable girl, Livvy Johnston, kept the flag flying in the Novice and Intermediate categories on Meridian and a couple of promising warmbloods.

Livvy was nowhere near as eye-catching, youthful or talented as Anna, but she was a fine rider who genuinely adored the horses she worked with. Unfortunately ambition made her a poor loser. When Casey finished ahead of her on Storm, she took it with terrible grace. 'Even a blind squirrel finds the occasional acorn,' she remarked loudly enough for Casey to hear.

It couldn't last. The only reason Casey's piggy bank enabled her to make it as far as Gatcombe in September was because she'd nearly killed herself working every available hour through the summer holidays. When she wasn't training Storm with Mrs Smith, she waited tables at the Tea Garden, shopped for groceries for the café's more infirm customers, walked dogs, nursed cats, babysat, delivered pizzas, washed cars, mowed lawns and cleaned windows.

Along the way there were unimaginably precious, pinch-yourself moments, such as riding in the hoofbeats of royalty at stately Gatcombe Park. Unfortunately, everywhere she turned someone seemd to be presenting her with a bill, and the money burned through her pocket likc acid.

Had it not been for the occasional injection of cash from her father, who periodically earned extra for working through the night to fill an order, Casey would have had to admit defeat and allow Mrs Ridgeley to use Storm in the school. As it was, the staff and more generous clients of Hopeless Lane organised a whip-round in order to get Casey and Storm to the last event of the year, the Woodstock Horse Trials in Wales.

It was not a success. The van blew a tyre on the way there and almost overturned. Amid catcalls from the crawling motorway traffic, they battled to fix it in driving rain, buffeted by a bitter wind. Moth, a mild-mannered man who'd been thoroughly entertained by his season on the event circuit, declared himself fed up. He could no longer justify the wear and tear on his van. As soon as they returned to London, he'd be resigning as Casey's driver.

Nerves frayed and head thumping, Casey was in no condition to concentrate when they arrived at Woodstock with barely enough time to warm up. Neither was Storm, who was stressed from the journey. In the cold drizzle, he performed a bad-tempered dressage and destroyed three show jumps.

The cross-country course was soupy with mud. There was a lot of ranting among the riders about the slippery conditions, but only Michelle Low refused to jump. Casey would have liked to join her, but she needed the qualifying points. In a whipping wind, she and Storm produced a desperately slow and scrappy clear round with 35 time faults. When the results were in, they were last among the qualifiers yet again. It wasn't the result they were looking for but it was progress of sorts.

It didn't help that Mrs Smith seemed distracted. She kept disappearing with Moth's phone at crucial moments, supposedly to call a sick friend. Casey would have given anything to talk to Peter, but he was with his father at a country fair on the other side of the country. There was no barbecue. No camaraderie. Larksong Manor might never have happened. At the end of the event, Casey found herself alone in the sodden lorry park with only a stale cheese sandwich for comfort.

Back home in Hackney, there was more bad news. A crisis in the Middle East had caused the price of petrol to leap during the week, blowing Casey's budget. She had no choice but to beg her father for the housekeeping money, condemning them to a week of baked potatoes and French onion soup without the trimmings. Casey wept as she gave Storm a bale of dusty hay. In the rush to leave Wales, she'd forgotten his bag of pony nuts. There was not a penny left to buy more.

She went on bended knee to Mrs Ridgeley. 'I know I'm a month behind with the feed bill, but is there any chance you could loan me some pony nuts and give me a few more weeks to get the money together?'

'No,' was the terse response. 'I can't. Why should I subsidise your pipe dreams? You've already had money off my instructors and clients. If you think you're getting more from me you've got another think coming. You have forty-eight hours to bring me proof that you are making strenuous efforts to sell your horse or I'm putting him to work in the school.'

On this decision she was immovable. The best entreaties of Mrs Smith only annoyed her further.

'I don't care if she has promise,' Mrs Ridgeley declared. '*I* had promise, *you* had promise, doubtless Casey's father and half the folk who walk through the gates of Hopeless Lane – yes, I know that's what you call it – had promise back in the dim and distant past. But life intervenes. And that's what Casey's up against now. Fantasy versus reality. Reality always wins.'

'Casey is not ordinarily gifted,' Mrs Smith said. 'She's exceptional. What's more, she has the work ethic to back it up. It's only a matter of time before she attracts the interest of a sponsor.'

Mrs Ridgeley cocked her head and gazed skywards. 'What was that . . . ? Oh, I thought I saw a pig fly.'

'It's tough ruvv,' Jin told Casey, after smuggling some pony nuts into Storm's stable. 'She thinks if she's hard on you, it will help your character, make you stronger.'

'It's not tough love at all,' Casey said furiously. 'It's jealousy, pure and simple. She gave up her dream so she thinks everyone else should give up theirs. Well, I'm not going to allow her to bully me into giving up Storm. He needs me and I need him, and it would take five hundred Mrs Ridgeleys to separate us.'

The morning after issuing the ultimatum, Mrs Ridgeley appeared to have a change of heart. She summoned Casey into her office with a benevolent smile. 'Case, girl, I'm glad to report that you're in luck. Roxanne Primley's come into some inheritance cash. She's keen on Storm. Thinks he's a super horse. In recognition of the schooling you've done with him, she's prepared to buy him.'

A chill went down Casey's spine. Roxanne Primley was not a gram under a hundred kilos and had hands like ham hocks. She held the reins as if she were wrenching the wheel of a juggernaut. Even Patchwork quailed at the sight of her.

Casey leapt to her feet. 'Over my dead body.'

'Don't be so ridiculous,' Mrs Ridgeley snapped, her patience evaporating. 'Honestly, I'm beginning to think that you and Angelica have lost your minds. On what, precisely, is your great faith in Storm and yourself based? Where did you finish at Brigstock?'

'It was our first event.'

'And at Longleat?'

'Well, we weren't last and we still—'

'And at the East Shore Classic and Aston Le Walls?'

'Last, but in between we had the amazing sixth place finish at Larksong Manor. That proves Storm has what it takes.'

'It proves nothing except that he's capable of being an also-ran,' was Mrs Ridgeley's cruel rejoinder. 'One swallow does not make a summer. Where did you finish at Woodstock, a mere seven weeks later?'

Casey stared miserably at the floor. 'Last.'

'I rest my case.'

14

THE LETTER WAS lying on the dining room table when Casey came home that evening, cheeks streaked with tears. Mrs Ridgeley had forced her to allow Roxanne Primley to 'test ride' Storm, a folly that had almost ended with Roxanne in A&E after Storm tried to crush her against the fence.

Unsurprisingly, Roxanne had withdrawn her offer. 'Mad brute,' she'd thundered at Casey, pulling up her jodhpurs to reveal a leg the size of a beluga whale. It looked as if a lion had mauled it. 'Do yourself a favour and take him back to the knacker's yard he came from before he kills you.'

Mrs Ridgeley was more succinct. 'You have forty-eight hours to find Storm a new home or I'll be going to Plan B.'

Casey dreaded to think what Plan B involved. She'd

cried all the way home and was still sobbing when her father walked through the door fifteen minutes later, puffed after a long day at work.

Nothing upset Roland Blue more than seeing his daughter in distress. He wrapped her in a bear hug and did his best to soothe her. 'I've no idea what's happened, Pumpkin, but if it's within my power I'll fix it, I can promise you that. I'll go to the ends of the earth if I have to.'

It all came out then. The sleepless nights, the bowing and scraping for pennies, the cough that Storm had developed from eating dusty hay.

Roland's jaw was set. 'I'll talk to Mrs Ridgeley and give her a piece of my mind. How dare she threaten you! I'll find the money for Storm if I have to ... if I have to ... Oh, never mind. I'll find it, that's all you need to know.'

Casey paled. 'No, Dad! Please, I don't want you finding anything. Storm's my responsibility and I—'

'What's this?' her father interrupted, picking up the letter.

Casey wiped her eyes. 'I don't know. I've been too frightened to open it. Probably a final demand from Mrs Ridgeley's accountant.'

'I doubt it. Final demands don't usually arrive in duck-egg blue envelopes. Debt collectors prefer the grimmer shades.'

Casey took it from him. There was no clue as to the sender. Her name and address had been neatly typed, but the postmark was illegible. She shrugged and ripped it open. 'Oh, well, it's not as if the day could get any worse.'

A moment later she let out a scream. The letter fluttered from her hand.

Her father snatched it up and read it. 'What the—?' He whooped and began whirling Casey round until the room was spinning and they were both laughing.

'I'm not going to say I told you so, but I did,' he said, beaming. 'True talent will out. Oh, my brilliant daughter, I'm so proud of you.'

While her dad whipped up a cheese omelette for their dinner, Casey read the letter again with shaking hands.

At the top of the pale blue sheet of paper was a deep blue letterhead on which a white eagle soared. Beneath the bird was a scroll containing the words *Ladyhawke Enterprises*. The only address was a box number. Casey's name had been written in an artistic hand, but the content of the letter was typed.

Dear Casey,

Let me start by saying that I had the pleasure of watching you and Storm Warning perform at Larksong Manor when you finished sixth. I've been known to be cynical about the gifts of unproven riders, but what I saw there led me to believe that, as a team, you and your horse have promise beyond your years and experience.

Allow me to be blunt. Your track record this season is hardly exemplary, yet I have followed your progress from

144

afar and believe that your results do not reflect the advances you have made. I hope you will forgive the impertinence but I have made enquiries about your circumstances and about your coach, Angelica Smith, a highly regarded rider in her day. These have led me to conclude that if you had access to top class facilities, tack and feed, you might be a force to be reckoned with on the eventing circuit.

I am willing to sponsor you in this endeavour for eighteen months, in return for ten per cent of your winnings and the pleasure of seeing a deserving young rider have the opportunity to compete. There are no strings attached to this offer, but there is one condition. If you will not agree to it, we cannot, as they say, do business. My request is simply this: I want complete anonymity. We will correspond only through the PO box number at the head of this letter.

If you agree to this, please let me know by return of post. As soon as I have your acceptance, I shall authorise a payment to White Oaks Equestrian Centre in Kent. They have some of the best facilities in the country. Storm Warning's livery, feed, insurance and veterinary bills will be taken care of. The yard has a modest but adequate horsebox, which they have agreed to put at your disposal for shows. A driver will be available, should you need one, but I suspect that your Mrs Smith would make a fine chauffeur!

I'm sure you don't need me to tell you that it is vital that you compete in presentable attire and that Storm Warning has first class tack. As such, I have set up a line *of credit at Horse Heaven. Again, it is an amount that should prove sufficient for your needs. I hope you will indulge me if I ask that you use a saddlecloth embossed with the Ladyhawke logo.*

For monthly subsistence, I suggest I send an amount to be agreed to Mrs Smith. There is a vacant cottage across the lane from White Oaks. It is simply furnished but it will be at your disposal from December onwards, leaving you free to choose whether to stay close to Storm Warning and be home-schooled or to commute and stay at your existing school. I respectfully leave those decisions to you and your father, and, indeed, your coach. Whatever works best is agreeable to me.

In conclusion, I am aware that I am a perfect stranger and that you will want to think about this. Should you decide to accept my offer, I appreciate that you might have livery obligations that do not allow you to move to Kent for a month or two. I have enclosed a cheque to cover this and any unforeseen expenses. Please accept it with my compliments, regardless of whether or not you are prepared to take me on as your sponsor.

In anticipation of your earliest reply, I am,
Yours sincerely,

Beneath an indecipherable signature were the words:
Director, Ladyhawke Enterprises

Casey opened the envelope. Tucked inside was a cheque that equalled her father's monthly salary. It seemed impossible that her heart could beat any faster, but it did then.

When Roland Blue set the omelette before her she was crying again, but this time her tears were not sad ones. They were, her father said teasingly, 'liquid joy'.

15

THE TREES THAT lined the driveway of White Oaks
Equestrian Centre were over three centuries old
and had roots like dinosaur feet. Over the years their
branches had knitted and formed a tunnel of dappled
green and dancing sunlight, in which red squirrels
played. Casey thought of the avenue as enchanted. On
either side of it were fields that sparkled with dew or
hard frost in the early mornings, one of which was
dotted with cross-country jumps.

When they'd first arrived shortly before Christmas
on an unseasonably warm day, she'd turned Storm out
for several hours. The way he'd raced around in circles,
bucking and throwing up his heels, had brought it
home to her that in all probability it was the first time
in his entire nine years that he'd known real freedom.

In a sense, the same was true of Casey. It was not

until she and Mrs Smith relocated to the Kent countryside that she realised how oppressive London was. It weighed down on her. The greyness of it; the muggy, polluted air; the hostile, unsmiling pedestrians; the aggressive billboards; the angry, hooting cars; the ear-splitting din – everything was designed to sap her energy and her spirits.

The pavements of Hackney had teemed with harried mothers, overworked office employees and cheerful criminals. Aside from the resentful idle, everyone seemed to be on a deadline. Rush, rush, rush. Casey rarely used the tube, which cost a king's ransom, but when she did people tore up and down the left side of escalators, shoving tourists who didn't know better out of the way, as if saving ten seconds was a matter of life and death.

But in the country things moved at the pace of nature. The laying of eggs, the birthing of lambs, the snuggling down of badgers in their winter dens – each happened in its own sweet time. It couldn't be hurried.

When Peter and his father had stopped by to visit on their way to a fancy equestrian centre near Tunbridge Wells, the kind of place where, Peter told Casey, clients dropped in to visit their horses by helicopter, she understood why they were so in tune with horses and why their smiles reached their eyes. They'd stayed for a pancake brunch and left soon afterwards, but not before Peter had shod Storm. He'd refused, as usual, to take payment.

'What part of "We're friends and I'm not going to

take money from you" do you not understand?' he said in mock frustration. 'Besides, Mrs Smith's pancakes alone were worth their weight in gold.'

'And what part of "I have a sponsor now and would really like to repay you for your generosity last season" do *you* not understand?' she retorted. 'We're practically rich.'

But Peter only laughed and said, 'Enjoy. It's completely deserved and I'm happy for you. See you down the road.'

She felt the usual sharp pang as he drove away but forgot about him almost as quickly. Storm took all her attention.

The facilities at White Oaks were everything the anonymous director of Ladyhawke Enterprises had promised and more. They could never be described as 'fancy' but they were spotlessly kept by Morag, the stable manager, and, to Casey's mind, perfect in every way. The outbuildings were of creamy stone, with flagstone floors, but somehow they blended well with the roomy modern stables and indoor school. Unlike Mrs Ridgeley, Morag did not believe in economising on wood shavings or quality food. The horses of White Oaks lived like kings.

At the height of winter, when pillowy snow lay knee deep on the Kent fields, Casey could relax at night knowing that Storm was snug in his stable and wrapped in his new blue rug embroidered with the eagle logo of Ladyhawke Enterprises. The regime at White Oaks suited him and he grew more sleek and shiny by the day. The rug showed off his dark silver colouring. When she opened the stable door to groom him each morning, she could not get over how handsome he was.

The move had not been without its hiccups. After his initial elation, her father had put a ban on her taking up any sponsorship without making further enquiries about Ladyhawke Enterprises.

'Why does this director person want to remain anonymous?' he demanded. 'Why is there no evidence of Ladyhawke Enterprises anywhere on the Internet? And there's no way I'm going to allow my little girl to go off to live in the country. You might be sixteen but you're still a child. You belong here, with me. Now don't get me wrong. I'm not saying no. I realise this might be the opportunity of a lifetime. All I'm saying is we must be wary.'

In the end, it was Mrs Smith who smoothed things over. Summoned to No. 414 Redwing Tower when the argument between Casey and her dad had become heated, she'd resolved the situation in under an hour.

It was simple, she said. As the victim of a con artist herself, she was well qualified to spot dodgy dealers. She'd made some enquiries on the equestrian circuit and there was talk of a wealthy benefactor who was passionate about eventing and liked to be involved in some way, but was a virtual recluse and did not want publicity or attention.

She promised to act as a buffer between Casey and Ladyhawke Enterprises. Casey was not to correspond with her sponsor at all. They would proceed with the utmost caution, taking things step by step. Their first move should be to use the sponsor's cheque to pay Mrs Ridgeley full livery fees for Storm to remain at Hopeless Lane until at least December. That way, she could impose no conditions on his stay. If the cheque proved genuine and didn't bounce, they could go to stage two: inspecting the White Oak Equestrian Centre and the cottage. They could ask lots of questions about whether or not this sponsor was known or someone to be trusted. Next they could see if they really were able to shop at Horse Heaven, and so on.

If at any point the company behaved suspiciously, by trying to tie them into a legal contract or impose bizarre conditions, such as changing Storm Warning's name to Ladyhawke Enterprise's Storm, they'd sever all contact.

At every stage things had not only worked out, they'd worked out beyond Casey's wildest hopes. Storm had brand new, top-of-the-range tack: a bridle, martingale, two saddles, boots and the Ladyhawke logo-embossed rug and a couple of numnahs. In addition, Casey was kitted out from top to toe in properly fitting competition clothes and everyday riding wear.

Peach Tree Cottage was darling and within five minutes' stroll of White Oaks, but it was rather ramshackle. The floorboards creaked like a bridge on the verge of collapse, the bath was stained with rust. Flushing a toilet at night woke up the whole house, and there was no heating. During the worst of the snow, Casey spent a big portion of the day either shivering on the Aga or virtually camped in the hearth. At times, she considered moving in with Storm.

And yet there was something wonderfully romantic about it all. At the end of a long day of riding, Casey loved nothing more than to lie in bed listening to the squawks and cries of the night creatures. She'd curl up around a hot water bottle and read horse books by lamplight, dreaming about the season ahead. Waking to a dawn chorus of birds instead of the cacophony of London traffic was the next thing to heaven.

Perhaps most importantly, she enjoyed living with Mrs Smith, something that almost didn't happen. As Casey had anticipated, the sticking point had been her education. Her father was adamant that she had to stay with him in London, continue going to school and could only train Storm at weekends. Casey was equally adamant that, in order for her to have any chance of qualifying for Badminton, she had to work with Storm every day. Living in the cottage and either quitting school or being home-schooled was the only answer.

Once again, she had Mrs Smith to thank for the outcome.

'Don't forget I'm a country girl at heart,' Mrs Smith told Roland Blue. 'I can't think of anything I'd like more than to return to my roots for a while. Nothing keeping me in London but the strays, but I know that Ursula from the café would be only too glad to take over the feeding in return for a place to stay for six months or so. She's just split up with her husband.

'As for the home schooling, it would be fun for me to put on my teaching hat again and help out. Better than that class of horrors she's in now. What, Casey didn't tell you that I spent nearly twenty of my best years teaching? How else do you think I keep my feline army in cat food?'

They worked through every one of Roland Blue's objections until he laughingly conceded defeat. There was enough money in the budget Ladyhawke Enterprises had allocated Mrs Smith for a weekly rail ticket for him. Every Friday, when Roland Blue had finished work at the Half Moon Tailor Shop, he'd catch the train to Kent. He'd stay the weekend with his daughter and Mrs Smith, wake at the crack of dawn on Monday and head back to London.

'That way,' Casey said, 'we're only really apart three days a week.'

At Christmas, Ravi Singh granted her father a two-week paid holiday. Roland Blue packed his suitcase and moved into Peach Tree Cottage for the duration. He enjoyed long, bracing walks across the wintry landscape with Casey, helped out at the stables and took turns with Mrs Smith to cook. In the evenings, the three of them played scrabble, or listened to Bach or Radio Four. There was no television. After a week, Roland Blue looked ten years younger.

On Christmas morning, they took a bag full of treats to Storm and the other horses before walking across the snowy fields to church. There, they lit a candle for

Casey's mum. Afterwards Mrs Smith and Roland Blue prepared a vegetarian Christmas dinner with every imaginable trimming, including cranberry and almond stuffing and Yorkshire puddings. They wore silly hats, pulled crackers and ate until they could barely make it to the sofa.

In contrast to the gifts they'd received from Casey's aunt – Santa Claus socks for her brother and a school supplies voucher for her niece – the presents they exchanged were simple but meaningful. Casey gave Mrs Smith a CD of the Dalai Lama's speeches and her father a grow-your-own herb kit. Roland Blue presented her with a showjumping jacket he'd made with his own hands. When Casey went into raptures over it, he said again: 'Wait till you see the coat and tails I'm going to make you when you qualify for Badminton.'

Casey and Mrs Smith had jointly baked a Christmas cake for Peter and Evan, sending it by recorded delivery to Peter's grandfather's farm in Wales. The postage had cost as much as the ingredients. The Rhys's had replied with a Christmas card featuring a zebra in a Santa hat. Inside was a hand-drawn voucher for '20 Free Farrier Sessions for Storm'. Peter had written on the card: *Now can we stop having conversations about money!! Have an awesome country Christmas. Love, Peter & Evan.*

From Mrs Smith, Casey received a first edition of *National Velvet*. She was deeply moved. 'My father gave it to me when I was a girl,' her friend told her. 'There's nothing I'd like more than to pass it on to you.'

Sitting in front of a blazing fire with the two people she loved most, knowing that Storm was nearby, equally warm and content, Casey thought she'd never been happier.

Later that afternoon, when a little voice at the back of her mind started saying, 'It's all too good to be true; nothing ever stays this perfect,' Casey excused herself and walked across the fields to see Storm. The stable-yard was deserted, the horses having been bedded down early. She stood for a long time looking at her beautiful new saddles in the tack room and thinking about how fortunate she was before going into Storm's stable next door.

As always, her heart gave a little skip when he started towards her as eagerly as if he hadn't seen her for a week, his whole being radiating trust and pleasure.

'You only love me for my sugar cubes,' she told him gruffly, knowing that nothing was further from the truth.

Wrapped in a spare horse rug, she sat in the corner of the stable and read Storm extracts from *National Velvet*, wondering as she did so if fortune would smile on her and Storm in the way it had on the unlikely combination of teenage Velvet and the piebald she'd won in a raffle. Velvet's dream had been to race 'The Pie' in the Grand National but, as Casey explained to Storm, things hadn't turned out quite the way she'd imagined.

'I wish I had a crystal ball,' Casey said out loud, but as she spoke she realised that she wouldn't want to see into the future even if she could. If it was going to be bad she couldn't help but try to influence the outcome. If she knew it was going to be wonderful she'd become too fixated on the happiness that lay ahead to enjoy today. Best to live in the moment.

That settled, she stood beside Storm's warm bulk and gazed out at the slowly descending dusk and, in the distance, the yellow lights of the cottage, twinkling through the snow-laden trees. Suddenly, Storm's head lifted and his ears pricked, and she saw what he saw – two deer crossing the white fields in graceful bounds.

As moments go, it was pretty perfect, and she decided then and there that, while it was true that perfection didn't last for ever, she'd enjoy every second while it did.

16

THE FIRST EVENT of the season was at Aldon in Somerset in the third week of March. The plan was to get up at 3 a.m. and leave as soon as Storm had been fed, groomed and had his mane plaited by Mrs Smith. They hadn't factored in the possibility that Storm might refuse to get into the White Oaks horsebox. It was a nice horsebox, albeit not a luxurious one, but it was small and wobbly. The ramp sagged and squeaked when Storm put his foot on it.

The horse took one look at it and decided that, if he couldn't go in Moth's familiar van with the benign, comforting presence of Bonnie the donkey, he would not be going anywhere at all. Within minutes he was rearing and wild-eyed, ready to kick to pieces anyone who threatened to force him in. Even Mrs Smith's usual failsafe methods proved fruitless.

'He thinks he's going back to the knacker's yard,' said Casey in distress. 'Poor angel. Well, I'm not going to upset him further. We'll have to withdraw from the event.'

'Why don't you put Willow in the horsebox and see if that helps?' suggested Morag, indicating the yard cat, a plump tortoiseshell, washing its whiskers after an unexpected crack-of-dawn breakfast. 'He seems to spend a lot of time in Storm's stable. We've taken him to shows in the past and he's been a great help with nervous horses.'

It seemed unlikely that a cat could calm Storm in his present state of high anxiety, but it worked like a charm. No sooner was Willow installed in his bed at the back of the box than Storm dropped his objections, gave a big shuddering sigh, and strolled in as meekly as a spring lamb.

By then they were running forty-five minutes late, and a heavy fog on the motorway delayed them further. When they arrived at Deacon Rise mist shrouded the park, settling in smoky layers around the trees. Riders flew like ghosts over practice jumps.

The only space left in the lorry park was two trailers away from Anna Sparks' vast, sponsors' logo-emblazoned wagon, too close for comfort in Casey's opinion. It made the White Oaks horsebox look like a toy. As they drove past, Livvy Johnston was putting a white numnah on a resplendent Meridian. An open storage compartment on the side of the lorry revealed rows of gleaming tack.

Casey's nerves escalated. The morning's delays had left her with barely twenty minutes to unload Storm and trot him over to the dressage. As a result they performed a test riddled with errors and were lucky to escape with a worst-case-scenario 49. Watching from their cars, the judges shook their heads. After a stern talking-to from Mrs Smith, Casey pulled herself together for the showjumping and was going well until a car alarm went off as they approached the combination. Storm did three circuits of the ring before she was able to stop him.

Casey was in the horsebox, changing for the cross-country and feeling utterly despondent, when she heard the unmistakable voice of Anna Sparks. It was so close that Casey panicked that Anna might be about to open the door of the horsebox. Leaning past Willow, she found that she was able to see Anna in the wing mirror of the van. The young star was with Livvy and Raoul, the sinewy groom, and they were looking at Storm.

'What a stunning horse,' Anna said. 'I'd like a BMW in that exact silver. A bit podgy after the winter and his topline needs building up, but he's a class act. Who does he belong to? Why weren't we offered him?'

In the horsebox, Casey almost fainted. For a second she forgot that Anna had proved to be a heroine with giant feet of clay. All she could think was, 'One of the most beautiful and talented riders in Britain thinks my one dollar horse is stunning.'

Raoul laughed. It was an unpleasant, oddly

menacing sound. 'Don't you remember him? He belongs to that donkey van girl. We saw him being offloaded at Brigstock last year, looking like a woolly mammoth. You called him a knackered old mule. She didn't appreciate that one bit.'

Anna did a double take. 'Tell me you're having me on. It can't possibly be the same horse.'

She approached Storm. Ears pinned to his head, he lunged to snap at her, missing her arm by millimetres. She giggled as she skipped nimbly out of range. 'Ooh, got a bit of an attitude problem, have you, handsome? Raoul, you'd soon put a stop to that, wouldn't you?'

Raoul bared his teeth like a hyena.

Livvy said petulantly: 'His looks might have improved but he's still a no-hoper. He and that Casey girl were bottom feeders in virtually every event last season – well, except for Larksong Manor, but that was an aberration – and this one's started the same way. They did a woeful dressage test this morning and entertained everyone by tearing round the showjumping ring as if it were a rodeo circuit. It was hilarious.'

'That means nothing,' said Anna, ice-blue eyes locked on Storm. 'What hope has he got with that fruitloop riding him? She looked like a scarecrow. When she started going on about Badminton, she sounded quite unhinged. Didn't she have some geriatric for a coach? Keep an eye on him. If his form improves, let me know. It might be an idea to buy him while he's cheap.'

Inside the horsebox, Casey was boiling with fury. The arrogance of the girl beggared belief.

'Take no notice of her,' counselled Mrs Smith when she came to find out why Casey was taking so long to get ready. 'She's grown up believing that money and beauty can buy everything. It'll be a shock to her system when she discovers they can't. Take it from me. I learned that lesson the hard way.'

Casey was so determined to prove that she was the right rider for Storm that she put her heart and soul into the cross-country. They went clear again, but racked up time faults. That, coupled with the disasters of the morning, meant that they were, as Livvy Johnston put it, among the bottom feeders at the end of the day. It was scant consolation that, by some miracle, they'd gleaned a few more qualifying points. Their overall performance had been so poor that Casey dreaded to think how they'd do in a tougher event.

'I have no excuses,' she said to Mrs Smith as they crawled in single file traffic through the greens and golds of Somerset. The fog had burned off to reveal a cloudless cobalt sky. Fluffy-tailed lambs shared fields with strutting pheasants. Cherry trees sprinkled their blossoms like confetti on the emerald lawns of thatched cottages. But somehow the extravagant beauty of the afternoon added to Casey's misery.

She glanced at her friend. 'I've let you down again. I'm sorry. You must be ready to give up on me.'

'Everyone has an off day,' Mrs Smith said mildly.

'But I've had an off year. I mean, Anna Sparks is right. I don't deserve Storm. At least when I was at Hopeless Lane I could blame the lack of an indoor school, or dusty hay, or Moth's van, or the pressure of being broke all the time, or Mrs Ridgeley for always making it so hard for us to train, or the bad tack, or inexperience. But now I have experience and everything I could possibly need, and White Oaks and the cottage are a total dream, and yet I've still managed to mess it up. Ladyhawke Enterprises are going to withdraw their sponsorship immediately. We'll have to go back to London and sell Storm after all.'

Mrs Smith accclerated onto the motorway. 'I can't see them being so hard-hearted. You could learn one lesson from today, however. As John Lennon famously said, "Life is what happens when you're making other plans." Stuff happens. Tyres get punctures, bridles break, horses play up, miss strides and demolish jumps, and car alarms go off at inconvenient moments. Get used to it. The top riders are not necessarily the best riders. Sometimes they're simply the ones who know best how to go with the flow.'

Despite this sage advice, Casey spent another twenty-four hours fretting that Ladyhawke Enterprises would snatch away their sponsorship and she'd be reduced to begging Mrs Ridgeley for Storm's old storeroom at Hopeless Lane before a letter arrived with the Ladyhawke emblem on it. Unlike the previous ones it was handwritten and postmarked Somerset.

'You open it,' she told her friend. 'I can't bear it.'

163

Rolling her eyes, Mrs Smith read:

Dear Casey,

I hope you are finding the facilities at White Oaks satisfactory and that Peach Tree Cottage meets your needs. As you can imagine, I followed your progress at Aldon with interest. Obviously, the outcome was not ideal. I fear that the thought of having a sponsor breathing down your neck may be putting pressure on you. I wanted to reassure you on that score. Please know that I am committed to you for the season, for better or for worse. Should you finish last in every event, I will not withdraw my support. I'm supremely confident that glory will come to you, but I'm quite content to wait. I understand that these things take time. In the meanwhile, I wish you every good fortune.

Yours truly,

There was the usual scrambled signature below.

Perhaps it was because every scrap of pressure was now taken off her and she'd resolved to do as Mrs Smith suggested and go with the flow. Perhaps it was simply because Storm's favourite farrier was there and was unapologetically pleased to see her. Either way, Casey arrived at the Burnham Market International in Norfolk feeling fit and, if not exactly confident, then at least more quietly positive than she'd been in the past. Since worrying only seemed to make things worse, she'd decided to give it up.

Burnham Market itself was one of the prettiest villages she'd ever seen, all delicatessens, antique shops and art galleries filled with sea paintings, arranged around a green with a Celtic cross. She and Mrs Smith stayed in the attic rooms of a pub creaking with atmosphere. It served hearty vegetarian roasts and a chocolate pudding that sent Casey into a coma-like sleep on the first night. She was so relaxed next morning that Mrs Smith was concerned she might flop from the saddle.

She needn't have worried. For the first time, Casey and Storm's performance in the dressage mirrored their very best performance in training at White Oaks. Mrs Smith had plaited the horse's mane and dabbed him with baby oil, setting off his pewter colouring, and she noticed with pride that several heads snapped round as he went by. And it wasn't just Storm who attracted attention. The country air had done Casey the world of good. She had the peachy skin of a farm girl and was as fit as a young athlete. Mrs Smith had insisted she keep up her running, stretching and weight training.

Peter came over with a spare coffee when he saw Mrs Smith waiting by the collecting ring for Casey to jump. 'Nervous?'

'Only for Casey. I have every faith.'

'She's fortunate to have you. She says you've changed her life.'

'Perhaps,' said Mrs Smith, 'but then she saved mine. Terrible thing, ennui.'

Before Peter could ask her what she meant, Casey came in on Storm. He couldn't believe the transformation in the horse, or in the girl. It was hard to believe he'd once considered her nondescript. Not that she was conventionally pretty even now. As many people would pass her on the street without noticing her as would have done so a year ago. But anyone whose gaze lingered on her for more than a minute would notice that she had something much more sustaining and valuable than, say, the in-your-face, take-your-breath-away beauty of Anna Sparks – a shy charisma that sneaked up on you and knocked you for six when you weren't looking. She had that very rare thing: presence.

Storm gave such huge leaps over the first two fences that Casey was almost unseated. He approached the oxer way too fast and rammed one of the poles. It oscillated madly but settled in the cup. After that, he seemed to settle, sailing effortlessly over the double and the rustic poles. He was striding towards the second element of the combination, ears pricked, when a toddler close to the ropes let out a piercing screech.

Storm's ears flattened, but Casey said something to him and he twisted himself up and over. Swishing his tail like a furious cat, he popped over the last element and turned to face the wall. The toddler was now in the midst of a full-blown tantrum.

'We've been doing a lot of work on this,' Mrs Smith said, 'coping with distractions.'

Peter wondered if that was a hint, although he couldn't see how he could be considered a distraction. Casey barely noticed him. They were friends but she only had eyes for her horse. He decided he was being paranoid. Angelica Smith was the straightest talker he knew. If she didn't want him around, she'd say so.

Storm arched over the wall with room to spare, popped over the final two jumps and was home clear. As they trotted out of the ring, Casey patted him ecstatically.

'Tell her well done for me,' Peter said, and was gone before Mrs Smith could ask him to stay.

'Wasn't Storm a star?' cried Casey, jumping off him and giving him half the packet of Polos produced by Mrs Smith.

She laughed. 'You were both stars. Your first ever clear round in the showjumping. That's quite an achievement. Enjoy it, savour it, then focus on the cross-country. It's a big, bold course. It'll need all your concentration.'

It was good advice but she needn't have worried. Casey was in a zone. Her mind felt sharper than it had in a year. Storm was keyed up and ready to run, but because his mistress was so calm and her hands especially soft on his mouth, he didn't feel the need to fight or flee. Burning up the course, he jumped for sheer joy.

As fence after fence flew beneath them, Mrs Smith's words came to Casey as clearly as if her teacher had been perched on her shoulder. 'Slip your reins so he can lower his head and get a good look at the trakehner. Good, now approach the bank square on. Give Storm plenty of time to read every situation. He's amply qualified to get round this course if he has enough information, as are you. But don't rush it.'

It was over too quickly. When the finish line and cheering crowds came into view, Casey had to drag herself into the present, as if from a beautiful dream. Mrs Smith had to repeat herself several times before Casey could take in what she was saying.

'You're among the leaders. Half the field have still to go, but it's hard to see your score being beaten.'

Ultimately, Casey was eighth. Within minutes of her finishing, a rain shower accompanied by a capricious wind blew in out of nowhere and numerous big names came to grief, pushing her up the leaderboard. Her East London birthplace and unusual horse attracted the attention of the *Telegraph* correspondent, who wrote a sidebar on her headed: 'From Joker to Ace.'

Riders who mocked 16-year-old Casey Blue and her dark grey, Storm Warning, a knacker's yard wreck only a year ago, are this morning laughing on the other side of their faces after she notched up an incredible eighth place finish in the Intermediate class in the Burnham Market International yesterday. Not only did she draw praise from the winner, Canadian Alex Lang, she also upstaged the reigning queen of young eventing, Anna Sparks, who finished tenth on her bay mare, Meridian.

Casey and Mrs Smith celebrated with a chip butty dinner at a cosy fish and chip shop overlooking the sea. Casey would have loved Peter and his father to join them, but they had a long drive back to Wales and she didn't like to ask. Peter was obviously thrilled for her, though, and had insisted on shoeing Storm before they left so that his feet would be in tiptop shape for their next event.

Only one thing happened to mar the day. Returning to the stable to collect Storm prior to loading him that evening, Casey was startled by Raoul, Anna Sparks' groom.

'Congratulations,' he said in faintly accented English. Argentinean or Brazilian, Casey guessed. He leaned against the stable door, regarding her with a smarmy smile. 'Quite a performance you put on today. Anyone would think your horse was on something.'

Casey went still. 'What did you say?'

'Oh come on, it's not often that horses make such a dramatic improvement without, you know ... help.'

Casey gave him a look that would have shrivelled a lesser man. It was water off a duck's back to Raoul. He enjoyed goading those he considered weaker than himself and was pleased to have got a rise out of her.

'What exactly are you implying?'

He grinned and put up his hands as if to ward off a blow. 'Nothing, sweet Casey. Nothing at all. I'm only observing that it's unusual to see a horse undergo such a transformation "naturally".' He emphasised the last word.

To cover her shock and anger, Casey made a fuss of putting on Storm's rug. 'Has it crossed your mind that the change in him might be down to love and great nutrition and training? Not that you'd know the first thing about love.'

He laughed unpleasantly. Storm showed the whites of his eyes. The man had an odour that reminded him of the knacker's yard.

Casey opened the stable door and pushed past the groom, deliberately swinging Storm's hindquarters so that Raoul was forced to jump out of the way.

'Haven't you forgotten something?'

Casey turned to see Raoul holding up the plastic soft drink bottle containing Janet's potion. Every two weeks Janet couriered a supply of it to Peach Tree Cottage. Their sponsor had actually encouraged them to keep using it. A little chill went through Casey as it suddenly occurred to her that she had no idea what was in the liquid. They'd been using it for so long and Storm seemed to derive so much enjoyment and benefit from it that giving it to him had become second nature. Now it struck her that it was entirely possible it contained some performance-enhancing drug. The Federation Equestre Internationale (FEI) had a long list of banned substances. What if Raoul had taken a sample and Casey and Storm were banned from ever competing again?

'Is this the magic formula that explains why Storm's suddenly gone from carthorse to wonder horse?' Raoul asked slyly, watching with amusement as Casey's face turned ashen. 'Nothing illegal in it, I hope.'

She snatched it from him. 'Don't be ridiculous. It's a vitamin drink.'

Sensing hostility from the groom, Storm let fly with a hoof, only just missing him.

'Is that what they call it these days?' Raoul said, watching them go.

17

'JANET WAS QUITE aggrieved at having to disclose one of her secret recipes,' Mrs Smith said, 'but under the circumstances she completely understood. She says here that her Potion Fifty-Nine contains the finest grade of spirulina – a high-protein algae superfood; powdered wheatgrass; B vitamins; Co-Q 10, an energy-boosting enzyme; linseed oil; omegas three, six and nine; iron and magnesium, made palatable with carrot and apple juice. A mutual chemist friend of ours has tested it and written a certified letter to that effect.'

She removed her reading glasses and looked at Casey. 'So Raoul can make all the allegations he likes. He's the one who'll wind up looking silly.'

Casey exhaled. 'That's a relief.' A small frown creased her brow. 'All the same, we need to watch our backs.

If Raoul can stoop to that, who knows what he's capable of.'

But she refused to dwell on it. As Mrs Smith was always telling her, she needed to let her riding do the talking.

Confidence boosted by her top ten finish at Burnham Market, Casey found that the eventing world was a very different place when you had a modicum of proven talent, nice clothes, a reasonable horsebox and a mount that other riders coveted. It helped too that she and Mrs Smith were friends with Peter and Evan, both enormously popular on the circuit. The camaraderie Casey had glimpsed at Larksong Manor widened little by little to include her and her coach, although they were still regarded as eccentric.

Most riders she met were defiantly down to earth. The high-risk nature of the sport, the likelihood of serious injury or death, meant that even the best were routinely humbled. It was a sport that attracted passionate amateurs from every conceivable walk of life. They were, Casey found, a cheery bunch of obsessives. At weekends, they left behind their day jobs as accountants, teachers, nurses or actors and spent crazy amounts of money for the pleasure of racing hell for leather across the countryside over death-defying jumps in mud, gales and heatwaves.

Judging by the gossip, some of the pro riders, who risked their necks nearly every week of their lives, liked to let off steam with wild parties. Casey was mystified as to how they found either the time or the

173

energy. She loved her new life, but it was draining. The combination of training and taking care of Storm, home-schooling, and running and doing yoga for fitness meant that she fell into bed each night, tired to the bone. But it was paying off.

Towards the end of April, she and Mrs Smith went to the Badminton Horse Trials in Gloucestershire. On the one hand it was exhilarating to be there. On the other, it was terrifying. The standard of the dressage seemed impossibly high, the fences mountainous. Storm was filling out nicely but he was still on the lean side. It was hard to believe that in a year's time he'd be a match for the horses that competed at Badminton Park, muscles writhing like snakes beneath their glossy coats, and even harder to believe that she'd be a match for the lithe, golden men and women who strode by in their immaculate top hats and tails: the greatest equestrians on the planet.

Not for the first time, she began to have serious doubts about the task she'd set herself. Every rider to whom she'd spoken had confirmed what Mrs Smith first told her, that on average it took a minimum of five years to get a horse to Badminton, so arduous was the qualifying procedure.

'The days when an amateur barely out of their teens could show up and win Badminton are long gone,' Alex Lang's groom told Casey. 'You'd have more chance of winning the lottery. A very rare exception would be someone like Anna Sparks, who has both a world-class horse in Rough Diamond and about ten years of competition experience. She'll have a good shot at it next year and I know she's obsessed with becoming the youngest winner of Badminton since Richard Walker won it on Pasha back in 1969, aged eighteen and two hundred and forty-seven days. Alex will have to look to his laurels.'

Sitting by the water jump with Mrs Smith on cross-country Sunday, feeling gauche, naive and every bit the fantasist Mrs Ridgeley had accused her of being, Casey said in a small voice: 'Is my dream an impossible one, Mrs Smith? Should I give up now before it goes any further and costs Ladyhawke Enterprises any more of their sponsorship money?'

'If you're starting to think that way then, yes, you should,' Mrs Smith said bluntly. 'If, however, you still have the champion's heart you did when I met you, then the answer is no. Champions don't compare themselves with others. They see themselves succeeding.

'When you rescued Storm, you had no idea where you were going to keep him or how you were going to manage, but in the face of all opposition you did it anyway. You were focused on a positive outcome. You pictured it and you did it. You also backed it up with hard work. If you want to compete at Badminton, you need to do the same. Watch these riders and visualise yourself being among them. See Storm leaping high and proud. Dream it and you'll believe it.'

Thus inspired, Casey finished twentieth at Cedar Hill in May. Two weeks later, she achieved a major milestone by qualifying for the Advanced level at the three-day Houghton International in Norfolk, despite incurring 35 time penalties and 20 jumping penalties in the cross-country after Storm skidded to a halt on the approach to the water.

At Mrs Smith's insistence, they took a six-week break from competition after that, with the aim of returning for the East Shore Classic in Devon in mid-July. It meant that Casey could spend time relaxing with her father, who missed her terribly, catch up on a couple of school projects and concentrate on Storm's dressage.

'Harmony and balance, these need to be your watchwords,' Mrs Smith told her as Casey made a mess of a collected canter in the indoor school at White Oaks. 'Let's see some transitions and shoulder-ins. Think about your hands. Klaus Balkenhol always says that contact that's not been correctly established from the hindquarters is not contact at all.'

The balance of relaxation and rigorous schooling paid off in the dressage section at the East Shore International, Casey's first two-star event, where she scored an impressive 37, as well as in the showjumping, where Storm escaped with just one pole down.

They were on course for a good cross-country round

when he slammed on the brakes at the water jump again, this time depositing her in the drink for 65 penalty points. Dripping and filthy, she hauled herself back onto a disdainful Storm and completed her round, but not before someone – she suspected Raoul – had videotaped her humiliation and posted it on YouTube. By the following morning, nearly five thousand people had viewed her crawling from the pond resembling a mud wrestler.

Peter watched it and found it side-splittingly funny, something he unwisely shared with Casey. 'This is why I love eventing,' he told her. 'It brings everyone down to earth. What? No, of course I didn't mean that your head's in the clouds. I only meant ... Casey, wait a moment ... Case ...?'

'Happens to the best of us,' Mrs Smith said unsympathetically. 'You have to laugh about these things. Whoever put it on the Internet is only jealous because you're on course to do something that usually takes years to achieve. If you so much as stay in the saddle at Aston le Walls, you'll qualify for the three-star at Hartpury.'

Casey went one step further. She wiped the smile off the faces of Raoul and Livvy Johnston with a top twenty finish in the event where she'd done so atrociously the previous year, causing a stir among the reporters. It was particularly satisfying to beat Livvy, who had a run-out on Meridian in the cross-country and was eliminated.

She was hosing Storm down in a happy daze, and

admiring his wet coat, which flashed like foil in the light, when Raoul and Livvy walked past.

'Well done,' muttered Livvy with a scowl that didn't match her words.

Casey was amused. 'Thanks.'

Raoul stood unnecessarily close to her and ran a critical eye over the horse. 'Is Storm still taking the vitamin drink? You might want to be careful in case the FEI do a random blood test. I'd hate to see your Badminton plans derailed.'

The smile left Casey's face. 'I bet you would. Well, they can test away. Last time I checked, carrot juice and wheatgrass powder were legal.'

'All I'm *saying*,' Raoul went on, 'is that when a horse comes out of nowhere and rockets through the ranks, people get curious. Badminton is a long way away. It would be a shame if something had to happen to Storm in between.'

Instinctively, Casey moved to shield her horse. 'Are you threatening us?'

The groom gave his eerie hyena laugh.

Livvy giggled. 'Don't mind Raoul. He's only giving you some friendly advice.'

'Save your advice for yourselves,' Casey said. 'You're the ones who need it.'

They leapt away as she splattered them with the hose.

Changing out of her breeches in the horsebox, Casey found she was shaking. Her bravado was only skin-deep. The joy she felt at competing and making small gains on the horse she adored, with her friend and teacher by her side, was always tempered by the fear that something would happen to Storm. Foul play, an injury, a broken bone, a fall that caused one or both of them to lose their nerve – the possibilities were endless.

So caught up was she in these dark thoughts that when she emerged from the horsebox to find a diminutive old man offering something to Storm, she thought for a second she was imagining it. Then he moved. He had his back to her and didn't see her. Talking to the horse in a low voice, he stretched out a cupped palm. Storm snorted loudly, but he didn't move away. Goggle-eyed, he fussed and fretted on the end of his lead rope.

A hundred horror stories about fixers, people who'd been paid by rivals to drug or nobble horses, raced through Casey's brain. She sprang forward. 'Get away from him,' she cried. 'What do you think you're doing?'

The man stiffened. He seemed to fold into himself like a beaten mongrel. When he turned, Casey's breath caught in her throat. His face was purple with illness. It was a warm day but he trembled constantly, inhaling in shallow gasps. His shabby suit hung in folds from his wasted frame.

'Can I help you?' she asked more gently. If he was a fixer, he was a very sick one.

His rheumy eyes met hers. 'Too late for that.' With effort, he tapped the right pocket of his jacket in which a packet of cigarettes nestled. 'Coffin nails they called these when I was at school. Should have listened. Course, you never do at that age. Think you know best. Think you have the world by the tail.'

He jerked his wizened chin towards Storm. 'I knew a horse like this once.'

The penny dropped. Casey knew at once who he was. A wave of terror went through her. All she could think was: what if he's come to claim ownership of Storm? What if he's come to take my precious horse from me and there's no legal way I can stop him?

She said carefully, 'What was his name, this horse?'

He pulled out a cigarette and lit it with shaking yellow fingers. 'Silver Cyclone.' He exhaled on the second word, blowing out smoke in a steam train plume. 'Greatest horse I've ever known. Had him X-rayed once when he was under the weather. The vet came to me in shock. He said, "Lev, Silver Cyclone's heart is twice the size of that of a normal horse!"'

Casey stared at him. 'What does that mean?' She had visions of Storm dropping down dead from a heart attack if she pushed him too hard.

The old man had a coughing fit. It went on for so long and was so violent that Casey started to think he was about to collapse. She looked around for help. A stable boy she knew hurried by. She was on the verge of asking him to call an ambulance when the old man got his breath back.

'Apologies,' he muttered. 'Damn nuisance, this disease.' He drew on the cigarette.

'You were telling me about his huge heart,' Casey reminded him. 'Is ... I mean, *was* it a bad thing?'

'Oh, no. It's the very best thing. Ever heard of Eclipse, the iconic American racehorse? A four-legged bolt of lightning. Eclipse had a heart twice the size of that of the average horse, and he passed that gene – they call it the X-factor – down through his dam line. Phar Lap, the legendary Australian racehorse, also had a double-sized heart. And what about the red stallion, Secretariat, the greatest racehorse who ever lived, a virtual machine? Won the Triple Crown by *thirty-one* lengths, a record that's never been broken. When he died, they found his heart was two and a half times that of an ordinary horse. So when I learned that Silver Cyclone had a king-sized heart, I thought it was an omen.'

Casey was mesmerised by the thought of these super-horses burning up the track with their giant beating hearts. 'And was it?'

He sucked on the cigarette again, bringing on another attack of choking and wheezing.

Recovering he said: 'Perhaps, but I chose the wrong destiny for him. I rescued him once, so he has that to thank me for, but in my own way I was worse than the circus I saved him from. I was hell bent on racing him and he wanted no part of it. He broke my heart and cost me my fortune so I turned on him. Tried to destroy him. It's painful to admit, but I wanted him to suffer. *Really* suffer. My family begged me to get rid of him, but I wanted to destroy his spirit. I tried beating him, tried starving him, but no matter what I did to him the look in his eyes, accusing me, condemning me, never died.'

Tears began to flow freely down his face. 'For what it's worth, I'll take my shame to the grave. I will never forgive myself.'

Casey didn't know what to say. In the weeks after she'd rescued Storm from the knacker's yard, she'd ranted at his previous owner on numerous occasions in her head. She'd called the man she considered a monster every name under the sun, and wished he could experience a fraction of the torment he'd inflicted on the horse. Now it was obvious he'd experienced that and worse.

The man stamped out his cigarette with a scuffed shoe and gazed at Storm with infinite sorrow. 'I came here because I saw a picture of your horse in a newspaper a while back and thought I was seeing a spectre. I've not been able to get that image out of my head ever since. You see, Silver Cyclone, he meant more to me once than my own family. If I thought ...' His voice cracked. 'If I thought that he was alive somewhere, that he was being taken care of, if I knew he was content, I could die in peace.'

Casey went to Storm, pressed her cheek against his and stroked his nose. The horse was trembling, but under Casey's touch his breathing calmed. 'I don't know about your Silver Cyclone,' she said. 'But I can tell you that I love *my* Storm more than anything on earth. I'd face down lions to protect him.'

She added defiantly: 'Nothing and no one will ever take him from me.'

A ghost of a smile touched the corner of the man's thin, sad mouth. 'Thank you. Thank you, Casey Blue. That's all I needed to hear.'

And with that he turned and stumbled away.

Casey knew even then that it was the last she'd ever see of him.

On the drive home from Northamptonshire, she said triumphantly to Mrs Smith: 'I know the identity of our mysterious sponsor.'

The Land Rover swerved, causing the trailing horsebox to sway alarmingly. Mrs Smith leaned on the hooter. 'Some people shouldn't be allowed on the road.' She looked sharply at Casey. 'You do?'

'Okay, I'm not certain he's the person behind Ladyhawke Enterprises, but I'm ninety-nine per cent sure.' And she told Mrs Smith about the old man.

At the end of the story, her friend was silent. Casey prompted: '*Well*, what do you think?'

Mrs Smith flicked on the left indicator and changed lanes. 'Not sure. Seems unlikely if he's in such a poor state of health and it doesn't sound as if he could afford it if he's walking about in a threadbare suit. Besides, what would be in it for him?'

Casey hid her exasperation. Surely it was obvious. 'He feels guilty. He wants to make up for past wrongs.'

Mrs Smith's mouth twisted. 'If there's one thing I've

learned in my sixty-three years, it's that no amount of money can erase the past.'

'But it helps,' Casey pushed.

Her friend smiled. 'Yes,' she acknowledged, 'it definitely helps.'

18

IN THE EIGHTEEN months that Casey had been on the horse trials circuit, Roland Blue had never once been to an event. It wasn't, he explained, that he didn't want to see her ride. There was nothing he enjoyed more than watching her school Storm at White Oaks. It was just that he was terrified of seeing her fall.

'If I'd seen you floundering around in the lake at the East Shore Classic, I wouldn't have been able to stop myself from diving in to rescue you. Besides, I can hardly tell one end of a horse from the other. I don't want to embarrass you.'

'You're not going to embarrass me,' Casey said. 'Just don't go diving into any lakes to rescue me. And who cares if you don't know much about horses? I certainly don't. I'm inviting you to watch, not take a quiz.'

He laughed. 'Okay, okay. I'll see you in Cambridge.'

'Oxfordshire, Dad. The Blenheim Palace International Horse Trials are near Oxford.'

'Right. See you there.'

Now, two weeks on, she stood with Peter in the shadow of Blenheim Palace, birthplace of Winston Churchill, awaiting her dad's arrival. As he came into view and she watched him approach across the lorry park, accompanied by Mrs Ridgeley, Moth and an assortment of clients from Hopeless Lane, she was ashamed to feel her intestines writhe with embarrassment.

Mrs Ridgeley led from the front, like a stocky general, her thatch of hair more yellow than ever. Roxanne Primley came next, a hulking lieutenant, followed by a nut-brown Moth, dressed like an undertaker, Gillian in her best riding clothes, Jin in an 'Over, Under and Through' eventing T-shirt, and several riding school regulars in a variety of ill-fitting or plain bizarre outfits. Sue Dodd was in black trousers and a silver sequined top – 'In honour of Storm,' she later explained. Her father, in his customary head-to-toe denim and cowboy boots, brought up the rear. They'd all driven up in a hired minibus.

At that moment Casey had an insight into how she, Moth and Mrs Smith must have appeared to Anna Sparks and her entourage when they rolled into Brigstock all those moons ago. Half a lifetime seemed to have passed since then. Peter, who'd been looking forward to meeting Casey's father and had, therefore, deliberately ignored her hints about him probably having 'loads of horses to shoe', murmured: 'Here comes the cavalry.'

'Hello, Casey,' said Mrs Ridgeley. 'You're looking very grown up and rudely healthy. Got yourself a fancy pair of breeches, I see.'

Casey flushed. 'I ... yes, thanks.' She resisted the urge to say, 'I think.'

There was a split second of awkwardness then Gillian broke the ice by throwing her arms around Casey. 'You look fantastic,' she said. 'We're so, so proud of you.'

'Are you?' Casey was genuinely surprised. Her exit from Hopeless Lane had not been an amicable one. Mrs Ridgeley had grudgingly agreed to let Storm stay at the riding school for a couple of months in return for Ladyhawke Enterprises' five hundred pound cheque, but had continued to make it difficult for them to train and to snipe about the lunacy of their endeavour. Finally, Mrs Smith had snapped and accused her of being jealous of Casey because 'the girl has the gumption to do what you would like to have done but did not. At sixteen, she has the courage of her own convictions. She also has the sponsor you refused to believe she could get.'

The ensuing row had resulted in them moving Storm a fortnight before they'd planned to. Much to Mrs Ridgeley's annoyance, Moth had insisted on driving them to White Oaks. She'd all but accused him of being a traitor. Such was her displeasure that when Casey went to say goodbye, she'd barely looked up from her accounts.

Nonetheless, Casey had never forgotten that if it hadn't been for Penelope Ridgeley's kindness at the start, she'd never have been able to afford to keep Storm, let alone compete him. She'd also benefited enormously from her time as a volunteer at Hopeless Lane. For that reason, she could forgive the riding school owner almost anything. When her father had called a week earlier to say he'd bumped into Mrs Ridgeley on the street and she'd immediately suggested they make a day of it and support Casey at the Blenheim Horse Trials, Casey had been touched. She was especially pleased to see Jin.

'Yes, we are proud of you,' said Mrs Ridgeley warmly, and she too hugged Casey. 'Immensely. I can't get near my computer at Hope Lane for the queue of people watching your performances on YouTube – yes, including the one where you're scrabbling around like a drowned rat.' She chuckled. 'Well, you can't have it your way all the time, you know. Seriously, girl, I take my hat off to you. You've proved me wrong. You've taken on one of the toughest challenges in sport and you're making a go of it. Long may it continue. Watching you go head to head with Anna Sparks in the CIC three-star at Hartpury was quite something. Shame she pipped you to the post, but then she's a rare talent, isn't she? She and Rough Diamond are a dream combination.'

'Well done, Casey,' interrupted Roxanne Primley, crushing Casey's hand. 'Great to see a local gal giving the toffs a run for their money. All the same, I should have bought Storm when he was cheap. Don't know what I was thinking. Gillian would have sorted him out in no time.'

Her eye fell on Peter, standing a little way back, watching the scene with a smile: 'Is this the boyfriend? He's certainly cute.'

Casey wanted to sink into the ground. 'I'm sorry, I should have introduced you earlier. This is Peter.'

'The love interest?' Roxanne persisted, wringing Peter's hand until he wondered if he'd ever be able to shoe a horse again.

'I'm a friend and I'm a boy,' he said with a grin. 'As to whether I'm a boyfriend, you'll have to ask Casey.'

Casey went scarlet. She was saved from having to reply by her father, who stepped forward and, having been subjected to one of Roxanne's bone-masticating greetings himself, shook Peter's hand with consideration. 'Very pleased to meet you, son. I've heard so much about you. Casey never stops talking about you.'

'Really?' Peter said innocently. 'What sort of things does she say?'

Casey decided that if she were made to feel any more uncomfortable, she'd explode. 'I tell him you're the best farrier in the world.' She grabbed her father's arm and smiled at the assembled troops. 'Now I'm sure you don't want to waste your day in the lorry park. How would you like to see some cross-country action?'

At ten to three, Roland Blue stood forlornly watching the show jumping in the Marlborough Arena. Mrs Ridgeley and crew had gone off in search of sustenance and Casey was tacking up Storm. He was proud of his little girl, could not have been prouder. When she'd emerged from the horsebox wearing the showjumping jacket he'd made for her, she'd looked so grown up and beautiful that he'd welled up and had to pretend he had a stone in his boot until he'd regained control of his emotions. He'd have given anything for her mother to see her then.

He was proud too that he had encouraged her to follow her dreams, even though he'd been afraid for her many times, especially when the anonymous sponsor had appeared on the scene. Yet the Ladyhawke Enterprises director had been as good as his or her word, generous to a fault and always paying on time. What's more, the company had demanded nothing in return except that Casey displayed their logo on her saddlecloth and did her best at all times.

So Casey was happy. Unfortunately, he could not say the same about himself. He was lonely. Some parents couldn't wait for their children to leave home. Roland had always been the opposite. He'd secretly hoped that his daughter would be one of those girls who was still living at home when they were thirty. Instead she'd been whisked away far too young into a world where he couldn't follow. One morning at Blenheim Palace had proved that.

Oh, it's not that the place wasn't spectacular. When they'd come up the drive that morning, it had been bathed in a dreamy grey-pink light and the glory of it was such that he felt deeply patriotic and nostalgic. It was an architectural marvel, a feast for the senses. A long time ago, on what would turn out to be the only splurge of his brief married life, he'd taken Dorothy to Paris on their honeymoon with the express aim of seeing *le Chateau de Versailles*. Blenheim was every bit as grand. It made Buckingham Palace, that fabled residence of British royalty, look like a nuclear bunker.

But its opulence made him feel small, and the confident, tweed-cloaked country folk striding its manicured lawns with their pedigree wolfhounds and golden retrievers rendered him more inadequate still. The last time he'd felt this intimidated was on his first night in Wandsworth Prison.

These were his thoughts when he suddenly became aware of his neighbour's gaze.

'You look like I feel,' said the man, who seemed vaguely familiar. He smiled, revealing expensive porcelain teeth, white against his tan. 'I always end up feeling like a cello player at a heavy metal concert at these events. Or should it be the other way round? Don't dress right, don't sound right, don't understand the terminology. Is it four faults for a refusal and three for a pole down or the other way round? Or is a refusal now four?'

Roland Blue laughed. 'I wouldn't know. I'm a dunce when it comes to horses. I can only just cope with golf. My daughter's the expert.'

'Don't worry. I'm always embarrassing my daughter with my ignorance of the equestrian world. She bans me from coming to most of these things.'

'I know what you mean,' said Roland Blue, a trifle bitterly. He'd noticed the embarrassment flicker across Casey's face when he and the Hopeless Lane crowd had approached her in the lorry park and been hurt by it.

'My wife is the same,' the man was saying. 'Appalled by my line of work. That's why she kept her maiden name, Sparks. We compromised by agreeing that Anna would have her name and our son should have mine. That was a mistake. The less said about him, the better.'

'You're Anna Sparks' father?' Roland Blue cried delightedly. Not having been briefed by Casey on the subject, he was oblivious to the fact that he was consorting with the enemy. 'Your daughter beat mine at Hartpury in August. You must have been as proud as punch when she won. They were neck and neck after the dressage and showjumping, but Casey finished well down the field after racking up time faults in the cross-country. She said something about playing it safe by taking the long route.'

The white teeth flashed again. 'You're Casey Blue's dad, I take it? Lionel Bing. An honour to meet you, sir.'

'Roland. Likewise. A pleasure to meet you. What line of business are you in?'

Lionel spread his arms. There were sweat patches under the arms of his cream linen suit. 'Lionel Bing, the Carpet King, at your service.'

It was then that Roland Blue placed him. Lionel Bing was the suave, used-car-salesman type who flogged luxury carpets and wood floors on television. He was good looking in a satellite channel news anchor way, although his overlong black and white-streaked hair could have done with a trim, but Roland had always thought his Carpet King adverts quite horrible. 'Oh,' was all he said.

He was relieved when Casey entered the warm-up area with Mrs Smith at her side, diverting the conversation away from floor fittings. Lionel had offered him a twenty-five per cent discount on Norwegian Walnut. Roland tried to imagine the faces of his neighbours at Redwing Tower if he told them he was replacing the torn linoleum at No. 414 with exotic hardwood, and the expression on Lionel's when he brought his lackeys round to fit it.

'A fine animal,' Lionel was saying as Casey guided Storm over a practice jump. 'You'll be looking to sell him soon, I suppose. That's what people do in the equestrian business, and make no mistake it is a business. No room for sentiment if you want to rise up the ladder and pay for the upkeep of these creatures. Riders are continually trading horses. They use the money to buy talented youngsters and pocket the difference. A gifted rider like Casey can make any horse a success.'

'I don't know,' Roland said doubtfully. 'She's very attached to Storm. Loves him to bits.'

'They're not pets,' barked Lionel Bing. 'That's the first thing eventers have to learn. That's where you and I, as parents, sometimes have to step in. These beasts eat money. Anna is fond of Rough Diamond too, but she knows that if she wants to conquer the world, tough decisions have to be made.'

'Yes, but Storm's not just any horse. He's Casey's friend. She saved him from the knacker's yard, you see. Bought him for a dollar.'

Lionel Bing whistled. 'A dollar? You're kidding me. I take it you mean one British pound?'

'No, I mean one US dollar. It was the only money I had on me at the time. I'd left my wallet at home,' he added quickly, in case Lionel mistook him for a pauper.

But Lionel was more concerned with Storm than the state of Roland's finances. 'So let me get this straight. Your daughter saved the horse, but you paid for it, so technically it's yours.'

Roland frowned. 'I've never thought of it like that. I was the one who signed the transfer of ownership papers at the knacker's yard so I guess that's true, but, you know, I'd never—'

Lionel exhaled a minty breath. 'Oh, wow. You must be thinking that this eventing lark is a licence to print money, what with Storm's value going up in telephone numbers.'

'Oh, I wouldn't say that. It seems a very pricey sport if you ask me ... What do you mean about his value? A woman at the London stables where Casey used to keep Storm offered her a few hundred pounds for him, but she turned it down.'

Lionel Bing's laugh was incredulous. 'A few hundred! How much do you think he's worth now?'

'A couple of thousand?' suggested Roland, hoping he hadn't made a fool of himself.

'Well, speaking for myself, I'd pay a quarter of a million for him tomorrow. Or today, for that matter. Cash.'

Roland Blue went white.

'A two hundred and fifty thousand pound return from one dollar,' marvelled Lionel. 'That's some investment. I could do with a man like you in my business.'

Roland recovered his powers of speech. 'Could you?' he said hopefully. He was passionate about his job and having the time of his life working with Ravi Singh, but it was always good to have options.

'Yes,' Lionel Bing assured him. 'I could.' He took a silver case from his pocket and removed a card. 'Really nice talking to you. Why don't you give me a buzz some time? We could go for a drink at my club.'

As Casey's name was announced and she cantered into the ring, Roland Blue decided that he was enjoying himself after all. He felt inordinately pleased to have held his own in a conversation with such an eminent businessman. Perhaps he should go to more of these events. Ravi was always telling him that networking was the key to getting ahead.

19

CASEY WAS ON her way to warm up Storm for their 3.20 p.m. start when Mrs Smith suddenly staggered and clutched at a stirrup leather for support. The blood drained from her face. Casey was on the ground in an instant. Looping Storm's reins around one arm and supporting Mrs Smith with the other, she led her to a bench in the shade.

'I'm fine,' said Mrs Smith. 'Don't make a fuss. You're jumping shortly and you need to focus. This is one of the most important days of your life.'

'I don't care. Nothing's more important than your health. Will you be all right here while I run to the First Aid tent and get help?'

The colour was returning to Mrs Smith's cheeks. 'It's not help I need, it's the answer to a question, but don't concern yourself with it now. I want you to start warming up.'

'I'm not going anywhere until I'm sure you're okay,' Casey said firmly, 'so you might as well ask me the question now.'

'Very well. Who is that man speaking to your father?'

Casey shaded her eyes. On the far side of the collecting ring, her father was deep in conversation with a man who had the look of someone who'd attended many sumptuous banquets. When she recognised him, she almost passed out herself.

'That's Anna Sparks' father, Lionel Bing. The only reason I know is because he roared into Hartpury in his Jaguar to drop something off for Anna and Peter pointed him out. I'd like some answers myself. Why is he talking to Dad? What could they possibly have in common?'

Mrs Smith's cheeks were deathly pale again. 'Lionel Bing is Anna Sparks' father?'

'You don't look well at all,' said Casey, surreptitiously glancing at her watch and noting with panic that she had less than five minutes to warm up. 'At the very least, let me get you one of those rehydrating sports drinks.'

Then, as her friend's words sank in: 'Why? Do you know him?'

'No. That is to say, our paths did cross once or twice many years ago, but I don't think I'd have recognised him if I fell over him. It's silly but I thought he was someone else – a ghost from the past. My eyesight must be going. Why do you suppose he and Anna have different surnames?'

'Who knows? Maybe he's her stepfather or something. Well, if you're sure that you're feeling all right, I'll have a practice jump.'

'Never better.' Mrs Smith summoned a smile with effort. 'Showing my age, that's all. Now go into that arena and shine.'

Head spinning, Casey cantered Storm in a serpentine. Mrs Smith had been lying, she was sure of it. Lionel Bing was the ghost from the past. But what had happened between them to cause such a reaction?

Ordinarily, Mrs Smith was the definition of cool and collected. 'Unflappable,' Morag called her. Yet the sight of the man had almost caused her to collapse. And Casey was sure it was he who was responsible and not exertion as her teacher had claimed. Mrs Smith was as fit as she was. So what was the big secret?

From the glimpse she'd had of Lionel at Hartpury, he was attractive in the plastic, slightly sleazy way of television chat show hosts. He'd made her skin crawl. At a guess, he was five or six years younger than Mrs Smith, which ruled him out as a candidate for Robert, her wastrel ex-husband. But as horrifying as the prospect was, it was not beyond the bounds of possibility that she could have dated him at some point. Her judgement in men had not been the best.

Anna Sparks trotted into the warm-up area, lighting up the grey day with her blonde hair and sunny smile. The fiery flash of the horse beneath her drew almost as many admiring glances. To Casey, Rough Diamond appeared more world-weary and disenchanted with life than ever, but she and Peter were alone in that opinion. The chestnut received as much fan mail as his rider.

Casey had been planning to do a couple of practice jumps but with the arrival of the Anna circus she couldn't face it. Instead she patted Storm, whispered some loving things in his ear and headed in the direction of the collection ring steward. John Stanley, the rider before her, was making matchwood of the combination. She had to put Mrs Smith from her mind and concentrate. Storm had performed a dream dressage and clocked up only eight time faults on the cross-country. If they had a clear round now, they were guaranteed to finish in the top twenty-six per cent of the field, which would mean Storm would leave Blenheim Palace close to becoming a four-star horse.

Waiting for the fence to be reassembled, Casey glanced over at her father. When she saw he was still talking to Lionel Bing, she nearly fell off Storm in astonishment. Whatever it was they were discussing, it couldn't be good. Either Lionel was filling her father in on her feud with Anna, or ... Or what? Lionel was beaming like a crocodile.

Casey's heart started to pound. What could her father possibly have said to him? A man like her dad, who always looked for the best in people and was, though she hated to admit it, easily led, would be no match for Anna's carpet baron father. Surely he wouldn't be naïve enough to mention his prison past?

The commentator's words filtered into her consciousness: 'Casey Blue riding Storm Warning ...'

Sadly, Casey knew her father was precisely that naïve. His trusting nature was the reason he'd got into trouble in the first place. He had a childlike faith in the essential goodness of humankind.

As she bowed to the judges and nudged Storm into a canter, a wave of nausea overcame her. She stared blankly at the fences. Walking the course was suddenly a distant memory. Her carefully rehearsed lines, angles and stride counts were lost in the fog of her brain. She barely remembered the way to the first jump. Storm was going too fast but she didn't have the strength to hold him. With little choice in the matter, she gave him his head.

'It's up to you, boy,' she said as he gathered himself. 'You're the only one who can save us now.'

For weeks after the Blenheim Palace Horse Trials, all anyone could talk about was Anna Sparks' performance in the show jumping. Unfortunately, it was for the wrong reasons. Some whispered that it was Anna's fault. When Rough Diamond refused the double, she'd whipped him with rather too much enthusiasm, drawing shocked gasps from the crowd. Most blamed the chestnut, who, they said, had experienced a nervous breakdown. He'd crashed through the first and second elements of the combination, bolted towards the third and come to a sudden, violent stop, launching Anna high over the jump.

Her fall was broken by a flower display. Scrambling to her feet, she'd approached him in an attempt to soothe him. Inexplicably he'd hurled himself away with white, terrified eyes, demolishing the wall. At that point he had appeared to lose his mind. He'd begun a panicked gallop around the arena, desperately seeking an escape route, rearing or striking out if confronted. It was a sheer miracle that none of the officials or spectators who tried to grab him was trampled.

The resulting chaos and destruction to the course had caused a lengthy delay, putting a lot of riders off their stride. In addition, many horses were unsettled by Rough Diamond's screams of rage and the chaotic arrival of Raoul, a hysterical Livvy Johnston, and a veterinary team. Rough Diamond was sedated and taken away for 'further evaluation'.

Peter's theory was that the chestnut would be kept well away from Anna until he was reasonably sane again before being quietly sold to an unsuspecting foreigner in some far-flung land. In the meanwhile, Rough Diamond had had his revenge. As an indirect consequence of his actions, Casey Blue's name moved higher and higher up the leaderboard as the afternoon wore on.

The commentator became progressively more excited. When it began to look as if Casey and Storm would win the Blenheim Palace Horse Trials, he mined every conceivable idiom.

'Well, this is a turn up for the books. Oh, this really will set the cat among the pigeons. The fox is in the henhouse now, and who would have thought it would be the unlikely figure of Hackney's Casey Blue, seventeen years old next week, on her knacker's yard horse.'

In fact, the very last competitor of the day, Alex Lang, had jumped superbly to snatch the trophy. Even so, when her runner-up place was announced, Casey had been almost smothered by the ecstatic hugs of the Hopeless Lane crew, her father, Mrs Smith and Peter. She'd been bubbling over with happiness. But she'd since found it hard to erase from her mind the barely concealed look of hatred on Anna's face as she passed her on the way to the media centre.

'See you at Badminton, donkey van girl,' Anna had said under her breath.

To Mrs Smith's annoyance, most reporters preferred to talk about why media darling Anna had lost as opposed to Alex Lang's victory and Casey's coup in finishing top young rider. They made excuses for her, blaming 'ill-conceived fences' and a 'rowdy crowd', and said that, for all his superficial perfection, Rough Diamond had always exhibited signs of being a 'wrong 'un'. People would be queuing up to offer her a replacement four-star horse before next season, they said. It was inconceivable that the brightest star in the young eventing firmament would not compete at Badminton.

A rare exception was Jackson Ryder of *New Equestrian* magazine. He'd grown to dislike Anna Sparks intensely after she'd arrived two hours late for an interview with him, spent most of their session texting her friends and stormed out calling him an 'imbecile who knew F-all about horses' when he'd challenged her on the bit she used on Rough Diamond. When he'd objected, she'd threatened to call her sponsors and have them pull their adverts from his magazine.

Though he wasn't brave enough to write about the incident, reasoning that being sued by Anna Sparks' father, Lionel Bing, was tantamount to career suicide, he took great pleasure in chronicling what he called the 'rise and rise of Casey Blue'. The soon-to-be-seventeen-year-old was, he was convinced, the heir apparent to Ms Sparks' crown. 'Can't happen a day too soon,' he muttered to himself as he typed.

He signed off with his favourite line: 'We've seen the future of eventing and it's beautiful.'

20

O N A D A N K, rainy February morning, Casey woke stiff and cold in her bed at Peach Tree Cottage. The deluge outside made her want to pull the covers over her head and go back to sleep, but Storm would be hungry and wanting his breakfast. Sighing, she dragged herself out of bed and into the shower. Five minutes later, she emerged racked with shivers. Morag had used all the hot water again.

Nothing had been the same since the third week of January when Mrs Smith had announced, in the middle of a dressage lesson, that she'd be returning to London for a month or two. She hadn't been feeling well, she said, and her doctor had advised her to undergo some medical tests. She also had one or two business matters to attend to. Casey would be admirably taken care of by the good people of White

Oaks. Morag could coach her and Storm, and was prepared to move into Peach Tree Cottage to keep Casey company during the week.

Casey was aghast. Mrs Smith had not been herself for quite some time, but she'd never so much as hinted that she felt ill. Apart from the occasional headache, the only outward sign that anything was amiss had been her emotional state. She'd been subdued and lacking her usual *joie de vivre*. Often when Casey was speaking to her a faraway look came over her face, as if she'd gone somewhere else in her head.

Initially, Casey had blamed it on Anna Sparks' father. Mrs Smith had been out of sorts since the Blenheim Palace Horse Trials the previous September when she'd reacted so strongly to the sight of Lionel Bing. When Casey had tried to probe her about it, Mrs Smith had laughed and repeated her line about having run into him 'once or twice about half a century ago'.

'It would be like someone asking you in fifty years' time if you remembered Anna Sparks. You wouldn't.'

'Oh, yes I would,' Casey said. 'I'd still remember her in a hundred years. I'd wish I didn't, but I would.'

But her friend would not be drawn.

After Blenheim, they'd decided to give Storm a long winter break to ensure that he was well rested for the next season. Casey had announced on her seventeenth birthday that she was done with school for ever. That meant that both she and Mrs Smith suddenly found themselves with tons of spare time on their hands and not much to do with it. When Mrs Smith seemed restless, Casey put it down to the unaccustomed inactivity, although that in itself was out of character. Usually her friend valued the quiet periods for the opportunity they gave her to meditate or read up on subjects as varied as Egyptology, global warming and Buddhist philosophy. She still went through the motions, but Casey had noticed that she spent more time looking out the window than at the pages. Once, she spent an entire hour pretending to read a book that was upside down.

Christmas was not nearly as much fun as it had been the previous year. If anything, her father was even more distracted and listless than Mrs Smith. His attempts to be perky were unconvincing. Casey had the impression that he was worried about something, but again and again he reassured her that he loved his job at the Half Moon Tailor Shop, was managing fine without her at Redwing Tower and would be making her the best dressage coat and tails she'd ever seen for Badminton.

She didn't believe he was okay at all. If it hadn't been Christmas she'd have tried to pluck up the courage to ask if his agitation was anything to do with Big Red and the rest of the crooks at the Gunpowder Plot pub. It was well over a year since she and Mrs Smith had seen him drinking with them, but because he'd never mentioned the encounter she'd never lost the fear that those meetings had continued. She rarely visited him in London. He and Big Red could be hanging out on a nightly basis and she'd have absolutely no idea. Nor did she want to ask him about it.

The mood of despondency in Peach Tree Cottage infected Casey, but it wasn't the only thing getting her down. She'd grown accustomed to receiving texts from Peter between events. He was witty and insightful about the people and horses he met and places he visited as he and his dad toured the yards, country fairs and championships of Wales and England, and she always looked forward to reading them. Half the time she forgot to reply because she was absorbed in something to do with Storm, but they never failed to make her smile. Then in mid-October they'd stopped.

She'd waited a week before sending him a casual, 'Hey you, how's it going?' text. When he didn't respond, she'd been sure that some technical glitch had prevented him receiving it, especially since he almost always messaged her back within the hour. Her next was more effusive. 'Hi Peter, how's it going in sunny Wales? Freezing in Kent wilderness. Dead quiet 2 after highs & lows of the season. Considering moving into Storm's stable for warmth and entertainment!'

She spent an age debating whether or not to write 'Love Casey' on the end. The word she'd once used so casually now seemed charged. Eventually she settled on two kisses and pressed send before she could change her mind.

When he didn't reply, she spent half a day complaining to Mrs Smith that her mobile was broken because the truth – that Peter was too busy enjoying himself to get back to her or, worse still, was deliberately ignoring her – was too difficult to face. When she received a text that evening, she smashed a coffee cup trying to get to her phone only to find it was from Morag. The White Oaks manager was doing her monthly horse feed order and wondered if Casey had any special requests.

The obvious conclusion was that Peter had a girlfriend. Casey was surprised by how much the thought bothered her, and not merely because a new relationship might jeopardise their friendship – already had if his silence was anything to go by. It gnawed away at her. She found herself lying awake at night wondering who the girl was. A couple of times she woke from fevered dreams where she'd confessed to him that she was a little bit in love with him and he'd laughed at her and told her that he only dated beautiful, sophisticated girls. In her dreams, he'd walked away with his arm around Anna Sparks' friend, Vanessa.

In reality, Casey knew that Peter couldn't bear vacuous, bitchy, over-made-up girls like V, but that didn't stop her imagination from working overtime. Was he besotted with some wholesome farm girl from his local village in Wales? Could it be another eventer? There was a drop dead gorgeous Irish rider who everyone seemed to swoon over. Or had the daughter of one of his father's wealthy stable owner clients caught his eye?

If she was honest, the whole issue of what to do

about Peter had plagued her since Blenheim. He'd come to talk to her while she was preparing Storm for the journey home after her second-place finish. She'd been so sure that he was going to make some crack about her dad's comment that she talked about him all the time, or follow up on Roxanne's blunt, 'Are you a boy *friend* or a boyfriend?' that she'd had a whole speech prepared. She'd decided to break it to him gently but firmly that she'd never, ever be his girlfriend. That their friendship meant the world to her and she cared for him deeply, but only in a platonic way.

Unfortunately, things hadn't quite gone as expected. Peter had congratulated her on her success and been very happy for her, but he hadn't said a word on the subject of being her boyfriend. He'd seemed preoccupied. He'd helped her load Storm, and that, as Casey saw it, was when disaster stuck.

They'd both moved to secure the lead rope at the same moment. Somehow they'd ended up centimetres apart, so close that Casey could feel the heat radiating off him. Peter's pupils had darkened almost to black and she'd been sure that he was about to kiss her. What had shocked her was how much she wanted him to. The detachment she'd felt just moments earlier, as she rehearsed telling him she had no feelings for him, vanished in an instant. She'd been weak with longing. She'd wanted nothing more than to be wrapped in his arms.

For a split second, they stood suspended in time. Then Peter said: 'Casey, there's something I need to tell you, something I've been dreading telling you.'

Unable to speak, she'd simply nodded.

'I'm not going to be able to shoe Storm until next season – not until February or later. We've had an insanely busy year and Dad's pretty exhausted. To be honest, I wouldn't mind a break myself. Would it be okay if I recommended a good farrier close to White Oaks?'

Casey's disappointment had been so great it had taken her breath away. Minutes later, Peter was giving her a rather impersonal hug goodbye. 'See you next year!' he'd said blithely before striding away across the lorry park.

It wouldn't have been so bad if Storm had been working and taking up all her time and energy, but she'd had far too much time to think. She'd been mightily relieved when January had rolled around and she was once more occupied with training Storm.

Then Mrs Smith had dropped her bombshell.

Casey was furious with herself for not noticing that her friend was unwell, but there'd been no obvious physical signs. What Mrs Smith's extended absence would mean for their Badminton preparations, she dreaded to think, but she could hardly say that. A three day event was nothing compared to the health of her best friend, even if it was the greatest three day event in the world.

What she hadn't reckoned on was how isolated she'd feel without Mrs Smith's support. Morag was a lovely woman and a fine teacher, but she was conventional.

She didn't quote from *The Way of the Peaceful Warrior*, W.H. Auden and *Zen and the Art of Motorcycle Maintenance* in the course of a single lesson the way Mrs Smith did, while wearing an overcoat that made her look like a Tibetan nomad, or a floaty batik top in which she resembled an elegant groupie from the Summer of Love.

Morag wore riding clothes every day of her life, including Christmas. She'd even worn them on her wedding day, which her ex-husband had cited as a specific cause of their divorce.

Like Mrs Smith, Morag believed Casey had bags of talent. She also found the girl tremendously dedicated, likeable and well-mannered. But unlike Mrs Smith, Morag had long regarded Casey's riding style as idiosyncratic and flawed, and Storm as being perpetually on the brink of bolting out of control. She'd been very much looking forward to 'fixing' the pair.

The fixing did not go to plan. Casey and Storm quickly became mutually mutinous. What Morag found weird was that the girl and horse had almost identical personalities. Both were a complicated mix of intensity, sensitivity, waywardness, stubbornness and rebelliousness. Both had been grievously wounded in the past. They needed careful handling to bring out their abundant natural reserves of talent and goodness.

Unfortunately, Morag's day couldn't revolve around Casey and Storm the way Mrs Smith's had. She had dozens of pupils. The horse was full of beans after his long rest, which didn't help. Things soon began to unravel. Watching the pair career around Deacon Rise, Casey bruised and sore after being bucked off by Storm twice on the way to the dressage, Morag came to the conclusion that the chances of them competing at Badminton in less than three months were precisely zero.

It particularly annoyed her that Casey blamed their atrocious performance on losing a rose brooch that had belonged to her mum. While Morag sympathised with the loss of something both irreplaceable and of undoubted sentimental value, she abhorred superstition.

'You'll never get to the top unless you take responsibility for your own actions,' she counselled Casey sternly. 'It's not about bad luck or good luck. You can't blame the sudden downturn in your fortunes on lost jewellery. You rode badly today; it's as simple as that. Your heart wasn't in it and Storm picked up on that. My strong advice to you would be to put Badminton out of your head for four or five years or maybe for ever. Be realistic. The harsh reality is that only the crème de la crème make the cut at Badminton. The rest of us have to learn to accept that the closest we'll ever get to it is on television.'

21

MARCH BROUGHT RAIN. A lot of it. Setting out to see Storm one morning, Casey attempted to use a mini umbrella as a shield, but it crumpled beneath the weight of the downpour. She had to abandon it before she reached the end of Peach Tree Cottage's garden. She trudged across the fields, head bowed, getting colder and wetter by the minute. If Deacon Rise had been a disaster, Riverton in late February had been even worse.

Her dad had offered to come. Even if he hadn't sounded so half-hearted she'd have discouraged him. She didn't want him to see her humiliate herself. Which she had done – in more ways than one. The only saving grace was that Raoul and Anna Sparks had not been at either event, and she'd managed to avoid Livvy. Anna's non-appearance was not a surprise. She rarely emerged before the first daffodil, people said, and there was a rumour circulating that she'd not yet found a suitable horse for Badminton.

What Casey had looked forward to most was seeing Peter. It was to be the first time she'd seen him in five months. When she spotted him across the lorry park not long after arriving, her heart had started flapping wildly against her ribs, like a bird trapped in a cage.

She'd told herself not to be so ridiculous. It was only Peter. *Just* Peter. Prior to the horsebox incident at Blenheim, she'd never had the slightest interest in any boy apart from the occasional cute one in a movie or music video, those in her school being mostly obnoxious, swaggering, fully paid-up gang members, or scrawny, acne-speckled worms. Now hormones had disrupted everything.

Not wanting Peter to see her looking all flustered, she ducked behind Mark Todd's wagon and watched from a distance while she recovered.

Peter's looks were not the kind to turn heads. He had brown, muscular arms and the kind of pecs that grace the pages of men's health magazines, but most of the time his body was hidden under baggy T-shirts or a fisherman's jumper with holes in the elbows. His teeth were white but not even, and his face was open and pleasant without being pin-up handsome.

No, what made Peter gorgeous was Peter. His languid movements; his gentleness with animals and respect for them; the way his melty, dark eyes crinkled at the corners when he smiled, and the way he listened and really looked at her as if she was the only person in the world.

Why had it taken her so long to notice these things? Why had she taken him for granted? For the nearly two years she'd known him, she'd treated him like a brother. That was certainly not how she felt about him now.

Casey started forward eagerly, but before she reached him a stylish girl with swinging dark hair, a scarlet overcoat and thigh-length black boots swept up to him. She gave him a lingering kiss. An animated conversation ensued. Casey caught sight of Morag hunting for her. She was supposed to be getting Storm ready for the dressage and trying to repair his untidy plaits, but she was determined to speak to Peter before she rode.

The girl took such an age to leave and touched Peter's bicep so many times in the interim that Casey was in a foul mood when she finally approached him.

'Is that your new girlfriend?' she said, making no attempt to greet him.

The look of surprised delight that had come over his face when he'd seen her was replaced by a sardonic one. 'Happy New Year to you, too, Casey Blue. Not that it's any business of yours, but that was Lavinia Gordon.'

'Is she your girlfriend?' Casey asked again.

He grinned. 'Why, are you jealous?'

She glared at him. 'Don't flatter yourself. I've told

you all along that I have no time for boys, least of all farriers' sons.'

The smile left his face. 'Not good enough for you, am I?'

Realising she'd gone too far, she said hastily: 'Peter, that's not what I meant and you know it.'

But he was already walking away.

The bird that had been thrashing around Casey's chest seemed to have damaged something. The pain was quite extraordinary. A line from a Janis Ian song went through her head, something about learning the truth at seventeen that love was meant for beauty queens ...

Morag came running up to her, panting great balloons of white air. 'Casey, where on earth have you been? You're late for the dressage. If you don't get there in the next ten minutes, you'll be disqualified.'

Leaning into the icy rain as she crossed the Kent fields to White Oaks Equestrian Centre, Casey felt profoundly grateful for Storm. In this time of turmoil, he was all she could truly hold on to. She loved him more with every passing day. Casey rarely thought of Storm in terms of good behaviour or bad. Whether or not they were making progress in their training, Mrs Smith had taught her that it was the rider's duty to understand the horse, not the other way round.

'Storm experiences the whole gamut of emotions

217

and has his reasons for reacting a certain way, just like you do,' her teacher had told her in one of her weekly calls. 'You and he are not dissimilar. Neither of you trust people easily, but once you do you're loyal to a fault. It's a nice quality.'

Whenever Casey felt she couldn't cope any longer with Mrs Smith being gone, the Peter situation, and every other thing that seemed to be going wrong, she'd get a rug and lie on the thick bed of shavings on Storm's stable floor, with Willow the fat tortoiseshell cat tucked under one arm. Being with her beloved horse seldom failed to cheer her.

Storm liked it best if she read to him. Her presence and the sound of her voice seemed to soothe him. More often than not, he'd stand over her and doze. One afternoon, he'd lain down beside her and the cat, and the three of them had fallen asleep together. The stable girls were still talking about it days later. They said it was the cutest thing they'd ever seen.

The thought lifted Casey's spirits and she quickened her pace. There was no sign of Morag or the girls. She supposed they were having breakfast in the White Oaks office. As she hurried towards Storm's stable, she registered something strange. There was a bay horse, not a dark silver one, hanging over the door. She didn't panic. No one ever handled Storm except her or Mrs Smith, but there might have been an urgent reason to move him. A leaking tap or something. But if that was the case, why was there a horse in his stable?

She told herself to calm down and that there must

be a logical explanation, but couldn't help breaking into a run as she crossed the stable-yard to the office. Inside its warm interior, Morag was in a huddle with two of the girls, Lucy and Renata. They started guiltily when Casey came in.

Casey glanced from one to the other with mounting unease. 'What's going on? Where's Storm?'

Renata shifted on her flat feet. 'Didn't your dad tell you? They've taken him.'

'My *dad*? What do you mean? My dad's in London. What's he got to do with anything? Who's taken Storm? You're kidding, right? You've put him in a different stable or something.'

She felt slightly hysterical, but was trying to keep a lid on it. It was a simple misunderstanding. Everything would be fine.

'Can someone tell me where Storm is? Morag? Why are you all staring at me like that?'

'Casey, before you start blaming anyone, I can explain,' Morag said defensively. 'It's not the girls' fault. The men came late last night with all the necessary paperwork. They claimed that you'd specifically asked not to be woken. The girls thought it was because you felt you'd be sad to see him go. I confess, I was stunned to hear that Storm has been sold, but I assume that you and your dad decided that it was time for you to upgrade horses or at least get one a bit safer. The good news is that you are now the proud owner of Meridian, the wonderful bay mare Livvy Johnston was riding last year.'

Casey stared at Morag as if she were speaking Cantonese. Any second now, she'd wake in her bed at Peach Tree Cottage and be overwhelmed by the relief that comes with realising that a hideous nightmare dissolves into nothing with the coming of daylight.

Somehow she managed to get her lips to move: 'I haven't spoken to my dad. What men? Who has Storm . . .' Her voice broke. 'Who has Storm been sold to?'

'Anna Sparks' father,' Morag said. 'He's been sold to Anna Sparks' father.'

22

ROLAND BLUE SAT at the pine kitchen table of no. 414 Redwing Tower, building a castle with one hundred thousand pounds in crisp notes. Outside the window it was pouring with rain. The weather added to his feeling of impending doom.

Somehow he'd believed that the money would fix everything. That the minute he had it in his grasp the future would take on a rosy glow. He'd feel taller and more significant. He'd be able to give Casey the sorts of things he'd always wanted for her – nice clothes, a beautiful home, meals without any of the ingredients missing. Only yesterday such an amount had been an unimaginable fortune to him. Twenty-four hours on, it seemed a paltry sum. Ironically, he'd felt richer, and happier, when he only had the dollar.

Sure, he could blow the money on Caribbean

holidays and the BMW he'd always fantasised about, but he'd eventually have to return to Redwing Tower, where they'd turn on him for being flash and probably steal his car. Alternatively, he could buy a flat in one of the more run-down or remote areas of London, but he wouldn't get much change. And theoretically, at least half the money was Casey's because she'd trained the horse to be as good as he was.

His stomach heaved as he imagined his daughter's reaction to the sale of the creature she loved with all her heart. 'Storm's not just any horse. He's Casey's friend,' he'd told Lionel Bing, but somehow Anna's father had convinced him that Casey was better off without Storm. That the horse was dangerously unpredictable and had no proper grounding for serious competition, and that he, Roland, would be irresponsible in the extreme if he continued to stand by and do nothing.

'No disrespect to Casey's coach, Mrs Smith, but she's old,' Lionel had told him. 'Dare I say it, she's out of touch. According to Anna, she and Casey are approaching Badminton as if it's a fairytale. Get it into your head, Blue, it's not. Badminton is for the big guns. It's serious business. I can't emphasise enough that if a young girl like Casey competes there on a horse that's not only unreliable or poorly trained but potentially explosive, she's not just risking her neck, she's risking her life. Do you really want that on your conscience?'

By the end of the speech, Roland had convinced himself that the money had nothing to do with his

222

decision. Getting rid of the horse as soon as possible was his sacred duty as a parent. With hindsight he saw that he'd been bullied into making a quick decision when the least he could have done was consult Mrs Smith, but he'd temporarily seen Casey's coach through Bing's eyes, as a pensioner dazzled and out of her depth in a hardcore sport.

Not that he blamed Lionel. It was his responsibility and his alone.

He checked that his mobile was switched off. 'Give her time to cool down and realise that she's got her hands on a real treasure with Meridian,' Lionel Bing had suggested. 'A marvellous mare. Safe as houses, but still game to tackle any fence. Next year or the one after that, Casey will have her chance to win Badminton. *This* Badminton belongs to Anna.'

Roland Blue began pacing the kitchen miserably. None of this would have happened if he hadn't lost his job at the Half Moon Tailor Shop, and for something that wasn't his fault. Two days before he'd been due to join Casey and Mrs Smith at Peach Tree Cottage for Christmas, Ravi Singh had summoned him to his office and accused him of stealing money from the till.

To say that he was devastated was putting it mildly. Not only had Roland considered Ravi his best friend, he'd been passionate about his job. Ravi had spent a lot of time telling him that he was a born tailor and he'd come to believe it. Making suits was an art form. Creating order out of the chaotic jumble of cloth, buttons and threads in the back room of the Half Moon

Tailor Shop was every bit as satisfying as seeing the customers' faces light up when they tried on one of Roland Blue's hand-stitched jackets.

In vain, he'd pleaded his innocence to Ravi. At the same time he understood that the tailor had no choice but to fire him. For months Ravi had turned a blind eye to small sums of money disappearing from the till, but when three hundred pounds had vanished at a time when Roland was alone in the store he had to act.

Roland Blue hadn't been able to bring himself to ruin Casey's Christmas by telling her he'd been accused of stealing yet again. Part of him was afraid that she might doubt his word. He'd decided that the best course of action would be to find a new job and then make out that he'd left the Half Moon Tailor Shop of his own accord. It didn't occur to him that he'd still be out of work two months later. Or that he'd be forced to tell white lies on a daily basis. Pretending to Casey that things were going well with Ravi had become a terrible strain.

One evening, as he'd contemplated yet another baked potato dinner, he was surprised to receive a phone call from Lionel Bing. There had been no pleasantries.

'I'll get straight to the point,' said Lionel. 'I'm prepared to pay you two hundred thousand pounds for Storm.'

'He's not for sale,' Roland Blue had responded automatically. Then, after a moment's hesitation:

'I thought you said you'd pay a quarter of a million.'

'That was before he trailed in with the losers at Deacon Rise. Now he's worth fifty thousand less. Horses drop in value as well as go up, you know. You should have taken my offer while you could, Blue. I told you that the horse business was no place for sentiment. If Storm Warning does poorly at Riverton, he'll be worth even less. Well, are you going to part with the beast or not?'

'He's not for sale,' Roland Blue said quickly, and hung up before he could change his mind.

A week later, Casey and Storm had put in a dire performance at Riverton in Cambridgeshire and were fortunate to collect any points at all. When Casey called home after the cross-country, she sounded depressed.

'It's not working at the moment, Dad. Storm and I, we're not clicking. Maybe it's because Mrs Smith's not here or because we're still a bit rusty after the winter, but we can barely do a thing right. Our dressage today was farcical. I'm riding poorly and Storm's playing up at every turn. Finishing second at Blenheim seems like something that happened to somebody else in another lifetime. Sometimes I wonder if I'm the right rider for Storm. We've done the incredible and qualified for the Badminton Horse Trials, but if our form doesn't improve it will all have been for nothing. All that money, all that faith, all Mrs Smith's time straight down the drain.'

That evening, Roland Blue went out with the boys and had more to drink than usual, thanks to a newly arrived social security cheque. When the pub closed and the boys declared themselves tired, he made the fateful decision to go to the Gunpowder Plot. There, he ran into Big Red and the gang – the mates who'd set up the job that had landed him in prison.

He was aware that Casey disapproved of them, and with good reason. Admittedly, their criminal activities were a drawback. However, she also maintained that they only liked him because he'd taken the rap for them and hadn't squealed about it. He refused to believe it. The phrase 'honour among thieves' always came into his head when he saw them. It had been pure bad luck that they'd got away from the mansion before the police arrived and he hadn't. And even worse luck that the householder had woken up and tried to bludgeon him to death with a poker, like something from an Agatha Christie film. He'd had to knock the man out with a lamp to save himself. The fellow was up and shouting in under a minute, but the incident had added significantly to Roland's jail time.

'We tried to signal to you,' Noel 'Foxy' Fox had insisted later. 'Didn't you hear my owl hoots?'

Spared a prison sentence of his own by Roland Blue, who'd not ratted on his mates as expected, Big Red felt extremely well-disposed towards the man. When he spotted Roland at the Gunpowder Plot, he bought him a drink, put his arm around him and regarded him in serious, kindly manner, as if he were a father giving advice to a favoured son.

'Blue, I have a business proposition for you. We

should talk about it – at your convenience, of course.'

And even though butterflies started fluttering in his stomach because Big Red's business propositions were only ever illegal, Roland had found himself grinning like a schoolboy simply because it was nice to feel that someone was interested in hiring him. 'I'd like that, Big Red. Would next Thursday suit?' He was free before that, obviously, but he wanted to give the impression he was in demand.

He immediately regretted agreeing to a meeting, but by then it was too late. Big Red had been swallowed by a horde of merry Saturday night revellers. Roland was feeling rather isolated when a friendly man offered him a seat at a corner table. As the night wore on and his new pal generously plied him with whisky, Roland found himself pouring out his troubles.

It was only next morning, when he woke up with a volcano smouldering in his skull, that he realised that it might not have been wise to tell a total stranger about Ravi Singh's accusations and his own prison past. Worryingly, the man had kept scribbling notes on a paper napkin. When Roland Blue had asked what he was doing, he'd claimed to be writing poetry for his girlfriend. Through the haze of drunkenness that had seemed plausible. Now he prayed the fellow hadn't been a reporter.

He consoled himself with the thought that, with Casey and Storm doing so badly, none of the papers would be interested. Much more concerning was Storm's catastrophic loss of form. With every lacklustre performance his value was plummeting. Perhaps it was time to step in before the horse was once again worth only a dollar. He was the parent after all. And even Casey had admitted that she might not be the best rider for Storm. It entered his head that with the horse gone, he might once more be the focus of his daughter's life, but he crushed the thought immediately. If he did the unthinkable it would be for Casey's sake, not his own.

On Monday, Roland dialled the number on the business card Lionel Bing had given him. Bing came on the line at once, but was hostile.

'What can I do you for, Blue? Make it quick if you can. I'm up to my neck.'

'It's about Storm. We're willing to sell him after all.'

'*We*?'

'Well, I am. I haven't told Casey yet. But as you said, sometimes we parents have to take the tough decisions. The horse is not right for her. I'm genuinely afraid for her safety.'

Lionel Bing became a lot more jovial. 'Good call, Blue. Good call. I can get you the money today. One hundred and fifty thousand in cash.'

Roland Blue was taken aback. 'Last time we spoke you said two hundred thousand, down from a quarter of a million.'

'That was before Storm Warning jumped the cross-country at Riverton like a mule with a bad hip. Now one hundred and fifty thousand is generous. Casey will need a replacement horse too. I have just the thing. Lovely mare called Meridian. A one-star horse. Quite

228

a sensation she caused on the circuit this year. Not a bad bone in her body. Gentle as a kitten. Far more suitable for a young girl than that temperamental knacker's yard beast. I'll let you have Meridian for fifty thousand. That's ten thousand less than she's worth, mind you, so you're getting a bargain, but I wouldn't feel right charging full price to a friend.'

'As you're aware, I don't know the first thing about eventing,' said Roland, who was beginning to feel out of his depth, 'but I do know that Storm is now eligible for four-star events. Casey has her heart set on winning Badminton this year. She'll need a horse that can take her there.'

'Don't be soft, man,' Lionel Bing roared down the line. 'Seventeen-year-olds don't win Badminton. Most of the winners are in their thirties, forties or even fifties. It's terrifying, neck-breaking stuff. Do you really want your little girl to end up in a wheelchair?'

'But what about Anna?' Roland protested. 'Aren't you concerned about her?'

'Anna's *ex-per-ien-ced*,' Lionel said, drawing out the word as if Roland was a foreigner who had difficulty with English. 'She's been competing for over a decade. She's one of the best riders in the world. If any eighteen-year-old can smash the record and become the youngest winner ever of Badminton, it's my daughter. Frustratingly, her horse Rough Diamond has been diagnosed as lacking the mental stamina for top-flight championships and has had to be dispatched. He is on his way to Dubai as we speak.

Storm Warning is not in the same league as Rough Diamond at all, but he has a certain mongrel tenacity and there may be time for Anna to work her magic on him.

'Now, Blue, I'm a busy man. Do we have a deal or not? If the answer is yes, you can collect one hundred thousand pounds in cash from my office this afternoon. We'll exchange Meridian for Storm when we pick him up. The transition will be seamless. Trust me, when Casey gets to know this special mare, she'll forget about Storm in no time.'

Roland felt a stab of conscience, but the thought of being able to leave his lonely flat in grim Redwing Tower at lunchtime and return an hour or so later with more money than he'd earned in his entire life was too much to resist.

'We have a deal,' he said, suddenly euphoric. He was hoping for an invitation to Lionel Bing's club – perhaps a nice lunch while they hammered out the details of the sale – but the man was suddenly all business.

'I'll leave the money and legal papers with my PA,' Bing told him. 'You'll be able to pick up the package any time after two p.m. Our people will collect the horse on Wednesday evening. Oh, and Blue, the less said to Casey before that time the better. If there are any ugly scenes that prevent us taking the horse, my men will be visiting your apartment to repossess my money – *with* interest.'

Roland Blue dealt his one hundred thousand pound castle a savage blow. The previous afternoon he'd come to his senses and put in a frantic call to Bing to try to stop him taking Storm. After multiple appeals to the flooring magnate's PA, Bing himself had come on the line and told him in no uncertain terms that the sale was final. He'd made it clear that it was more than Roland's life was worth to dial Carpet King's number ever again.

All Roland could do now was wait for the eruption he was sure was heading his way.

There was a pounding at the door. He only just had time to scoop up the money and shovel it into a drawer before Big Red, discovering the door was unlocked, let himself in. He was wearing a scarlet tracksuit and carrying a rolled up newspaper under one arm. His bald pate was shiny with raindrops.

'What are you up to?' he asked, looking round suspiciously.

'Nothing,' Roland Blue lied. 'I was planning dinner.'

'At three in the afternoon? You're like an old woman. You need to get out more, mate, and I've got the ideal job for you. A nice little earner. Warehouse with next to no security. In and out. No mess, no fuss.'

Roland Blue felt hot under the collar. The man was a virtual giant – six foot four and beefy with it. His brawny arms were black with tattoos. What if he took a refusal badly? 'Thanks, Big Red, I really appreciate it. You've no idea how much. But the burglary was a one-time thing only. I keep my nose clean these days.

My daughter, she's doing well with her riding, and I don't want—'

Big Red laughed, setting the coffee cups rattling. He unfolded the *Sun* newspaper and spread it out on the kitchen table. On the centre pages was a large photograph of Casey kissing her Blenheim Palace Horse Trials trophy. Alongside it was a smaller picture of a beaming Roland Blue, drunk at the Gunpowder Plot pub. Across the top of the page was a banner headline: 'Blue-Faced Liar: Star Rider's Burglar Father Accused of Stealing.'

'Going straight, are you?' jeered Big Red. 'Keeping your nose clean?'

There was the sound of keys in the lock. Before Roland Blue could muster the strength to stand up, Casey walked in. She was soaked to the skin and her face was so swollen with crying she could barely see.

She ran to her father and threw her arms around him. 'They've stolen Storm, Dad,' she sobbed. 'Anna Sparks and her evil entourage, they've taken my precious angel. All season long, they've been trying to sabotage our Badminton chances, and now they've done it. Dad, you have to help me. At White Oaks, the stable girls claimed ... Oh, Dad, they said you were responsible. They claimed you'd sold Storm to Lionel Bing. I told them you'd never do that, not when you'd helped me save him, not when you know how much I love him.'

It was at that moment that the enormity of his crime hit Roland Blue.

Suddenly conscious that they were not alone, Casey pulled away from him. She gave Big Red a contemptuous glare. 'What's *he* doing here?'

Before either man could answer, her gaze fell upon the tabloid open on the table. Her hand went to her mouth. 'Oh my God. Oh God. It *wa*s you, Dad, wasn't it? *You* betrayed me. You sold Storm.'

She backed away from him, her face stricken with horror.

Roland Blue said weakly: 'I can explain ... You see, back in December, Ravi accused me of stealing. Case, you must believe me that it wasn't true, but I lost my job. Money was tight and, you know, Lionel convinced me that you were too inexperienced to compete at Badminton and that Storm's unpredictable temperament could get you both killed. He said his value was dropping because you weren't doing well and ...' His voice tailed off.

Casey's grey eyes had the searing intensity of a lightning bolt. Even Big Red shifted nervously in his chair. She'd stopped crying. All of a sudden she looked a lot older than her seventeen years. 'I don't want your excuses, Dad. I don't want your so-called love. I don't want anything except my horse. I don't know what you were paid for him and I don't care. If you ever want to see me again, you'll get him back. If you fail, well, this is goodbye.'

And with that she walked back out into the rain.

23

CASEY DIDN'T STOP running until she reached the Victorian house in which Mrs Smith had an apartment. She felt dizzy, sick and as chilled to the bone as she'd been on the snowy February day when she first saw Storm, a little over two years earlier. Her eyes were dry, but her vision was blurred from the rain and too much crying. London was a culture shock – gloomy, loud and aggressive. It came at her in a series of assaults. Each added a fresh layer of pain.

As she stumbled through puddles, she kept saying like a mantra, 'Mrs Smith will make everything all right. Mrs Smith will know what to do. She always does.'

She didn't think about her father. She never wanted to think about her father ever again.

There was no answer when she rang the doorbell

of the ground floor apartment, although a couple of hungry cats rushed up and mewed hopefully. After all she'd been through it was the final straw. Casey leaned against the door and slid slowly to the ground. She curled up on the mat like a stray animal.

Next thing she knew she was being shaken awake. An old lady with the tiny, bright brown eyes and spindly limbs of a robin was peering down at her. 'You gave me quite a scare, dear. I thought for a minute you were dead.'

'I wish I was,' said Casey.

'Wishing one was dead is a privilege of youth. The older one gets, the more one clings to life.' She frowned. 'You're Casey, the horse girl, aren't you? Mrs Smith is so proud of you. You're all she ever talks about. It's Casey this, Casey that . . .'

Then, as if she'd only just noticed, 'You're wringing wet, dear. You'll get your wish sooner rather than later if you don't get out of those clothes. Angelica's at the hospital having some test or other and it could be Christmas before she's home if my experiences are anything to go by. I know she won't mind me letting you in. She'll not forgive me if I let you catch pneumonia.'

The apartment was as spotless as always, but it had an odd, unlived-in feel. Ursula had moved in with her sister just before Christmas and Mrs Smith had obviously been too preoccupied with hospitals and tests to make it the sunny, peaceful home it normally was.

Casey fed the pleading cats, but despite her promises to the neighbour, she didn't have a hot bath or make tea. She knew Mrs Smith wouldn't mind – quite the opposite, but her friend was such a private person that somehow it didn't feel right. She did, however, go in search of aspirin. Her head felt as if someone had sawed off the top without an anaesthetic.

She found the tablets in the second kitchen drawer she looked in. They were sitting on top of a stack of pale blue paper. Casey was swallowing a pill with a glass of water when something struck her. She nearly spat it out.

As if in a dream, she opened the drawer again. There was a knot in her chest. The paper was printed with the Ladyhawke Enterprises' deep blue and white soaring eagle logo.

The gears clashed and grinded in Casey's tired brain. Something was wrong, but what exactly? Why did Mrs Smith have her sponsor's stationery in her kitchen? Did that mean she knew more than she was saying? Did she know the director's identity?

On her desk in the living room, a schoolmaster's one reclaimed from the scrapheap, was an old laptop and printer. Casey moved in slow motion towards it. Beneath the table was a wastepaper basket filled with balls of pale blue paper. She picked a few out. They were all addressed to her.

Dear Casey,

As your sponsor, I was naturally interested in your pre-

*Badminton warm-up events. Please don't worry that you
didn't perform well . . .*

Dear Casey,
  *I hope you're well. I know you must be a little
disappointed with your performance at Riverton, but I just
wanted to say that your results did not reflect your fine
riding or the huge progress you and Mrs Smith have clearly
made with Storm's training . . .*

Dear Casey,
  I wish I could just . . .

There was a faint sound. Casey glanced up. Mrs Smith
was gripping the door handle as if it were the only thing
preventing her from falling down. Her face, usually so
radiant, was grey.

Casey held up one of the aborted letters. Her voice
was flat and emotionless. 'It was you all along, wasn't
it? There was no Ladyhawke Enterprises. Storm and
I never had a sponsor who believed in us. White
Oaks, Peach Tree Cottage, the saddlecloths and rug
with the logo on them – everything was fake. *You*
wrote the letters; *you* set up the tack store accounts;
you pretended to pay yourself a salary. Every single
thing was a lie.'

Mrs Smith started forward. 'Casey, I can explain.'

Casey laughed scornfully. 'Get in the queue. You're
the third person who's said that to me today. You,
Morag, my dad – you've pretended to care for me but

237

you've done everything for your own selfish reasons. You and my father, you're the same. You're fantasists. Well, I hate you and I hate your stupid dreams. I never want to see you again.'

Evading Mrs Smith's hand, she grabbed her wet coat and strode towards the door.

'You hate me for helping you find a home for you and Storm when Mrs Ridgeley would have had you both out on the street?' Mrs Smith's voice was so low that Casey barely heard her.

Casey stopped dead. She turned reluctantly. 'No. No, I don't.'

'You hate me for believing in you?'

Casey sank into the sofa and buried her face in her hands. 'Of course not. You and Dad believed in me when no one else did.'

Mrs Smith sat down beside her. 'Well then?'

Casey lifted her head. 'But you lied to me. Deceived me. You created a fantasy world in which a mythical sponsor had spotted that Storm and I had talent and believed in us so much that they were prepared to sponsor us all the way to Badminton. Do you know how much that meant to me? Because they believed in me, I believed in myself. And the money. You've always appeared to have so little. I'd never have taken one penny from you had I known.'

Mrs Smith nodded. 'I suspected just as much. So what would you have had me do, Casey? What would you have done in my position? The summer after you rescued Storm I had to stand by and watch you worry yourself sick about how you were going to afford to keep him. You were working twenty-hour days, not sleeping and getting more gaunt and hollow-eyed by the hour, and you were barely breaking even. It was obvious that there was going to come a tipping point when you'd be forced to sell Storm, either because you couldn't afford the vet or feed bills, or because Mrs Ridgeley had made your – *our* – position at Hopeless Lane untenable.'

'I'd have managed,' Casey said, but without much conviction. 'Somehow. I'm sure I'd have thought of something.'

Her teacher gave a wry smile. 'Doubtless you would, but that wasn't the destiny I wanted for you – one where you were scraping by, unable to afford decent tack or train, feeding your precious horse on dusty hay. Over the months I'd had ample opportunity to observe you and Storm and what I saw astounded me. You're furious with me because the sponsor who believed in you was a figment of my imagination, but the words of the director of Ladyhawke Enterprises were my words, Casey. *I* believed in you. Still do believe in you. That will never change.'

Casey let out a strangled sob. 'I know and that makes me feel even worse. What a waste. All that faith and all that expense, and everything's been for nothing.'

Mrs Smith misinterpreted her words. 'But don't you see that it hasn't been? Casey, when I met you I was dying inside. I'm not good at the mundane, the humdrum. For the past thirty years I've been suffocating slowly. At times I've felt as if I were being buried alive, creeping toward the grave by degrees. Men I could do without, but I missed horses and the buzz of competition so much it was like a physical ache. You and Storm, well, it's no exaggeration to say that you've saved my life by giving me a reason to go on. When Mrs Ridgeley threatened to put an end to that, I felt I had to step in – for my sake as well as yours.'

'The money – where did it come from?'

Casey had the sudden awful thought that her father might have stolen it to give to her teacher, and that he and Mrs Smith might be in this together.

Mrs Smith read her mind. 'Not by any sinister means, of that I can assure you. Do you remember me telling you that while my ex-husband got his hands on most of my money, he didn't get all of it?'

Casey dried her eyes and nodded.

'I knew within weeks of my marriage that I'd made a mistake and that Robert was not, shall we say, the best money manager. How I wish I'd realised then that he was a crook, plain and simple. Perhaps instinctively, I hid two things from him: a one thousand pound rebate I unexpectedly received from the taxman, and a painting – my father's favourite – which I'd put in a safety deposit box. The money is what saved me when Robert gambled away everything I owned. It's what helped me start a new life in London. I had no idea of the value of the painting until the day after Mrs

Ridgeley issued you with the ultimatum, when I took it to the auction house, Sotheby's.'

'No!' cried Casey. 'Please tell me that you didn't sell your father's picture so I could keep Storm? I couldn't bear it.'

Mrs Smith smiled. 'I did and I have no regrets. I can say without hesitation that he'd have approved. He always did have a soft spot for noble causes. Suffice to say that it's entirely thanks to him that you and I have been supported in our goal of getting to Badminton. I know you're angry with me for deceiving you. No doubt your father will be livid too. But I had no choice. You're both so proud. As you've just admitted, you'd never have taken a penny from me. I'd have had to stand by and watch you suffer as your dreams came crashing down. This way, I've been able to make you and Storm happy, plus experience a sense of exhilaration and accomplishment far greater than when I competed myself. You'll never know how much that's meant to me. I feel alive again.'

She took Casey's cold hand. 'If you can find it in your heart to forgive me, we can go on as before. If you and Storm do as well as I expect you to do at Badminton, you won't need my help any longer. You'll find plenty of real sponsors.'

At these words, the morning's events returned to Casey in an express train rush. She leapt to her feet. 'There'll be no Badminton because I have no horse. Storm was the best thing that ever happened to me and now he's gone, sold to a girl who'll probably send him back to the knacker's yard when she's done with him.'

Mrs Smith stared at her in confusion. 'What do you mean, Storm's gone? What's going on? What girl? Who bought him?'

'Anna Sparks' father. He's been bought by Anna Sparks'—'

Casey got no further because Mrs Smith had collapsed in a dead faint. She regained consciousness in under a minute, but her skin stayed bloodless and she shook as if she was in imminent danger of hypothermia.

Casey grabbed a rug off the bed and wrapped it round her. 'Don't move,' she ordered. 'I'm making you a cup of sweet tea. No, don't try to talk just yet.'

After a few sips of hot, sugared Darjeeling some of the colour returned to Mrs Smith's face, but she couldn't stop shaking. 'This is all my fault. This is my doing. Oh, why didn't I warn you?'

Casey felt weak again. The layers of betrayal went deeper and deeper, like a never-ending onion. 'Warn me about what?'

'Anna Sparks' father, Lionel Bing – I wasn't wholly truthful when you asked me about him. I *do* know him. Until I saw him across the collecting ring at Blenheim Palace I hadn't seen him for thirty years, but once I knew him far too well. We were arch-rivals on the dressage circuit. He claimed to your father that he was ignorant about horses, but that was merely another of his million lies. It was he who bought my horse,

Carefree Boy, from my ex-husband and his groom who killed him. Had Carefree Boy lived, Lionel planned to take my place at the Olympics. As it was, my beloved horse died. That prompted an investigation into allegations of mismanagement and cruelty at his stables. Nothing was ever proved but shortly afterwards he vanished from the dressage scene and reinvented himself as an entrepreneur. That, I suspect, is the real reason Anna Sparks is careful to play down her carpet baron father's equestrian past. It surprises me that the media has never stumbled on the connection, but then again perhaps they have and are either afraid of him or reluctant to upset such a talented young rider.'

Casey was reeling. She'd had enough shocks to last a lifetime. Thirty years on, history was repeating itself, only on this occasion Lionel was using his riches to snatch a horse for his daughter, not himself. Briefly, Casey told Mrs Smith about the ghastly day she'd had since arriving at White Oaks to find Storm missing.

Mrs Smith covered her eyes. She was silent for so long that Casey wondered if she'd fainted again. At last she looked up. Her expression was grimly determined. 'Do you trust me to help you?'

Casey gave her a long, hard look. One by one each of the adults she had trusted had let her down – Mrs Ridgeley, her father, Morag and now Mrs Smith. The difference between Mrs Smith and everyone else, however, was that since the day she and Casey had discovered a mutual obsession with horses at the Tea

Garden, every tiny thing she'd done had been with Casey's best interests at heart. Her motives were utterly unselfish. Everything had been done with love.

'Yes,' Casey said, 'I do.'

24

MRS SMITH RODE the escalator out of Liverpool Street Station with one hundred thousand pounds in cash in a reusable shopping bag. Roland Blue's money was wrapped in brown paper and covered with an old sweater, and the thieves of the City were unlikely to guess she was carrying a king's ransom, but that didn't stop her from imagining that every passenger on the tube was eyeing it with a view to mugging her and making off with it.

After six weeks of being poked and prodded by specialists and used as a pincushion by nurses, she was in no condition to face her nemesis, but for Casey's sake she would do it. She would get Storm back if it killed her. For all she knew, it might.

The tests she'd had so far had been inconclusive. More had been done that morning, topping off an already traumatic week. Not that she'd gone into those kind of details with Casey, who had enough on her plate. She'd said only that it was hard to make sense of the gobbledygook spoken by the doctors, but as far as she could tell there was nothing to worry about. She wasn't about to tell Casey that she'd instructed the specialist that on no account was he to deliver this latest batch of test results until after the Badminton Horse Trials in the first week of May.

Mr Mutandwa had been horrified. 'Angelica, it is my strong opinion that such a course of action is not only ill-advised, but could have far-reaching consequences.'

'Mr Mutandwa,' she'd retorted, gently mocking his seriousness, 'it is my strong opinion that my body is my own and I have the right to decide its destiny. If my services are needed at Badminton, which, sadly, is a matter of some doubt, I shall require all my powers of concentration.'

Holding tightly to the shopping bag, but not so tightly that muggers would think she was carrying anything valuable, Mrs Smith consulted a map and struck out along Bishopsgate.

Poor, sweet Casey; she didn't deserve any of this. Angelica knew very well that Roland Blue would rather die than hurt his daughter, but he was, it had to be said, rather weak at times, not to mention impetuous, and what he'd done was incredibly foolish. It was by no means guaranteed that it could be undone.

She feared for their relationship if Storm was lost for ever. The scars inflicted in childhood could take a lifetime to heal. In the three days since the horse had been sold Casey had refused to speak to her father, let alone see him. Until the situation with Storm was resolved, she was sleeping on the sofa at Mrs Smith's flat.

The headquarters of Carpet King were on the thirty-eighth floor of a glass building shaped like an owl. The reception was laid with deep-pile bamboo carpeting in shimmering gold. In the corridors, strips of California Oak exuded the mingled fragrances of sandalwood and beeswax.

The receptionist, a cocoa-tanned blonde with unnaturally white teeth, was quite clear. No appointment, no meeting. 'Mr Bing is booked up for many weeks ahead, I'm afraid. I'm sorry if you've had a wasted journey.'

Mrs Smith made herself comfortable in a bespoke armchair. 'Oh, he'll see me. Make no mistake about that.'

'What makes you so sure?'

'Because,' Mrs Smith said tartly, 'I know where the bodies are buried.'

Moments later, the door to the inner sanctum opened and a hunched man with a grey, ratlike face scurried out. He cast a resentful stare at Mrs Smith before being sucked away by the lift.

The receptionist almost asphyxiated Mrs Smith with her perfume. 'Mr Bing will see you now.'

Mrs Smith had the greatest difficulty coordinating her limbs sufficiently to cross the sea of gold carpet to the boardroom. The door clicked shut behind her. Lionel Bing had his back to her when she entered. He was wearing black trousers and a pink shirt with a white collar and seemed fixated by something on the street below. When he turned and she saw his face and Brylcreemed badger hair close up for the first time in nearly thirty years, Mrs Smith had an overwhelming urge to run screaming from the room.

'So, Angelica,' he drawled, 'we meet again.'

Mrs Smith had rehearsed her speech carefully, but Lionel Bing, reclining now in his black leather chair, arms behind his head, got in first.

'Let me save you the humiliation of begging for the return of Storm Warning. That poor sap, Blue, has already done that and I sent him packing. The horse is not for sale. Not at any price.'

Mrs Smith put the shopping bag on the cherrywood desk. 'Here is the hundred thousand you gave to Casey's father. Not a penny is missing. You know as well as I do that you cheated him; Storm is worth at least twice that amount. However, if you allow us to collect the horse and return Meridian, who, if I'm not mistaken, was declared unsound by your vet at the end of last season – at our own expense – we'll say no more about it.'

Lionel laughed. 'You always did amuse me, Angelica. Three decades on and you haven't changed a bit. Still on the side of the underdog. Still treating horses as if they're equal to people. Like I said, the answer is no. That wild-child daughter of Roland Blue has about as much chance of winning Badminton as I have of riding a unicycle on the moon. Her father's a convicted burglar, for goodness' sake. Somehow she's lucked into a half decent animal. In my daughter's hands, Storm Warning will be transformed. Six weeks from today, Anna will become the youngest ever winner of the greatest championship in three day eventing.'

'When you die they'll open you up and discover you have a machine for a heart, Lionel. Or, perhaps, a tarantula. Don't you understand that Storm is not just a horse to Casey? He's not a thing that might help her break a record or win a championship. He's her best friend. I'll give you double what you paid for him. That's a profit of one hundred thousand in three days. Surely that's enough even for a man of your limitless greed.'

Lionel Bing had the air of a schoolboy watching a butterfly squirm on the end of a pin. He grinned. 'Sorry, Angelica. No can do. Storm Warning belongs to my daughter. Anna had her heart set on the creature. Casey Blue will simply have to transfer her affections to another horse.'

Unzipping the inside pocket of her coat, Mrs Smith removed a document and laid it on the cherrywood desk. 'I was hoping it wouldn't come to this.'

Lionel snatched it up and checked over both shoulders before reading it, as though a passing bird might be spying on him. His voice came out as a high-pitched squeak. 'Where did you get this?'

Mrs Smith smiled. 'Oh, there's plenty more where that comes from. When you helped Robert defraud me out of my fortune, you left a long paper trail. It makes for fascinating reading, although it's not for the faint-hearted. I'm sure the tabloids would be overjoyed to get their hands on it.'

'Are you blackmailing me?'

'Not at all. I'm merely playing you at your own game.'

The CEO of Carpet King knew when he was beaten. 'Throw in another thousand and you can have your precious horse. On one condition. I want the money now, before you leave my office. You can use my phone to call your bank and arrange it. Only when I see the money – every penny of it – appear in my bank account, and when I have your signed agreement that you'll never again speak of my dealings with your ex-husband and will deliver all compromising documents to me by noon tomorrow at the latest, will I authorise my stable manager to release Storm Warning into your care.'

Standing beside the man who'd ruined her life by destroying both Carefree Boy and her Olympic dream, in order to use his phone to enrich him further, was the hardest thing Angelica Smith had ever done. It was a measure of her love for Casey and Storm that she did it with her usual efficiency.

'Why are you doing this?' Lionel asked as she hung up. 'It won't bring back Carefree Boy.'

Mrs Smith's mouth tightened. 'No, but when Casey wins Badminton I'll have the satisfaction of wiping the smug smile off your face.'

Lionel laughed as he typed in his bank details. 'Dream on, Angelica. Dream on.' His eyes twinkled with glee as the money showed up in his account. 'A pleasure doing business with you, sweetheart. If all my customers were as generous as you, I'd be building gold skyscrapers like Donald Trump.'

'Enjoy it while you can,' Mrs Smith advised him, heading for the door at speed. She couldn't wait to be gone. She had a migraine. 'You can't take it with you.'

Lionel treated her to his crocodile smile. 'Don't be so sure. Oh, there's something I should tell you before you go. It's about Storm Warning . . .'

Mrs Smith flinched as if he'd struck her. 'Yes?'

'He went berserk when Anna tried to ride him. Threw her and would have trampled her if the groom hadn't beaten him off. After that, he went after Raoul like a rabid dog. The man is now in hospital with a broken arm, three broken ribs and a crushed foot.'

She turned on him in fury. 'You treacherous monster . . .' She could hardly get the next words out. 'The horse? What's happened to Storm?'

'Didn't I mention it? He's lame. Stepped on a nail when he was chasing Raoul. Vet says he'll be out for at least six months. There'll be no Badminton for Casey Blue.'

25

'I CAME AS SOON as I heard.'

Casey almost had a heart attack. The last person she'd expected to appear at Storm's stable door at White Oaks was Peter. When she didn't speak, he let himself in. Only then did she move, rushing to him and hugging him wordlessly – awkwardly at first and then tighter and tighter, as if she'd never let him go. In her despair, the solid strength of him was as welcome to her as a desert island would have been to the survivor of a shipwreck.

'I'm sorry,' he mumbled into her hair. 'I'm so, so sorry. I can't imagine what you must be going through.'

'I'm the one who's sorry,' Casey said, pulling back reluctantly. 'What I said the last time I saw you was unforgivable. I was an idiot.'

He smiled. 'Forget it. I have.'

Tentatively, he reached out a hand to Storm and the horse gave a low whicker of pleasure. It was a source of daily amazement to Casey that, despite the cruelty and betrayals Storm had suffered at the hands of humans, he remembered those who treated him well.

Her biggest terror when she'd gone with Mrs Smith the previous day to fetch him from the Sparks' stable-yard was that he'd never trust her again. That somehow he'd blame her for the hurt that had been inflicted on him. But even in the state of high anxiety in which they'd found him, he'd known her as his salvation. She was the only one he would allow to touch him, and the only person able to load him onto the horsebox.

Casey had hardly left his side for a minute since, not least because she was worried about his state of mind. He was depressed. Before his accident he'd lived to gallop and jump. Now he was like a bird with a broken wing. He craned his neck towards the farrier's son and tried to take a step, but managed only a crippled hop.

Peter couldn't conceal his shock. He stroked the horse tenderly. 'Poor Storm. Oh, poor boy. What have those monsters done to you?' He glanced over his shoulder. 'Needless to say, my dad and I will never ever shoe another horse for the Sparks, something for which I, for one, will be eternally grateful. Couldn't you sue?'

'I wish. We had to sign a confidentiality agreement as a condition of getting Storm back. But Mrs Smith says that karma exists to balance the scales of justice for those of us who can't afford lawyers.'

Peter slipped his hand down Storm's leg and carefully

lifted the horse's foot so he could study it. 'Let's hope she's right. What's the prognosis?'

Casey answered without emotion. In the past week she'd been through so much pain that she had reached a place of numb acceptance. All that mattered to her was that she and Storm were reunited. She'd deal with the future hour by hour.

'The prognosis is bleak. It seems that there was a delay of over twenty-four hours before the Sparks' stable manager called the vet, by which time Storm's foot was infected. There was a further delay before the nail was removed under sedation. Apparently, his foot has suffered serious internal damage. One vet says he'll need to be rested for six months and is unlikely ever to compete again; the other says he's out for the season and that, given his temperament, our best option would be to retire him if we can afford it or have him put to sleep if we can't.'

Peter could imagine how well that had gone down. He lowered the horse's hoof carefully. 'What does Mrs Smith say?'

'She said something to the effect of, "These quacks know nothing, and we should not get downhearted until we have the opinion of the kind of people who really understand these things."'

'And who might they be?'

Out in the yard, there was the sound of a car engine. 'Your name came up as one of them,' Casey informed Peter. 'I believe the others have just arrived.'

In the late afternoon sunshine, an odd trio was climbing from an ancient blue Anglia. First to emerge was Janet, maker of Storm's vitamin potions and the foul-smelling but effective concoctions that had helped save him on that first, bitter winter's night at Hopeless Lane. Casey had only met her once, but she was impossible to forget.

She was a not inconsiderable size, for starters, both tall and heartily built, with the ruddy complexion of a farmer's wife. No one would have guessed she'd spent a lifetime in the city. Like Mrs Smith, she had been through a hippy phase; unlike Angelica, she'd never left it. Her voluminous purple and mauve tie-dye skirt could have doubled as a tent. Her white blouse had more ruffles than a romantic poet. As she walked, her various bracelets, bangles and beaded necklaces jingled so much she sounded like a wind chime.

Jin, Casey's friend from Hopeless Lane, climbed out of the passenger seat next. She was still reed-slim and wearing old jodhpurs and a faded Hope Lane sweatshirt, but she'd blossomed. The glasses and braces had gone and she'd become delicately pretty, something her worn clothes strangely enhanced.

Casey was thrilled to see her. Throughout the battles with Mrs Ridgeley, Jin had always been on her side. The two girls embraced, giggling.

'What are you doing here?' Casey asked.

'Mrs Smith called me. She asked if I would bring my uncle.'

Before Casey could ask why, Mrs Smith arrived and there were excited greetings all round. A further delay ensued while Janet wrestled with the back seat, eventually releasing a stocky Chinese man with creased caramel skin and a grey-streaked ponytail down to his waist. He was wearing black martial arts pyjamas with a dragon embroidered on the pocket, and stepped from the car with great dignity. However, he seemed cross. After looking around the stable-yard, he directed a barrage of agitated Mandarin at Jin.

Jin replied in the same language. She was exceedingly deferential and bowed her head several times, but it was obvious she was trying not to laugh.

'Is everything okay?' Casey asked worriedly when she managed to get Jin alone for a minute.

'Yes and no. I mean, it will all be fine. My uncle – his name is Eric Wu – is very scared of horses. There was an accident when he was a boy and it left him with a big fear.'

'Then why is he here? I mean, why did Mrs Smith want to see him?'

Jin shrugged. 'He helped her once. She hurt her back and could hardly walk and he fixed her. He is an acupuncturist, a healer. In London, he is barely known outside the Chinese community, but back in Shanghai people speak about him with reverence. They say he is one of the best who has ever lived. His massages are legendary.'

'But does he know anything about horses?'

Jin shook her head. 'Not a thing. Like I said, he is afraid of them. And he speaks no English.'

The posse set off in the direction of Storm's stable, led by Peter.

Casey hung back and whispered to Mrs Smith: 'An acupuncturist who can't speak English and is terrified of horses? How's he going to help? What on earth were you thinking?'

Mrs Smith had a pleased smile playing around her lips. Eric Wu had started ranting again, but she'd never seemed less concerned. She took Casey's arm. 'I need to ask you to trust me one more time. Can you do that?'

Casey didn't see that she had any option. After Mrs Smith had done the impossible and got Storm out of Anna Sparks' clutches, she'd resolved never to doubt her teacher again. 'Yes,' she said. 'I can.'

But it was hard not to be nervous when Mrs Smith led her away from the stable, leaving Janet, Jin, Peter and Eric Wu alone with Storm. 'Peter will show them Storm's foot. He knows more than anyone about horse's feet and, if something can be done, he'll have as big a part to play as they do. If it can't, well, the sooner we know that the better.'

They sat side by side on the paddock railing, gazing out across the green fields, the smells of horses and sheep teasing their nostrils. Neither spoke. Mrs Smith was confident that she'd done the right thing in bringing Janet and Eric Wu to White Oaks, and she thanked whatever lucky star had caused Peter to drive all the way from Wales on that particular afternoon. But she was in agony, as she was so often these days. Biting her lip and praying it would pass before Casey noticed anything was amiss, she hoped that it would not be made worse by bad news.

Casey was trying, unsuccessfully, to be positive. She no longer cared that her Badminton dreams were in tatters. All she wanted was for Storm to be healthy and happy again. She couldn't bear to see him suffering.

The sun had solidified and become an orange ball, sliding behind the oaks, by the time Peter, Janet, Jin and Eric Wu emerged from Storm's stable and headed in their direction. Their faces were sombre. Casey's heart sank. If they couldn't help, Storm's last hope was gone. What would happen next, she dreaded to think. Mrs Smith had admitted to her that their financial situation was dire. She'd spent almost every penny she had buying Storm back from Lionel Bing. Casey's success at Blenheim the previous year had earned them a horse food sponsorship, which helped, and provided there were no big vet's bills, they could scrape by for another couple of months. Then, Mrs Smith acknowledged, it would be 'decision time'.

It was not until the group drew closer that Casey saw that Peter's body language was hopeful and that his mouth was turned up at one corner. Janet spoke on behalf of the group, jingling as she gesticulated. 'We've gone over your nag's foot with a fine-tooth comb,' was her opening comment. 'It's a right mess, no doubt about it. Never seen worse. But we think we can tackle it with a combined effort. Eric Wu refuses to touch the beast, but Jin here says she'll stick him full of acupuncture needles, as directed by her uncle. Eric is also going to show you how to massage Storm to keep his muscles toned. And I'm planning to dose him up with potions twenty-eight, thirty-three and one hundred and seventeen, plus apply a series of manuka honey-based poultices.'

'And I'm going to make him a sort of slipper,' Peter put in. 'Something sheepskin-soft, but which lets plenty of air in and takes all pressure off the frog. That way, he'll theoretically be able to put some weight on the leg.'

For the first time in a week, Casey felt as if someone had opened the dark room in her head and let in a chink of daylight. 'How long is this going to take?'

'A month,' Janet asserted. 'Peter and I will stay for the first week to set everything in motion. After that, he has to return to Wales to work with his father, and my husband will be getting antsy. I'll be back and forth as necessary. Jin and Eric Wu will stay for the duration. Morag came by when we were discussing logistics, and offered to lend them her caravan. They're good with that so we're all set.'

'Not so fast,' interrupted Mrs Smith. 'If Storm is to have any chance of getting fit for Badminton in two months' time, we need him sound and capable of putting all his weight on the foot in three weeks.'

Janet jingled her bracelets in agitation. 'Can't be done. A month is cutting it close.'

'Three and a half weeks, then.'

Janet gave an exaggerated sigh. 'You drive a hard bargain, Angelica, I'll say that for you. All right, we'll aim to have him up and running in three and a half weeks, but I'm warning you not to get your hopes up. Now, Jin, you can tell your uncle to put his cross hat away and look lively. We have work to do.'

26

TWO DAYS BEFORE the start of the Badminton Horse Trials, Mrs Smith sat in front of the Aga at Peach Tree Cottage sipping Chai tea with a healthy sprinkling of cinnamon in it. She'd stopped believing in divine intervention thirty years earlier when she'd lost her cottage, her Olympic dream and Carefree Boy all in one week, but her feelings on such matters had recently undergone a profound change. If not a miracle, how else could one explain how a horse with a devastating, career-destroying foot injury could, eight weeks on, go tearing around the White Oaks field, kicking and bucking like a yearling?

Two months ago, when she'd asked Janet, Eric Wu and Peter to assess Storm, she'd fervently hoped that their combined skills could give him, and by extension Casey, some semblance of a future. She hadn't expected his foot to heal so cleanly that when the vet came to X-ray it at the weekend it was impossible to tell that it had ever been harmed.

Of course, the real test would come at Badminton when she discovered whether or not her alternative training regime had given him the cardiac fitness he'd need to survive the five-mile cross-country course. His recovery had taken just over three and a half weeks in the end, which meant that Casey had been riding him for close to five. She'd done very little jumping but plenty of strength training. They'd also focused on Storm's weak points in the dressage: flying changes and perfect halts.

There'd been no money to send Storm to one of those specialised rehabilitation centres. They'd had to improvise. Morag's mother was disabled – or 'differently abled', as she put it – so the swimming pool in Morag's garden had a wheelchair accessible ramp. Such was her guilt over the Storm debacle that she was more than willing to let Mrs Smith have use of it. Within two weeks of Storm's injury, his foot had healed enough for them to be able to swim him in the pool. A fortnight after that, he was capable of doing a horse version of aqua-aerobics twice daily for forty-five minutes at a time.

Mrs Smith, meanwhile, had spent hours poring over scientific papers and the thoughts of fitness gurus who believed in using anaerobic training – intense bursts of activity lasting no longer than two minutes, repeated as many as ten times with as little as five seconds' break in between, to build strength and speed. It was what she'd aimed to do with Storm from the beginning, but now it had to be taken to extremes.

'Pushing the heart rate close to its capacity in brief bursts means that the body doesn't have time to send oxygen to the muscles,' she explained to Casey. 'That's what anaerobic means – without oxygen. It boosts the metabolism, increases bone strength and flexibility, and builds terrific power. Of course, aerobic – "with air" – exercise is important too for building endurance. Unfortunately, we're rather restricted in how much of that we can do, so we have to improvise.'

For endurance and toning, they had to rely on marathon pool sessions with Storm. Out of the water, they concentrated on dressage and jumping technique and hill sprints. After he'd been dried off, Casey massaged him under Eric Wu's instruction, with Jin translating. Three times a week he had acupuncture.

The results were astounding. Even at his fittest, Storm had never looked so sleek, so rippling with muscle. As he walked, the light flickered over him like the sun on a silver sea. But it was the change in his mindset that was particularly striking. To the amusement of the stable girls, Mrs Smith insisted on playing Storm Bach's *St Matthew's Passion* to keep him calm. And every day Casey would read him at least a couple of chapters from one of her favourite horse books. This extended regime of love, pampering and massage had given Storm a confidence he'd never had before. He positively strutted.

There was a knock at the cottage door. Mrs Smith checked her watch. It was barely six o'clock. Her stomach gave a lurch. Heaven forbid that something had happened to Storm.

It was the postman. "'pologies for getting you up, love,' he said, eyeing Mrs Smith's robe. 'Special delivery for you. They got me running from pillar to post today and I was worried that if I didn't drop this off now you might not get it till tomorrow. Took a chance you'd be up with the birds.'

Mrs Smith signed for the letter. 'Never apologise for being early, young man. It's lateness that's the real crime.'

Sipping tea in front of the Aga, she studied the envelope calmly. It bore the hospital postmark. So he'd tracked her down. The specialist, Michael Mutandwa, had tracked her down. She'd taken care not to give him a forwarding address to which he could send her test results, but somehow he'd located her. In the top left-hand corner of the envelope he'd written 'URGENT!' and underlined it several times.

She took a nervous sip of Chai. When the cottage phone rang, she started so violently that the tea slopped all over her robe. Grabbing a dishcloth and dabbing at the soaked fabric, she answered, glad of the distraction. 'Angelica speaking.'

'Mrs Smith, thank goodness! It's Roland. Sorry to call so early. I just had to speak to you. I wanted you to pass something on to Casey.'

Angelica Smith wiped the last of the tea splatters

from the chair and sat down, gazing ruefully at her ruined robe. She hoped it wasn't bad news. Casey had had that in spades. As it was, she'd not seen or spoken to her father since the day she'd discovered he'd sold Storm. They communicated entirely through Mrs Smith. Roland Blue was heartbroken, but he was also filled with such deep self-loathing that he understood his daughter's feelings. 'What kind of father does a thing like that?' he'd said over and over to Mrs Smith.

'A misguided one,' she'd told him. 'One who is trying so hard to do the right thing that he does the opposite.'

She'd neither encouraged Casey to speak to her father, nor discouraged her. Casey was old enough to make her own decisions on these things, and Angelica felt she'd meddled quite enough in other people's affairs for one year.

She took a deep breath. 'What is it, Roland?'

He sounded elated. 'The most wonderful, incredible, amazing thing in the world has happened. The only thing that could be better is if Casey won Badminton.'

Mrs Smith sighed. This could take a while. She caught sight of the hospital letter sitting on the kitchen table and shut her eyes to banish the image.

'Are you there?'

'Yes, Roland, I am. Are you going to tell me what this incredible, amazing thing is, or do I have to guess?'

'Sorry, I'll get to the point. Late last night, at about eleven thirty, there was this banging on my door and when I opened it, who should be standing there but Ravi Singh, who owns the Half Moon Tailor Shop where I used to work before . . . Well, anyway, he came in and I made him a coffee and he apologised about a million times—'

'The *point*, Roland . . .'

'Yes, the point. To cut a long story short, the business has been in decline since I left and money continued to go missing. Ravi installed CCTV to try to figure out what was going on, and guess what he found?'

Mrs Smith could feel a pounding headache coming on. 'I'm afraid I can't.'

'It was his own nephew. Can you believe that? His own nephew was stealing from him. The lad had worked out quite an ingenious system too. Ravi was furious, not only to find that this boy who he trusted had thrown it back in his face, but because he knew how much my job at the tailor shop and our friendship had meant to me and how devastating it would have been to me both personally and professionally to be accused of stealing again. Suffice to say that he's rehired me and given me a massive starting bonus – more than equivalent to the salary I would have received had I been working there for the past five months. Anyway, I'm not sure if it'll make any difference to how Casey feels about me, but I'd be grateful if you'd pass it on.'

Mrs Smith smiled. 'I'll be glad to do that, Roland. And congratulations. I could not be happier for you.'

A stair creaked. She only just had time to snatch up the hospital letter and put it in the pocket of her robe before Casey appeared at the kitchen door, tousled in pyjamas. She looked impossibly young. Once again,

Mrs Smith felt a twinge of conscience. Had she done the right thing encouraging a seventeen-year-old slip of a girl to take on the greatest challenge in three day eventing? Not that she could do anything about it now. The die was cast.

'Peach Tree's like Grand Central Station this morning,' mumbled Casey in the husky voice of the newly awoken. 'Who was at the door?'

Mrs Smith decided that partial honesty was the best policy. 'The postman. Wrong address.'

'Hmm, a lost postman? He might want to consider another profession. And who was on the phone?'

'Your father.' Mrs Smith relayed the conversation.

The change in Casey was immediate. 'I must go to him. Would it be okay if I catch the train to London this afternoon after we've finished working with Storm? I could stay the night in Hackney and come back tomorrow morning.'

Mrs Smith gave her a hug. 'Of course it would. We'll manage very well without you for an evening.'

When Casey returned upstairs, looking as if a burden had been lifted, Mrs Smith took the hospital letter from her pocket. She opened the Aga compartment that housed the wood burner and placed the envelope in the smouldering coals. It blazed for a few seconds before melting into ash. 'What the eye doesn't see, the heart doesn't grieve over,' she murmured to herself.

It had begun to drizzle. Mrs Smith hoped it would continue. They'd had the hottest April on record and a little rain might soften the going at Badminton. Reaching for the cinnamon, she prepared herself a fresh cup of Chai.

Ever since Casey had told her father that if Storm was lost for ever it was goodbye, there'd been a Dad-shaped hole in her heart. The agony a person could cause you appeared to be equally weighted with the amount you loved them, and since she didn't have a mum she'd always felt she loved her father double the usual amount. So the amount of pain he inflicted when he betrayed her was proportionate. The fact that he'd compounded it by telling a tabloid reporter about his burglary past and not telling her that he'd lost his job had been hard to forgive.

She was ashamed to admit to herself that part of her had believed he was guilty of the theft charges. Two months ago, she'd have staked her life on his innocence. But then she'd also have staked her life that nothing would induce him to sell her horse out from under her, and he'd not only done that without so much as a word to her, he'd sold Storm to her arch-rival.

But it was the company he kept that had ultimately caused her to cut off all contact with him. When she'd walked into No. 414 to discover Big Red sitting in her chair at her father's table, scarlet-faced and tattooed, acting as if he owned the place, her faith in Roland Blue had taken an extended holiday.

Now she felt awful. Her dad had been over the moon about his apprenticeship at the tailor shop. He'd told her at least a dozen times that he'd felt he'd finally found his niche in life, something he was good at. The exquisite show jumping jacket he'd made her had been ample testimony to that. She should have known that he'd never do anything to jeopardise the job that was his pride and joy. She shouldn't have doubted him.

The bendy bus on which Casey was travelling disgorged her in Hackney, virtually at the foot of Redwing Tower. Her nerves were shredded. She wanted so badly for her relationship with her father to be the way it once was, when it was just the two of them against the world. She wanted him to come to Badminton. Win or lose, it wouldn't be the same without him.

Climbing the graffiti-plastered stairwell, it suddenly occurred to her that her father might not even be there. She hadn't wanted to phone ahead because she'd wanted to surprise him. Now it occurred to her that he could be at the tailor shop, pub, or even the Singhs' house, and then she'd be stuck because she hadn't brought her keys.

When she reached the fourth floor, the hairs stood up on the back of her neck. For the hundredth time she told herself not to be so childish. There was no bogeyman in the corridor, no one lying in wait. There never was.

She was poised to knock on her father's door when a hand the size of a baseball mitt gripped her wrist. A voice purred in her ear, 'Come to visit Daddy, have we, little horse girl?'

Casey was filled with an equal measure of fear and fury. She tried to pull away, but Big Red had the strength of a comic-book super-villain. The blood slowly drained from her fingers. 'What are you doing here?' she demanded. 'Why can't you leave my father alone?'

The giant laughed. 'Don't tell me you believed all that stuff about how he was a changed man and would be going straight from now on? Oh dear, I can see from your face that you did. Sorry, love, it doesn't work that way. Didn't Daddy mention that he's agreed to do a little job for me in the next day or two? Don't look so shocked. You'll get a piece of the pie, I'm sure. Expensive hobby, horse riding. You'll be glad of the extra cash.'

'I'd rather starve than accept one penny of stolen money.' Casey practically spat the words at him.

He released her wrist and she shook it in an attempt to get the blood flowing again. 'Suit yourself. As you learned when your father sold your horse a couple of months back, he doesn't necessarily feel the same way. Take it from a man who knows: once a thief, always a thief. Now, are you going to knock, or shall I?'

'Actually,' Casey said, 'I was just leaving.'

27

INSIDE THE LORRY it was mercifully quiet. It was a large, comfortable, modern one on loan from a showjumping couple who boarded their horses at the White Oaks Equestrian Centre. As Casey locked the door behind her, slumped down on the bed and put her head in her hands, she sent out a silent thank you to them for providing her with a sanctuary from the crowds, smiles and questions at the Badminton Horse Trials.

For as long as Casey could remember, competing at Badminton had been her dream. And yet now that her dream was here, she could barely face it. Oh, sure, she'd be doing her best. For Storm and Mrs Smith's sake, for Peter's, and for Eric Wu and Jin's, both of whom had come to Gloucestershire – Jin to help Mrs Smith with plaiting and getting Storm show-ready, and

Eric Wu to be on hand in case of any injuries (he was still prone to outbursts of agitated Mandarin, but Casey suspected that he'd secretly come to worship Storm as much as Jin did).

So she'd be trying her heart out for them, but it was a heart that had been severely battered recently and she couldn't muster the will to care about the outcome for herself. If her father wasn't by her side, if he didn't love her enough to stay out of trouble, what did it matter?

The previous night she hadn't slept a wink. She'd tossed and turned for hours, tormented by the thought that, while innocent people were in their beds, her father might be engaged in Big Red's "little job". What was it this time? An armed robbery? Another millionaire who wouldn't miss a few thousand?

Her father was not the only man on her mind. The thrill of arriving at Badminton as a competitor was somewhat diminished by the sight, shortly afterwards, of Peter walking arm in arm across the lorry park with a beautiful blonde.

Casey's hopes had been raised when he'd broken up with Lavinia almost five weeks before, shortly after leaving White Oaks. During his time there, he and Casey had bonded again, although not quite in the way Casey would have liked. He'd been charming and supportive, but distant. She'd hoped that he might stay at least a week, but he'd driven away after just three days. She'd hoped too that he might spend his nights in Kent at Peach Tree Cottage and that on one of those nights he might forget about Lavinia and kiss her, but he'd booked himself into a local bed and breakfast and insisted the booking couldn't be changed.

Any fantasies Casey might have entertained about how he'd see her again and go back to looking at her in that special, slightly moony way – which had once irritated her but which she now found herself lying awake, longing for – were crushed in the telephone conversation where he told her about his break-up.

'It wasn't exactly a match made in heaven,' he'd said of Lavinia. 'Her idea of a good time is shopping for alligator-skin handbags, or drinking cocktails at the American bar at the Savoy. Mine is watching a lamb being born or having a picnic on a deserted Cornish beach.'

I'd like those things, Casey had thought wistfully.

'Anyway,' Peter went on, 'she and I realised at about the same time that I was in love with someone else.'

Eyeing the blonde across the lorry park, Casey could hardly blame him for falling for her. All the same, she'd have done anything to change places with the girl. For some reason, the thought that she'd blown her chance with Peter and that he'd never again think of her as anything other than a friend, was as agonising as anything her father had done. She felt sick.

A horse whinnied. Through the window Casey could see Jin putting the finishing touches to Storm's immaculate grooming. He looked majestic. Casey had to keep pinching herself. It seemed beyond miraculous that his foot had healed at all, let alone in time for the championship. As recently as the previous evening, when she and Storm had done the trot-up in front of stately Badminton House, she'd been convinced that the horse inspectors would detect something they'd missed, some niggling ache. But he'd passed with flying colours.

She glanced at her watch. It was quarter past three in the afternoon. In less than an hour she'd be performing a dressage test in front of thousands of people and she was still in jeans. Reluctantly, she put on her white breeches, sleeveless shirt and gleaming long boots, and started on her hair and make-up. She wished she had her mother's rose brooch. For some reason she couldn't explain, she'd drawn strength from it. And, if she analysed it, love.

Love. That was what everything boiled down to. Without it, all the riches and trophies in the world meant nothing. She'd known that all along but it was hard to believe it until she'd experienced it for herself.

There was a rap at the trailer door. Thinking that it was Mrs Smith or Jin, Casey called: 'Come in.'

In came her father, grey with tiredness, followed by an Indian man in a turban, immaculately, if impractically, dressed in a dark suit and pale blue shirt with a matching silk handkerchief in his pocket. He was carrying a sports bag. Her father was in his customary blue jeans, but was wearing a crisply ironed white shirt and a smart black jacket.

Casey dropped the mascara wand and leapt to her

feet. 'Dad! Ravi! What are you doing here?'

Then, remembering that she'd vowed never to see her father again: 'Look, this really isn't the best time. I'm about to do the dressage. I don't know why you've come. I've got nothing to say to you.'

'It's the dressage we want to see you about ...' her father began. He opened his arms to embrace her, but she moved out of range.

His face fell, but there were things he'd planned to say and he was determined to say them. 'Casey, I know that you're still mad at me about Storm, that you'll probably never forgive me—'

Casey turned on him. 'This is not about Storm. This is about what you did last night or the night before. I'm sure you'd prefer Ravi not to hear this, but I'm going to say it anyway. This is about you robbing houses or banks or whatever the hell you've been up to with Big Red.'

Her father was stunned. 'What are you talking about? That's insane. Whatever gave you that idea?'

'*He* did,' cried Casey. 'I had it from his own foul mouth. I was on my way to see you when he decided to enlighten me that you'd agreed to do a "little job" for him. He implied that you might give me a share of the stolen money for my horse-riding "hobby".

Roland Blue was a mild-mannered man, but at these words he shook with rage. 'I'd like to kill him,' he burst out.

Ravi rolled his eyes. 'Like that's really going to help.' He seized Roland's arm and more or less forced him to

276

sit down. 'If you'll forgive me interrupting, Casey, I think I might do a better job of explaining than your father.'

When Casey stayed silent, he put on the kettle and dropped teabags into three mugs. 'A couple of months ago, while drunk, desperate and at the lowest ebb of his life – a depression and desperation brought on by my false accusations – your dad agreed to a meeting with Big Red. It was something he immediately regretted, but as you're aware Big Red is not familiar with the word no. On the day that you rushed to No. 414 to confront your dad about the sale of your horse, Big Red had only just arrived. After you left, your father was in such a state that when Big Red asked if he'd drive the getaway car in a raid on a warehouse—'

'I said, "Yes, no, I don't know," to be precise,' Roland confessed. 'Part of me felt that I'd ruined my life so I might as well go the whole hog and destroy it completely; part of me was simply trying to get him out of the house so I could think.'

'Big Red interpreted that as a yes,' Ravi went on, handing Casey a cup of tea. 'I was with your father when he came round a couple of days ago and there was quite an ugly scene as we attempted to convince him that your father was not then, or ever, likely to rejoin his murderous crew. Fortunately or unfortunately, I was a gang leader in my teens and early twenties and I'm not easily intimidated.'

Casey tried to reconcile what she knew of this very refined, courteous man with the image of a thuggish

277

teenage tearaway. The only thing that hinted at another life was a curving black line above his collar at the back of his neck, which suggested a tattoo beneath.

Ravi put his hand on her father's shoulder. 'It's true that your dad has been up working for the past couple of nights, but he's been at the Half Moon Tailor Shop, not robbing banks. I know because I've endured two sleepless nights with him. One of the things that endeared Roland to me when I interviewed him a couple of years back was that he said he wanted to become a tailor because he had this dream to make you a coat and tails for the dressage when you finally made it to the Badminton Horse Trials.

'At that stage, you didn't even have a horse and I found it fantastically touching that a man could have such faith in his daughter. Of course, he planned to make the coat months ago. I put a spanner in the works by sacking him from his job. The least I could do was help him make it now.'

He unzipped the sports bag and removed a large parcel wrapped in brown paper. Speechless, Casey took it from him. While Storm was injured, she and Mrs Smith had been far too preoccupied with healing him to think about how they were going to get their hands on a top hat and tails for the dressage if they ever made it to Badminton. They'd managed to borrow both when they'd panicked and remembered them at the last conceivable minute, but the hat was loose and she worried that it was going to fall off, and the black jacket was three sizes too large. Casey resembled a circus ringmaster in it.

With a glance at her father, who was watching anxiously, Casey ripped open the package. Inside it was a midnight blue coat and tails lined with scarlet silk. It was the work of an artist, but that's not the only thing that made it special. Across the shoulders was a delicate line of embroidered red and pink roses, with a couple of matching miniature roses on each wrist.

Tears sprang into Casey's eyes. She knew at once what they signified and it made the gift all the more precious. It was as if her mother's love was sewn into every stitch. 'It's exquisite.'

'I helped your father cut it out and do the lining,' Ravi explained. 'The design, the roses and the hand-stitching, they're all your father's work. He's an exceptionally gifted tailor. It was his opinion that the traditional dressage coat and tails was a bit boring and I agreed. We thought it needed an injection of youth, fun and flair. After all, you are Badminton's youngest competitor.'

'Do you like it, Pumpkin?' Roland asked nervously. 'I was panicking that you might have already done the dressage. We were supposed to be here hours ago, but two trains were cancelled and we had to wait ages for a taxi from Bath.'

Casey gave him a bear hug. 'I love it, Dad. It's the most beautiful coat I've ever seen. I don't know what to say. I don't feel I deserve it.'

His voice was thick with emotion. 'I don't blame you

for doubting me after the things I've done. Eventually, you might forgive me for what happened with Storm, but I'll never forgive myself. However, I can promise you this, Casey. As long as I live, nothing on earth will induce me to steal so much as an apple. Please trust me on that. I want to make you as proud of me as I am of you, and thanks to Ravi I might actually manage that.'

'The hat,' Ravi remembered. 'Give her the hat.'

Roland reached into his backpack and carefully removed a top hat wrapped in tissue paper. He unwrapped it and handed it to her. She put it on before slipping into the coat and tails. Both fitted perfectly.

Footsteps sounded on the steps. Mrs Smith came rushing in. 'Casey, are you ready? We're running a bit late—'

She stopped. Her eyes went from Casey to Roland Blue and Ravi Singh and back again as she took in what was happening. She nodded to the men. 'Very good to see you both.' Circling Casey, she examined her from every angle. 'My dear, you look sensational. So, I might add, does Storm. If the two of you don't get extra marks for presentation I'm going to eat the borrowed top hat. Now, are you ready?'

For the first time in weeks Casey's smile reached her eyes. 'I'm ready.'

'Whatever happens, remember I could not possibly be more proud of you,' added Mrs Smith.

'Break a leg,' Ravi enthused before clapping his hand

to his mouth. 'No, whatever you do, don't break a leg! Good luck, I mean.'

Her father grinned. 'Go get 'em, kid.'

Some quirk of fate had seen to it that Anna Sparks was the rider who preceded Casey in the dressage at 4.10 p.m. Losing Storm had not impacted her Badminton preparations in the slightest. Far from it. The handsome profit Lionel Bing had made on the transaction meant that he was more than happy to hand some of it to the German Olympic silver-medallist Franz Mueller for the year-long loan of his champion horse, Best Man.

Mueller had suffered multiple fractures when a young horse he was training was frightened by a lunatic in a sports car. He was out for the remainder of the season and only too thrilled that a rider of Anna's calibre could now continue honing Best Man's substantial gifts.

Anna Sparks was equally delighted. The Storm Warning nightmare now seemed exactly that – a nightmare. In describing the incident to friends, she referred to Storm as a "donkey in thoroughbred's clothing" and claimed that her father had foisted him upon her. She wasn't mad at him, she told her best pal, Vanessa, because the very next week he'd found her a 'real horse', one more than capable of winning Badminton.

The last part, at least, was true. On Friday afternoon, her undoubted talent and Best Man's dressage skills combined to tremendous effect. A penalty score of 32.1 sent them straight to the top of the leaderboard.

When Casey entered the arena and saw Anna on Best Man, a showstopping bay with four white socks, the announcer was going into raptures. 'What a performance. *What* a performance. Thirty-two point one. That, ladies and gentleman, is what it's all about. That's why Best Man earned a silver medal at the last Olympics and why Anna Sparks is being touted as the hottest young talent in eventing. Well, it's hard to see anyone beating that score today.'

As she and Anna crossed paths, Casey hurriedly said, 'Congratulations. Great score,' before she was on the receiving end of one of Anna's looks. It took effort to be sporting under the circumstances, but Mrs Smith had drilled into her that it was important to maintain the moral high ground.

Anna was so taken aback she nearly fell off her horse. She reined him in. 'Thanks. Good luck. What was it that you said a couple of years ago? Something about seeing me at Badminton and that the best rider would win?'

'Something along those lines.'

Anna gave her a cold smile. 'Well, here we are. Let the best rider win.'

28

THE BADMINTON HORSE Trials have been held
on the 1,500-acre Gloucestershire estate of the
Duke of Beaufort since 1949, when they were billed
as the 'Most Important Horse Event in Britain'. Forty-
seven riders, most of them cavalry officers, entered in
its inaugural year, paying an entry fee of two pounds.
Six thousand spectators attended over the three days,
sitting on hay bales. The first prize was one hundred
and fifty pounds and the event made a profit of twenty.

It is said that the first cross-country course was
designed by laying it out in miniature on top of a
grand piano. The philosophy of many early riders when
approaching some of the more terrifying obstacles was
to shut their eyes, kick and hope. From 1951,
Badminton was 'open to the world' and threw up all
manner of interesting stories. The 1960 winner was an

Australian dairy farmer, Bill Roycroft, riding a 15hh stock horse. He and his compatriots, heading to Rome for the Olympics, schooled their horses on the deck of the ship on which they sailed.

When he saw the cross-country course, he said wryly: 'There are jumps out there that you could fall into, get buried in and never be heard of again.'

More unlikely still was the 'Galloping Nurse', Jane Bullen, who won Badminton in 1978 on the 14.3hh family pony, Our Nobby. Glamorous Sheila Wilcox won it for three successive years, and Lucinda Green won it six times. But experience didn't always pay. Top eventer Andrew Nicholson had ridden at Badminton every year for over three decades and never won.

As three day eventing became more competitive and professional, the qualifying process for Badminton became ever more draconian, with most riders taking a minimum of five years to get there. Age restrictions were imposed. Competitors were ineligible until they were in the year of their eighteenth birthday. The new rules meant that only a handful of the world's best riders made the grade. It had become the toughest challenge in equestrianism and those who underestimated it, or came ill-prepared, risked paying the ultimate price.

By the time Casey got to Badminton, ninety starters had been whittled down from one hundred and fifty entries, and the dressage took place over two days. During the course of the event, one hundred and twenty thousand spectators poured into the park. On

Thursday, the weather broke. After weeks of unrelenting heat, it felt like a release. Sodden crowds escaped the worst of the storm in the marquees selling equestrian gear, spices, horse art, polo shirts, dog beds and a lot of tweed.

Friday dawned damp and overcast. Between dressage competitors, people warmed up with cappuccinos and beer in front of smoking burger and cheese toastie bars. Some, like Mrs Smith, Roland Blue and Ravi Singh, carried pots of strawberries and clotted cream to the grandstand so they could be there when the announcer boomed: 'Next we have the youngest competitor in the field, seventeen-year-old Casey Blue, riding Storm Warning.'

After forty-eight hours on an emotional rollercoaster, Casey was shorter on sleep and preparation time than she would have liked, but as she entered the dressage arena at a collected canter, tingling with excitement and nerves, she was quietly confident. When she halted Storm and saluted the judges, her new coat felt like a glorious shield. The silk lining was a balm against her skin.

Mrs Smith often said that success in sport was all about overcoming psychological milestones. 'Until Roger Bannister ran the four-minute mile in 1954, nobody thought it could be done. Now every other weekend runner can manage it. Same with Edmund

Hillary. When he climbed Everest in 1953, it was an unimaginable feat. Now you can virtually rollerblade up.'

She'd repeated this theory when they were bedding Storm down on their first evening at the championship. 'What I'm saying is, don't let the pressure of being one of the youngest ever competitors at Badminton get to you. Remember that there are about a hundred obstacles – I'm including the individual movements in your dressage test – between you and the trophy. Any one of them can bring a rider's hopes crashing down around their ears. Put your whole focus on each of these obstacles and do your very best. If something goes wrong, move on as quickly as you can. Forget about the scoreboard and what others are doing. Good technique and the bond between you and Storm, those are the only things that matter.'

Casey's biggest fear was forgetting the test, but Mrs Smith had encouraged her to learn the rhythm of it, almost like a song. Now she found that each movement flowed naturally from the last. *Change rein in medium trot, Shoulder-in left, Circle left (eight metres in diameter), Half-pass left ...*

Beneath her, Storm felt as light as air. He'd had little competition experience since Blenheim nearly seven months earlier, but he was a relaxed, happy horse, a superfit horse, and one brimming with confidence. His ears were pricked and his dark eyes shone as they transitioned from an extended trot to a collected one. *Shoulder-in right, circle right ...*

Mrs Smith had once said that riding her Grand Prix dressage horse, Carefree Boy, was like riding a creature of myth. That was how Storm felt now, all power and grace. He seemed to float beneath Casey as she changed the rein in an extended walk, halted and reined-back five steps.

So far, so good, but Storm's natural exuberance meant that the collected canter that should have followed was at least two parts racehorse gallop. Recalling Mrs Smith's advice, Casey concentrated on trying to score a ten on the Serpentine of three loops, but Storm's blood was up and they messed up the first flying change.

Watching from the grandstand, Roland could almost see his daughter shift focus. Her body language and hands softened until she seemed to flow with the horse, become one with him.

'This is the toughest bit,' whispered Mrs Smith. 'A Serpentine of five loops, switching from true canter to counter canter, followed by a couple of flying changes, a real problem area with Storm.'

A minute later, she had to restrain herself from leaping up and cheering. 'They did it. I don't believe it – they did it. It wasn't perfect but it was close.'

Storm trotted down the centre-line and halted, immobile. Not even an ear flickered. Casey saluted the judges and left the arena at a walk on a long rein. Storm seemed to relish the applause, arching his neck and strutting a little.

'If confirmed, that'll give them a score of 44.5 and

put them in fourteenth place,' said the announcer.

'What does that mean?' asked Roland Blue as he clapped until his hands stung.

'It means,' said Mrs Smith with a smile, 'that a journey of a thousand miles begins with a single step.'

When Casey Blue's dressage result was posted, Jackson Ryder of *New Equestrian* magazine left the media centre with a temporarily granted all-access pass and went in search of her.

As he'd expected, she was hosing Storm down herself, dressed in jeans and a sweatshirt. A lot of riders left everything to their grooms, barely touching their horses until they mounted. He might have guessed that Casey wouldn't be among them. He watched from a distance as she bantered with her enigmatic coach and young Chinese friend. He noticed the farrier's son, Peter, come around the side of the lorry, stand for a moment looking wistfully in Casey's direction, then go away again. None of the three saw him.

When Casey left the group to lead Storm to the famous Badminton stables, he caught up with her and introduced himself.

'Good result in the dressage. How do you feel?' he said.

She gave him a grin of such unabashed happiness that he was reminded of how young she was. 'Like the most fortunate seventeen-year-old on earth. At the same time, it's all a bit surreal. I mean, look at this.'

She led him and Storm into the stable-yard that flanked Badminton House, where the family and ancestors of the Duke of Beaufort had been resident for four centuries. Gleaming horses grazed on its lawns. The stables were fit for royalty. She opened the door to one of them and Storm followed her in. A plump tortoiseshell cat jumped down from the window ledge and miaowed a pleased greeting. 'Willow,' Casey explained. 'Storm's stable companion.'

Storm dipped his head to accept a couple of mints from her palm, then nuzzled her and lipped at her pockets in an attempt to cajole a few more.

She gave him an affectionate shove. 'We've only been here a couple of days and already it's going to his head.'

Jackson had been wondering if being labelled Badminton's youngest ever competitor had gone to the head of the former 'donkey van' girl, but if it had it certainly didn't show. 'What's that?' he asked, as she lifted something from a bin bag in the corner of the stable.

'My sleeping bag.'

His eyes widened. 'You're sleeping here, with Storm? Not in the lorry or a hotel?'

She seemed surprised that he was surprised. 'This is a big deal for Storm and I don't want him to feel lonely or overwhelmed. I want him to know that we're in this together and I'll be taking care of him every step of the way.'

As he walked back to the media centre, Jackson Ryder tried to picture Anna Sparks sleeping on the shavings in the Badminton stables so that Best Man could feel comforted and taken care of. It was laughably unlikely. He reflected on how all the greats in every discipline, from flat racing to dressage, had formed an intense bond with their horses. Those who didn't often lived to regret it.

Back in the media centre, he kept his observations to himself. Much as they loved a heart-warming tale, the majority of his colleagues had written Casey off as too young, too green and too 'under-resourced' to make any kind of impact at Badminton. Had he owned one, Jackson Ryder would have been prepared to bet his house that they were wrong.

29

THE BBC COMMENTATOR, Lloyd Barton-Jones, crunched up his third successive lemon and honey throat lozenge and, when his producer cued him in, leaned forward with eager anticipation.

'The great Anna Sparks is off and galloping in the cross-country at Badminton,' he intoned. 'Just look at the crowds. The earlier cloud has burned off and the day's turned into quite a scorcher. It's brought eventing fans out in force. They're all here – from the grandmothers who fell in love with horses after watching Elizabeth Taylor in *National Velvet* to the mums and dads who saw Tatum O'Neal in *International Velvet* and their Pony Club kids. Most of them are pulling for Anna, rooting for her to become the youngest ever winner of these horse trials. Judging by the way she's flying over these early fences on Best

Man, Franz Mueller's Olympic silver-medal-winning mount, they're not going to be disappointed, although the cross-country course does have a habit of throwing up surprises.

'Over the last few years, we've seen the legends of the sport, Mark Todd and Mary King, not to mention Pippa Funnell and William Fox-Pitt, show that experience counts at Badminton. However, this week the youngest competitors in the field have served notice that there's about to be a changing of the guard.'

As the camera recorded Anna's progress, Lloyd Barton-Jones frantically signalled a runner for a glass of water. His throat was tickling him again.

'The youngest rider is, of course, Casey Blue, only seventeen and seven months. There's been a lot of controversy over her inclusion at the Badminton Horse Trials on health and safety grounds. No one can dispute that she and Storm Warning earned their way into the greatest championship in eventing on merit, but it is worth pointing out that most of that merit was last season. This season has been a catalogue of disastrous performances and injury for the pair. Still, she made it through Badminton's rigorous qualifying and that's what counts. Very creditably she did too in the dressage yesterday, finishing fourteenth.

'But the cross-country has a way of sorting the men from the boys or, should I say, the women from the girls. Anna Sparks might only be eighteen years and two hundred and twenty-five days old, but she's one of the most gifted young riders in the world with a wealth of competition experience to draw on. She's also riding a medal-winning Olympian, while Casey, famously, is on her one dollar horse, Storm Warning. The odds, one would have to admit, are very much in Anna's favour.

'Gosh, look at Anna negotiate fence ten, Robin Hood Hollow, as if it were nothing. A textbook performance over these flowerbeds, which have seen some thrills and spills this morning. Best Man's going like a train – a little too fast, perhaps, but Anna knows what she's doing, I'm sure.

'Through Vicarage Ditch and on to Colt Pond. The horse is hesitating, but she won't hear of it. They're splashing through. My goodness, she had him over this very tough, ten-out-of-ten-for-difficulty fence quite forcefully. Now he's going even faster. She's really driving him on.'

Lloyd Barton-Jones summoned the runner for another glass of water, He wondered if he could get away with sucking a lozenge on air. Privately, he was worried by the aggression and speed with which Ms Sparks was attacking the cross-country, but he wasn't about to share that with her fans.

'Experience and talent will always out,' he asserted. 'And few riders have as much as this young woman. Just look at how she pushed Best Man through the Sunken Lane. I hope he's got plenty of puff, this horse. They're really moving. But they've survived the Forest Quest and the leap over the red pickup trucks – a doddle for this pair – and are heading down to the infamous Lake complex. A huge crowd has gathered here today. There's picnic baskets galore, lots of happy dogs and burger smoke. Quite a carnival atmosphere, I'd say.

'Anna's made it over the first jumping effort, the Reed Ripple – ooh, bit of a scramble, could have been nasty. She's chosen the short route. They're turning sharp left to take the second Ripple into the lake and ... WOULD YOU BELIEVE IT, ANNA'S IN THE DRINK. Anna Sparks is in The Lake. She tried to turn her horse for the step out and he swerved and stumbled. Sort of tipped her in. If I didn't know better, I'd say he did it on purpose. She's unhurt, but a fall at the water jump – or indeed any jump – means automatic elimination. Anna Sparks' Badminton dream is over.

'She's on her feet, muddy and dripping – not her usual composed, sophisticated self by any means, but that's the cross-country for you, a great leveller. She is not pleased, that's obvious. The PGA Tour golfer, Chip Beck, once described a catastrophic loss as being "tested in the crucible of humiliation". That, I'd say, is where Anna Sparks is now.'

What happened next caused Lloyd to swallow his lozenge whole. Anna charged out of the water like some monster from the deep, her face streaked with black. There was something green dangling from her right ear, though whether it was slime or weed he couldn't tell. She grabbed Best Man's bridle and began lashing him with her whip. Barton-Jones was dumbstruck until he caught sight of his producer gesticulating wildly and remembered that millions of viewers would be expecting him to comment.

'Oh dear, this is not good,' he said inadequately. 'Not good at all. This does not set the right example to the tens of thousands of young riders who see Anna as a role model. Good grief, what is she thinking? This is too appalling for words. The stewards are intervening. They're rescuing the horse. I fear that the Badminton authorities are going to be deluged with complaints. There will have to be a full investigation. The Royal Society for the Prevention of Cruelty to Animals is going to have something to say about this. So, I would expect, will Franz Mueller, who'll be extremely upset about his horse being mistreated. My goodness, this is desperately disappointing.'

Much to Barton-Jones' relief, the cameraman suddenly recalled that there were other competitors on the course and zoomed in on Casey and Storm. He put another lozenge in his mouth. 'I've just been informed that young Casey Blue is being held at the tenth fence. That's the last thing she needs if she's nervous ...'

Funnily enough, Casey was thinking just the opposite. She had no idea what was going on up ahead, only that there'd been an incident at The Lake that would delay her by five minutes. Her first instinct had been to panic. They were through the warm-up fences and the first real tests, the FEI Classics Coral – 'long distance showjumping', she'd heard it called – and she had Storm in a good rhythm. The last thing she needed was to be stopped at a fence that was rated nine out of ten for difficulty: three 'flowerbeds' that made up Robin Hood Hollow – only they weren't flowerbeds at all, but high, round and skinny flower menaces with a ditch in between.

But as she waited it occurred to Casey that the delay could be a stroke of good fortune. Storm's fitness over nearly six and a half kilometres and thirty gruelling fences had yet to be tested and if she could somehow keep him warmed up and on his toes, the rest would allow him to recover. If she got the balance wrong, however, there was a real danger that Storm could refuse or run out, costing them twenty penalties a time. Worse still, he could misstep or misjudge the flowerbeds, with lethal consequences. Already today a rider had been helicoptered to hospital with life-threatening injuries after a fall at Colt Pond.

From the mini spectator stand beside the jump, Mrs Smith, sitting with Roland Blue and Jin, watched her charge anxiously. She too thought it was no bad thing if Storm had a small respite, even though he gave every appearance of being as sound as a bell. During his warm-up that morning, he'd been bounding around like a mustang newly in off the range.

But she was under no illusions about the dangers presented by a break in rhythm on the cross-country, especially when a rider had to jump one of the most hazardous obstacles on the course – a real pig in Mrs Smith's opinion – with only a short run-up. She uttered a silent prayer: 'Please let them be safe.'

Pain ripped through her abdomen. She gasped. Thanks to covert acupuncture sessions with Eric Wu, the last month had been blissfully free of such 'twinges', as she liked to call them, but he'd warned her that he could not keep the problem at bay for long. 'You go hoppital, Miss Smiss,' he'd told her, but she'd paid no attention and he hadn't pressed her. He was as sceptical about Western medicine as she was.

'Are you okay, Mrs Smith?' Roland Blue asked worriedly.

'I'm quite well, thank you. That ice-cream we ate earlier has given me toothache.'

Before he could press her further, the steward signalled and Casey was galloping towards the first flowerbed. Mrs Smith could hardly bear to watch, but Storm arched over the first two with ease and was through the ditch and popping up and over the last one as if they were daisies in a suburban garden.

Casey had a sense of unreality as she and Storm cleared the oxer over Vicarage Ditch. She'd been reading about the fence and other notorious jumping efforts like the Sunken Lane since she was a child. To fly over them on her own horse of fire was like being handed the keys to a favourite dream and told that you could live it.

The Farmyard fifteenth was the halfway point.

Storm was galloping steadily but at full throttle. Casey tried unsuccessfully to slow him as they took the long run to the water jump, leaping the Forest Quest and two red pickup trucks along the way.

Casey was one of the last riders on the cross-country track and a crowd tens of thousands strong had gathered around The Lake, drawn by increasingly lurid accounts of the Anna Sparks drama, plus some quite funny falls in which nothing was damaged except a few egos. The fish and chip and burger bars were billowing the mingled aromas of hot fat, chargrilled meat and vinegar, and Lady Gaga blared from some distant source.

As Casey and Storm approached, the cacophony came at them as if they'd opened the door on some underground club, and Casey felt Storm hesitate. She ran a soothing hand down his neck and urged him forward with her seat and her legs. A long buried memory stirred: herself at fifteen, gangly and horse-obsessed, her riding style more rodeo cowboy than future eventer, trying to coax a recalcitrant Patchwork over an assortment of junk shop furniture and Mrs Ridgeley's flowerpots on bleak winter evenings at Hopeless Lane. She'd fixated on winning Badminton without ever really believing it would happen. Knowing full well that a girl like her, a girl from a tower block in the inner city with a burglar for a father, had more chance of winning the National Lottery. She'd been carried along only by the faith of that father and, of course, later by that of Mrs Smith and Peter. She'd believed in Storm while struggling to do the same for herself.

And yet here she was, galloping down to the water jump in the hoof-prints of legends. The enormity of her achievement struck her with such force that she reeled in the saddle. Thousands of people were gathered and most were focused on her. Television cameras were at that very second beaming her progress into millions of homes around the world. Suddenly she felt ridiculously young and inexperienced. The jumps looked too high, too wide and too solid. The Lake was treacherous. Impassable. Storm was a one dollar horse, out of his league.

That's when she knew that winning didn't matter. It was enough that she was here. It was enough that she and Storm had saved one another, and that she was flying along on a horse who galloped so fast and so smoothly it felt as if he had wings. It was enough that she and Storm were trying their hearts out. If their best wasn't good enough, then so be it.

The first of the narrow, densely packed reed fences that led down to the Lake came at her almost before she was ready for it, and she had to grab Storm's mane to keep her balance. While walking the course, Casey had planned to go the easier route, but Storm veered left as they hit the water and almost lost his footing. They were now committed to the short, hard route.

'She's doing an Anna Sparks!' someone cried, but somehow Casey clung on and Storm recovered. Four strides and they were up, over and out. 'You brilliant,

brilliant boy,' said Casey, giving him lots of pats. 'You're a star.'

They might have escaped a dunking, but they were by no means home and dry. As they jumped in and out of Huntsman's Close and began the long gallop to the Quarry, Casey felt Storm tire dramatically. He was breathing hard – too hard, she worried. With the Quarry still to come, they could be in trouble. She glanced at her watch. They were making great time, but if she pushed Storm and he fell or was fatally injured because he was exhausted, she'd never forgive herself. It was an agonising decision but they were going to have to quit.

She pulled him up. He fought for his head but only feebly. He was shattered. A few strides on he'd slowed to a walk, his breath coming in gasps.

Watching in his booth, BBC commentator Lloyd Barton-Jones was beside himself. 'This cross-country has had more twists than a thriller,' he cried. 'Just when you thought it couldn't throw up any more surprises, Casey Blue, on course to be one of the leaders at the end of the day, has stopped. She appears to be concerned that Storm Warning is flagging. She's stroking him and preparing to dismount. A voluntary disqualification, that'll be. There'll be some questions asked about the wisdom of allowing such a young . . .

'Oh my goodness, I don't believe my eyes. Her horse has other ideas. He's surging forward and Casey has managed to stay in the saddle only by the skin of her teeth. Look at Storm Warning go. He's rocketing along

300

at the pace of a Derby winner. A silver streak, he is. Down the hill to the Quarry he goes. This is one of the toughest challenges on the course. It may yet defeat them. Oh dear, Storm Warning scrambled over that log like the tired horse he is. Is he in trouble? No, he's not. He's flying along like Pegasus. I've never in my life seen anything like it. He's cleared the Big Brush and he and Casey, who is laughing and patting him, are galloping into the main arena for the finish.

'Up in the grandstand, the crowd is on its feet. People cannot believe the evidence of their own eyes. Casey Blue, the youngest competitor ever to ride at Badminton, and her knacker's yard horse, Storm Warning, have not only survived one of the most treacherous cross-country courses on earth, they've set it on fire. It's a heroic effort, and it's hardly surprising that Casey's collapsed into the arms of her coach, Angelica Smith, her father, Roland Blue, and the farrier's son, Peter Rhys. Everyone is crying. There are people running from the grandstand ... I've just been told that they're friends from Storm's old stable-yard, Hopeless ... apologies, Hope Lane Riding Centre. They're hugging Casey, they're hugging the horse ...'

Lloyd Barton-Jones reached for a box of tissues and tried, discreetly, to blow his nose. 'Well done, Casey Blue and Storm,' he said in a muffled tone. 'Well done.'

At the end of the day, Casey was lying an impressive third behind a little-known American rider, Sam Tide, and Princess Anne's daughter, Zara Phillips, but all the reporters could talk about was Anna Sparks and the catastrophe at The Lake.

'Casey, earlier this year your horse, Storm Warning, spent some time at the Sparks' stable-yard. There are rumours that he was returned to you lame,' said the man from the *Telegraph*. 'Could you confirm or deny that?'

'No comment,' responded Casey.

'In that case, could you give us your opinion on what happened with Anna and Best Man at the water jump? Should she be banned from the sport for attacking her horse?'

'No comment.'

There were groans of disappointment.

Jasper Simmonds, the Badminton press officer, leaned forward and murmured in her ear: 'Casey, you're only just starting out in your career. Do you really want to go down the no comment route?'

Casey met his gaze. Colourfully attired in pink trousers, a white shirt, a horse-patterned cerise tie and tweed jacket, he was a genial and much-loved presence around Badminton. Whenever she'd seen him that week, he'd exuded the air of a man who relished his job. Plus he'd ridden Badminton himself, aged eighteen, back in the 'close your eyes and kick' days.

Realising that he was right, she turned to the reporter from the *Telegraph*.

'I'm not going to say anything about what happened with Anna and Best Man. There'll be plenty of people weighing in on it and most of them will be a lot more qualified to comment on it than I am. But I will say this: when I found Storm he was unloved and I gave him love and today you saw him return that love with everything he had.'

Epilogue

I T WAS A little after 8 p.m. on Sunday night when the lorry finally rolled up White Oaks' leafy drive, and close to nine before Casey could tear herself away from Storm. He'd been massaged, rugged up, had his legs encased in cooling clay, and been given so many carrots and mints that he was well on his way to a sugar high.

'If you give him one more treat, he'll be bouncing off the stable ceiling,' teased Peter, who'd more or less invited himself to White Oaks for the post-Badminton dinner.

'I know.' Casey gave Storm a last cuddle and bolted the door reluctantly behind her. 'It's just that I'm incredibly proud of him and I want him to feel adored and appreciated.'

'I think that right now he's feeling like the most adored, appreciated horse on the planet,' said Peter with a smile, momentarily wishing he could trade places with Storm.

But he knew very well that the 'One Dollar Horse', as the media were now calling him, deserved all the affection and treats he could handle. At 2.25 p.m. that day, Storm Warning had jumped a clear round to beat the New Zealander, Ian Brewster, by a fraction of a second, and carry Casey Blue into history.

By the time they'd reached White Oaks, Jackson Ryder's *New Equestrian* magazine article was already online and an ecstatic Morag had rushed out of the office to show it to them.

One Dollar Horse Wins Badminton Lottery

When Casey Blue rescued a starving horse from a knacker's yard, she had no idea that he'd one day reward her with the ride of her life. But according to the Hackney-born 17-year-old, the youngest winner of the world's toughest three-day event by more than a year, it's all down to love, massage, and the Tao of former dressage champion Angelica Smith, her coach . . .

With Storm settled and Willow suitably rewarded with a plate of smoked salmon, Casey and Peter took the path across the fields to Peach Tree Cottage. Night was drawing in and the oaks were violet against the darkening green of the grass and a sky in which a single star twinkled. Through the trees, the cottage had a honeyed glow.

Out of the corner of her eye, Casey watched Peter as he strode by her side, brown arms swinging. When he was warm the veins stood out on his hands in a way that made her go weak, and it didn't help that the muscles in his thighs strained at his faded blue jeans as he walked. The fact that he'd asked if he could come to her victory dinner, that she hadn't had to swallow her pride and beg him, had put a cherry on the cake of the most magical day of her life. But every time she pictured him walking with the gorgeous girl through the lorry park, a shard of glass stabbed at her heart.

'Penny for them,' Peter said as they crossed a field of sheep. 'Are you thinking about Badminton?'

'No. I mean, yes.' Casey took an uneven breath. 'Well, not exactly. I do keep thinking about what happened, but at this moment, no, I'm not.'

He laughed. 'Now I'm thoroughly confused.'

They'd reached a stile. Casey was hot with shyness. Her instinct was to make an excuse and change the subject, but if she did that she'd never know, and it was the not knowing that hurt so much. She said in a rush: 'This girl you're in love with. Is she good for you? Does she appreciate you and treat you the way you deserve to be treated? I mean, I'm happy for you and everything ... Well, maybe not over the moon exactly, but of course I want you to be happy ...'

Peter gave an incredulous laugh. 'Casey Blue, you may be a phenomenal rider but you're a complete dunce when it comes to romance.' He caught her hand. 'Don't you understand that it's you?'

Casey stared at him. 'What about me?'

'You really don't get it, do you? It's you I love. It's always been you. From the moment I saw you walking across the lorry park at Brigstock, all gawky and awkward and impossibly beautiful in this unconventional way, I've never been able to think about anyone else. And believe me, I've tried.'

'But the blonde girl at Badminton? I saw you arm in arm with her. You looked as if you were crazy about her. You were laughing.'

For a moment he looked blank, then comprehension dawned. 'You must have seen me with Kat – Katherine – she's my cousin. We grew up together. We're virtually siblings. She sent me a text to say she was visiting Bath with her fiancé and I invited them to Badminton for a drink and to watch you practice dressage. Neither of them have the slightest interest in horses so they left pretty soon afterwards, but it was great to catch up with them.'

'Oh.' Casey was glad it was too dark for him to see how much she was blushing. He loved her. The thought was overwhelming.

'Look, I know you'll never think of me as anything other than a friend or a sort of brother, but—'

He had to stop then because she was kissing him and her mouth, which he'd wanted to kiss for so long, was as soft and sweet as ice-cream. When he held her, she fitted against him like a glove.

When they were both dizzy, Casey said, 'Now that

we've established that I don't think of you as a brother, shall we go in?'

They walked into the cottage hand in hand. Mrs Smith raised an amused eyebrow, but wisely made no comment. Roland Blue got all agitated and made a big deal about last-minute dinner preparations, even though it was obvious that Eric Wu and Jin had everything under control. Mr Wu was positively beaming.

'Conglatulations,' he said to Casey. 'Storm velly good horse. Velly special.'

Roland Blue opened the door to the crowded living room. The table was laid with a cloth and candles and, in honour of Casey and Mrs Smith, a vegetarian feast. Eric Wu and Jin had cooked up some Chinese treats with rice, Ravi Singh and his wife had brought an Indian dhal, Morag had made a salad, Janet had contributed a fruit punch and Roland Blue had baked a cake in the shape of a horseshoe.

Casey was moved to tears. Winning the Badminton Horse Trials was the best thing on earth, but sharing her success with the people who'd helped make it a reality was every bit as wonderful. It had become a sort of joint celebration too, because Casey's rose-adorned coat and tails had been a big hit at Badminton. Her dad and Ravi, who'd had the foresight to take business cards with them, had already received ten confirmed orders for similar coats, plus thirty-eight enquiries. Ravi was talking about setting up a separate equestrian-wear business with Roland as director.

Casey put her arm around her father and smiled up at him. 'Looks delicious, Dad. I doubt that any Badminton winner has ever had a better celebration feast. Anything missing?'

Gazing down at his daughter's face, alight with joy, it struck Roland Blue that his horse-mad little girl had grown into a remarkable young woman. He'd never been prouder or happier than at that moment.

'No, Casey,' he said. 'Nothing's missing.'

Casey's story continues in

RACE THE WIND,
available from April 2013.

Here is a preview of the first chapter.

1

Long before any of the humans stirred, the horse saw the trouble coming. He stared out into the darkness as two pinpricks of light grew steadily on a country lane where cars rarely passed at 3.35 a.m.

Storm Warning shifted in his stable. His muscles ached, but not unpleasantly. The cheering of the crowd that had urged him on to victory hours earlier still roared in his ears. He had run until his great heart – twice the size of that of a normal horse – had threatened to burst from his chest, yet he'd do it again right now if he could. For if there was one thing he enjoyed more than leaping so high it felt as if he were flying, it was galloping. Storm loved to race the wind.

Impatiently, he jostled the stable door with his

shoulder. In another couple of hours, the birds would begin their dawn song and the sun would spin gold the leaves of the ancient trees that gave the White Oaks Equestrian Centre its name. Shortly afterwards the stable manager, Morag, a woman he didn't dislike but wasn't particularly partial to either, would arrive with a banging and crashing of buckets, and the grooms would descend, stiff and wild-haired, from their flat above the office.

But that wasn't why Storm was restless. He was hungry for the hour when the girl he adored would come striding across the dew-whitened fields, accompanied by the old woman who smelled of exotic places and had magic, healing hands. When Casey and Mrs Smith arrived at his stable each morning, all was right with Storm's world.

Today, however, something felt different. Felt wrong. As the car drew level with the boundary fence of White Oaks, it slowed to a crawl and turned off its headlights. Like a panther, it crept up the lane, halting outside Peach Tree Cottage. Three dark figures climbed out.

In a pocket-sized upstairs bedroom at Peach Tree Cottage, in the English Garden County of Kent, Casey Blue was dreaming. A smile played on her lips. She was reaching for the Badminton Horse Trials trophy, a magnificent sculpture of three silver horses mounted on a red and black base. Cheers and applause rang out all around her.

'This is a huge achievement for Casey Blue,' the announcer was booming. 'She is the youngest ever winner of one of the toughest championships in world eventing.'

He didn't say that impoverished teenagers from grim concrete tower blocks in London's East End, riding one-dollar horses rescued from a knacker's yard, were not supposed to overcome some of the world's greatest riders to become Badminton champions, but that, Casey suspected, was what he was thinking. And who could blame him? Yet the impossible had been made possible because on the final day, the show jumping round, Storm, who could have been weakened by the gruelling cross-country, had felt strong and sure beneath her.

In the dream, Casey was smiling so widely her face hurt. But as her hands settled on the trophy it was torn from her grip. A flurry of officials surrounded her.

'There's been a mistake,' said one. 'You are not the winner. You don't deserve to be Badminton champion.'

'What are you talking about? Why not?'

'Your father is a burglar. A common thief.'

'He's not!' Casey almost screamed the words. 'Don't say that. He made a mistake once, a long time ago, and he's paid for it. He went to prison and served his time. Haven't you ever made a mistake? And anyway, what does that have to do with anything? This is not about

315

my dad. It's about me and Storm. *We* did the dressage and cleared the cross-country. *We* achieved the times and put the scores on the board. This is *our* life. Isn't that what counts?'

But the officials were walking away, taking the trophy with them, and already the arena had almost emptied. The last stragglers cast disapproving glances over their shoulders.

'We did win,' Casey protested, tears streaming down her face. 'We did win, you know we did.'

An urgent hammering shocked her awake. She lay without moving, trying to separate the nightmare from reality. Had she and Storm won Badminton or hadn't they? Yes, they had. She'd gone to sleep at midnight after an evening of celebration. The trophy was on the kitchen table downstairs, in among the champagne glasses.

She sagged against the pillows, smiling with relief. Now she only had good things to look forward to. Top of the list was the Kentucky Three-Day Event in America. As a result of her Badminton victory, she'd received an automatic invitation. It had put the icing on the cake of the best day of Casey's life.

The hammering came again, and this time there was the sound of footsteps on the stairs and lights clicking on. Still Casey didn't move. It was pitch black outside – 3.46 a.m., according to the clock, and she loathed getting up at that hour, even when she was going to an event.

Besides which, there were plenty of other people to get the front door. Her father was an early riser, as was Peter, Storm's farrier, who was also her . . . boyfriend. She had to get used to that word. As of yesterday, he was her boyfriend. There was also Angelica Smith, her sixty-three-year-old coach, who was a bit of an insomniac and was often up all hours of the night, drinking chai tea.

In the kitchen below, the muffled voices grew louder. The stairs creaked. Peter spoke through her door: 'Case, are you awake?'

She sat up, pushing her dark hair out of her eyes. 'How could I not be?'

Light spilled in behind him as he entered. His shirt was unbuttoned, revealing a brown stomach ridged with muscle, hollowing as it dipped towards his jeans. Despite the uncivilised hour, Casey felt her own stomach lurch with longing.

She flushed as the events of the previous evening came back to her. He'd kissed her. He'd told her he loved her. But he didn't look loving now. He looked worried.

'What's happening?' she asked. 'Is it the farmer again? He seems to get a kick out of frightening us from our beds at the crack of dawn. Or is it Morag with some foaling disaster?'

'Casey, you need to get dressed and come downstairs. The police are here.'

'The *police?*' Casey was wide awake now. 'What do they want? Is Storm okay? Please don't tell me he's been stolen.'

'No, Case, they're here to see your dad. I think you'd better come quickly.' And with that he was gone.

Casey flew out of bed in a panic, hands shaking as she struggled to pull on her jeans. Her jumper went on inside out. A thousand thoughts tumbled through her brain.

She'd been fourteen when Roland Blue had been arrested and charged with burglary and assault. The fact that he was the world's most unlikely thief had, in a way, made it worse. The dad she knew had only ever been kind, funny and loving. In court, friends and former employers had lined up to vouch for him as honest and loyal.

But he was also lacking in self-confidence and easily led. His most likeable trait, an infinite capacity for seeing the best in everyone, was not always tempered with good judgement.

A few years earlier, he'd fallen in with a bad crowd. They'd convinced him that a multi-millionaire wouldn't miss a few hundred thousand. He'd agreed to join the gang on a robbery. It was unfortunate that he happened to be knocking the millionaire out with a lamp (the man had woken and tried to kill him with a poker) when the police arrived. In the chaos, his accomplices had fled.

After refusing to rat out his mates, Roland had been left to take the fall on his own. Hence an eight-month prison sentence.

Since then he'd been clean. He'd retrained as a tailor, a job that had become a passion. He was so gifted that

318

he'd hand-stitched Casey's top hat and tails for the dressage at Badminton, embroidering an exquisite rose design on the shoulder and cuffs to remind her of her mother, who'd died when she was two. Roses had been her mum's favourite flower. Casey, who worshipped her dad, flaws and all, could not have been more proud of him.

And now this.

She clattered downstairs and burst into the kitchen. Her first impression was of people frozen in a tableau.

Mrs Smith was leaning against the Aga in her old silk robe, wearing an expression of naked fury. That was the scariest thing of all because very few things in life had the power to upset Mrs Smith's equilibrium. Peter was beside her. He started forward, but Mrs Smith said something under her breath and he stopped mid-stride.

Facing Casey across the table on which the trophy still sat was a large man with blue-black hair and a pockmarked face underlined by several chins. Even unmoving, he exuded a sinister magnetism. His eyes slid over her as if she were of no more consequence than the refrigerator and moved to her father, who wore his rumpled clothes from the previous day.

Flanking Roland Blue were two more policemen – one black and athletic-looking, the other short, stocky and in his mid to late fifties, with an unruly grey mop and pupils the colour of coffee dregs. He had the unhealthy pallor of a man low on sleep and big on caffeine and takeaways, but there was an unmistakable intelligence in his level gaze.

'Detective Inspector Lenny McLeod,' he said, advancing with his hand outstretched. 'These are my colleagues, Constable Dex Higgins' – he gestured towards the black officer – 'and Detective Superintendent Bill Grady. You must be Casey. Apologies for the disturbance. It couldn't wait.'

Casey ignored his hand. Her instinct was to rush to her father's side, but something about the stances of the men discouraged her. 'What's going on?' she demanded. 'What couldn't wait? Leave my dad alone. He's done nothing wrong.'

'That's for a judge to decide,' snapped Grady. 'We have a ton of evidence to suggest otherwise.'

Roland Blue gave a short laugh. 'That's a lie. Evidence of what? That I've been gainfully employed as a tailor and a model citizen? What have you got on me? Did I drop a piece of chewing gum on Hackney High Street?'

Higgins frowned. 'It's a bit more serious than that.'

'A parking ticket? Is that it? Look, if you want a character reference speak to my boss, Ravi Singh. He'll tell you—'

'We already have.' Grady squeezed his bulk into a kitchen chair. 'Can you tell us where you were between midnight and 1.15 a.m. on April 27th?'

A creeping coldness enveloped Casey, as if a winter fog was invading her bones.

'I was at home in Hackney – number 414 Redwing Tower. Speak to Ravi. He and I worked round the clock for two nights running to finish a jacket for Casey. You can see it if you like.'

'Mr Singh did confirm he was with you on the 26th,' said McLeod. 'But he told us he left your flat shortly before midnight when he became too tired to continue. Apparently, you urged him to go home and get some sleep.'

'This conversation is not going any further without a lawyer present, detectives,' Mrs Smith interrupted. 'You've said quite enough. You're making a monstrous error and I'd advise you to leave before you do any further damage.'

Roland smiled. 'Thanks, Mrs Smith, but I have nothing to hide.' He turned to the men. 'So what if I did? Are you going to arrest me for showing concern for a friend?'

'We're rather more interested in a warehouse raid that took place during the hours when you were alone that morning,' Grady said. 'A raid in which a security guard was shot. He died yesterday. That makes this a murder inquiry.'

Roland went white.

Casey rushed forward with a cry, but Higgins grabbed her arm.

'Leave her alone,' Peter said angrily.

Grady rounded on him. 'One more step, boy, and I'll have you down the cells so fast you won't know what hit you. Now stay where you are and shut up.'

Mrs Smith regarded him with dislike. 'We have the

right to call a lawyer, detective superintendent, *and* to be treated with respect.'

Grady heaved himself to his feet and tossed a piece of paper on the table. 'Call all the lawyers you want, madam. Right now, our arrest warrant takes precedent. As for respect . . . we save that for thems that have earned it. Dex, read Mr Blue his rights.'

McLeod gave Casey a warning glance and steered her in the direction of Peter.

Constable Higgins intoned: 'Roland James Blue, I am arresting you on suspicion of murder. You do not have to say anything, but it may harm your defence if you do not mention when questioned something which you later rely on in court. Anything you do say may be given in evidence—'

'But this is insane! You have the wrong man. Casey, you believe me, don't you? I'm innocent.'

'I know you are, Dad. This is all just some hideous mistake. We'll fix it, I promise.'

'We most certainly will,' said Mrs Smith.

'Enough time wasting,' snarled Grady. 'Cuff him, Dex. Let's get him to the cells where he belongs.' He almost shoved the pair out into the darkness.

Casey's hands fell to her sides. It was as if someone had tugged at a thread and her whole life had begun to unravel.

McLeod glanced at the trophy on the kitchen table. 'I heard on the news that you won the Badminton Horse Trials yesterday, Casey. The youngest winner in history.

That's some achievement. I'm sorry this has spoiled things. Please understand that we're only doing our job. Uh, congratulations.'

The door slammed shut. The car engine roared and they were gone.

Acknowledgments

Writing this book has been a dream come true for me, partly because I've always wanted to write a book about eventing, but also because through Casey I got to achieve my childhood goal of riding at Badminton – at least vicariously! It was, from start to finish, pure joy.

Best of all, though, was doing the research. I'm grateful to Christine Knudsen, who was kind enough to let me ride her eventer, Lucky, and to Sharon Hunt and Anna Ross Noble, who graciously allowed me to watch them work. However, I'm particularly indebted to Badminton's long-time press officer, Julian Seaman (the inspiration for Jasper Simmonds!), a former competitor, for his help, advice and wealth of Badminton expertise. Huge thanks also to Paul Graham of British Dressage, who knows everything there is to know about eventing, and to Susan Lamb, about whom the same is true. Any technical errors in the book are my responsibility and mine alone.

This book would never have happened without the belief and enthusiasm of my amazing agent, Catherine Clarke, and my equally amazing editor Fiona Kennedy. Special thanks too to Lisa Milton, Jo Carpenter, Alex Hippisley-Cox, Nina Douglas, Jane Hughes, Fliss Johnston, Alexandra Nicholas and Sarah Vanden-Abeele at Orion Children's Books, the most dedicated and generally wonderful team of people you'd find at any publishing house anywhere. Thanks to my father, Mum and sister, Lisa, for being tirelessly supportive and for inspiring and encouraging my love of horses. Last but not least thanks to Jules for the rose illustration and for being there through thick and thin.

Lauren St John
London
December 2011